A Killer's Essence

BY THE SAME AUTHOR

The Caretaker of Lorne Field

Outsourced

Killer

Small Crimes

Pariah

A Killer's Essence

Dave Zeltserman

The Overlook Press
New York, NY

This edition first published in the United States in 2011 by
The Overlook Press, Peter Mayer Publishers, Inc.

141 Wooster Street
New York, NY 10012
www.overlookpress.com

For bulk and special sales, please contact sales@overlookny.com

Cataloging-in-Publication Data is available from the Library of Congress

Book design and typeformatting by Bernard Schleifer

Manufactured in the United States of America

ISBN 978-1-59020-321-7

For Mike Lombardi

Chapter 1

Back in 1972 I was seven years old and always tagging along after my older brother, Mike. This was before the attention you have today on child abductions and pedophiles—that evil existed, shit, it has probably always existed, but it wasn't on TV or the news much, if at all. You didn't have CNN and the Internet to focus on it twenty-four seven, and as a result a lot of parents didn't think about it. Back then it wasn't all that unusual for a seven-year-old and a bunch of ten-year-olds to spend their afternoons hanging around their Brooklyn neighborhood unsupervised. And that was what Mike and his friends and I used to do, at least when he and his friends couldn't shake me, and I was a tough little bugger to shake back then, just as I am now.

This one afternoon it was just Mike and me. We had just spent a half hour in Bob's Drugstore thumbing through the comic books until the owner got fed up with us and told us to buy something or leave. Mike spent a dime on a Sky Bar candy bar. He broke off the caramel piece for me, and we left anyway. While we were walking past the fish market a man came out and offered us five bucks to clean up the backroom. Mike wanted that five bucks, but something about the man made me grab onto Mike's arm and pull him back while shouting "No!" repeatedly as if I were demon-possessed. Mike looked at me as if I were nuts, and I thought he was going to punch me, but that wouldn't have stopped me from what I was doing. A couple of older men from the neighborhood wandered over to see what the commotion was about, and the man from the fish market started to look nervous. He told us to forget it and he went back into his store.

"What'd you do that for, Stan?" Mike demanded, his narrow face taut and angry. "Five bucks! You know what we could've bought for five bucks? Are you stupid?"

At this point I was crying. I couldn't explain to him why I did what I did. I couldn't say it out loud. I couldn't have him think I was even nuttier than he already thought I was. Anyway, all I wanted was for us to get away from there, so I kept pulling on his arm, using every ounce of strength I had to drag us away from that store. One of the neighborhood men gave me a concerned look and told Mike that he should take his little brother home. Mike looked pissed, but he did what the man asked him to. All the way home he kept asking what was wrong with me.

Later at dinner Mike told our folks what had happened and how I cost us five bucks. Pop asked why I did what I did, but I couldn't explain it to him. He shook his head, disappointed-like, and gave me a lecture about the value of money, but left it at that.

The next night while we were eating dinner, Mr. Lombardi from down the hall knocked on our door. Chucky Wilson, who was a year older than Mike, hadn't come home yet from school and he wanted to know if either Mike or I had seen him or knew anything. We didn't. He looked tired as he apologized for interrupting our dinner. Pop asked him if they needed any more help looking for Chucky. Mr. Lombardi thought about it, but shook his head and told Pop to finish his dinner and if they still hadn't found Chucky in another hour he'd let Pop know. After Mr. Lombardi left I told Pop that Chucky was with that man from the fish market.

"What?"

"That man from the fish market must've promised Chucky five bucks also. That's where Chucky is!"

"Stan, quit talking nonsense," Mom said.

"I'm not! I'll bet anything that's where Chucky is!"

"Stop it now!" Pop ordered. "Christ, I don't know how you get these ideas."

None of us had much of an appetite after that, Mike and me mostly pushing our food around our plates and Pop staring off into space. After a while of that he got up and left the table and then the apartment. He didn't bother saying anything to Mom about where he was going. She looked like she was fighting hard to keep from crying.

It turned out that Pop collected other men from the neighborhood and they visited the fish market. They broke into the store and found the man who had offered Mike and me five bucks. He was in the back room chopping up what was left of Chucky. I didn't learn that part until recently, but that's what they found. It was days after that when Pop asked me how I knew where Chucky would be. I couldn't explain it to him, so I shrugged and told him I just knew.

For years I convinced myself that none of that happened. That it was a dream I once had, or maybe a story I heard, or something from a movie or TV show that I saw as a kid. After meeting Zachary Lynch, I started remembering more about that day back when I was a seven-year-old kid and thinking that maybe it wasn't just a dream. I found the old newspaper stories about that man in the fish market and what he did to Chucky Wilson, and then dug out the police reports. My pop had died when I was twenty and Mom is in no shape these days to remember anything, but I talked with Mike and he confirmed what happened. All those years we never talked about it, both of us pretending it never happened.

"What did you see that day, Stan?" he asked.

I shook my head and told him I didn't know, and from the look on his face he seemed relieved to hear that. The fact is I did see something. When that man came out of the fish market wearing his stained apron over a pair of dirty khakis and even dirtier T-shirt, for a moment I didn't see a man but something ghoulish, something from out of a nightmare. It only lasted a second, if that, and then he turned back into a balding and scrawny middle-aged man, but for that moment I saw something else.

Later, after talking with Mike, I sat quietly and remembered everything I could about that day and wrote it all down. After all those years I finally accepted what I saw. I still have never told anyone about this other than Zachary Lynch, and he's the only person I know who would possibly understand.

Chapter 2

Wednesday, October 13, 2004

Bambi stood just inside the doorway, her expression revealing mostly skepticism as I approached the front desk at one of midtown's trendiest boutique hotels. The desk clerk was young, well-groomed, and had those pretty-boy Hollywood looks. The clothes he wore were probably worth more than my entire wardrobe. He gave me a bland smile that just bordered on condescending. With my scruffy looks and cheap suit I probably didn't look like I could afford their twelve-hundred-dollar-a-night room charge. I couldn't. Not even a tenth of it.

"Yes?" the desk clerk asked with a fake politeness.

"My name's Stan Green. Winston called to tell me that my room is ready."

He gave me an empty look, his bland smile showing some strain.

"Winston Harris," I said. "The manager of this hotel. Your boss. How about giving him a call?"

His smile faded. "One minute, please," he muttered under his breath. He turned his back on me to make a call. While I waited I placed my hands lightly on the wood surface of the front desk counter and felt its smoothness. It looked like polished maple but it also had designs made up from darker and richer woods ingrained within it. A lot of detail went into it. The length of the surface ran more than ten feet. My guess was it cost close to my yearly salary, at least after deducting my child support payments. The wall behind the desk contained a full-length built-in aquarium filled with different colored jellyfish. Blue, yellow, orange, red. It was all pretty spectacular the way these translucent creatures floated along, puffing in and out, looking more like colored plastic baggies than living things. Very exotic, and very expensive. Again, the tank and the fish probably cost more than I was worth.

Three weeks ago I had helped the hotel manager, Winston Harris, keep some nasty business quiet. The business involved a favored guest of the hotel caught with a hooker who had been trying to extort more than the agreed-upon price, at least according to this favorite guest. Winston showed his appreciation for my discretion by promising to set me up with one of his rooms for the night as well as room service on the house. I didn't take his offer seriously, and besides, that wasn't my reason for doing it. The hooker turned out to be a young college kid who was desperate for the extra cash. She was in well over her head with the game she was playing, and the john she was playing the game on looked like he was on the verge of a massive coronary, at least if this went on any longer. Add to that that I had already put in a long day with six hours of overtime and didn't feel up to the hours of paperwork that would've accompanied any arrest. So instead of dragging them both through the hotel lobby in cuffs, I lay down the law for them. At the time I didn't pay any attention to the manager's expression of gratitude and further ignored his request for my home number since I didn't expect anything to ever come of it. On this job people say things in the heat of the moment. You can't take it too seriously.

Bambi had left the doorway and was now standing next to me so that her hip brushed against mine. She rested one of her hands lightly on the small of my back, the other on my arm. She gave me a thin smile, then moved her stare back to the desk clerk as she waited for him to get off the phone. I first met Bambi sixteen months ago, which was only a few days short of the one-year anniversary of Cheryl leaving me. When Bambi first told me her name, I thought it had to be a stage name—that she was either a stripper or a wannabe actress—but nope, that was the name she was born with. Why any parents would do that to a kid I don't know, but I checked the records myself. She was absolutely gorgeous. Picture Eva Longoria at twenty-four. If Bambi wanted to she could've made a hell of a lot of money as a stripper, but fortunately she didn't want to, and instead worked as a salesgirl at one of Park Avenue's very ritzy women's clothing boutiques. I keep telling her she should work in a men's clothing store instead. What man could possibly resist buying a suit from her? Or a dozen? She'd clean up on the commissions. Whenever I suggested that she would just laugh it off and tell me she wouldn't want to make me jealous by putting her hands on some other guy's inseams, and besides they gave her a fifty-percent discount at the store she worked at.

After nine months of living together I still hadn't figured out whether it was gratitude or love on my part. A twenty-four-year-old as stunningly gorgeous as Bambi didn't have to settle for some rumpled thirty-nine-year-old cop with bad knees. She could be a handful, though. Putting it lightly. Three weeks ago when I told her about Winston Harris's offer, she damn near tore me a new one. Christ, she was furious.

"You couldn't give him your phone number? One night in a luxury hotel would be such a big deal?"

"It's a matter of principle, babe. Besides, I didn't do what I did in order to solicit a bribe."

"Yeah, no kidding. You let those two go because you were too *effing* lazy to fill out the paperwork!"

That stung because it was partly true. That's the thing with Bambi—when she wanted to she could be ruthless at zeroing in on whatever it was you were most sensitive about.

"It was my discretion," I said. "I thought I'd give them both a break. If I arrested them that girl would've gotten kicked out of college and probably would've resorted to hooking full-time. I think I was able to scare her from trying it again, and I'm pretty sure I scared the john just as badly." Trying to joke, I added, "Besides I think it was more my burning desire to be back home with you than laziness."

"Yeah, right. Stan, for once use your head! How would it be a bribe if you didn't ask for it? For Chrissakes, he was offering it to you! You don't have to be so *effing* squeaky clean all the time!"

"It still would've been a bribe," I argued stubbornly.

She was too mad to say another word. She stood glaring at me for a long moment, her lips mouthing something not very nice. Then she turned on her heels and made sure to slam the bedroom door behind her hard enough to shake the apartment. Needless to say I slept on the sofa that night. And the next two nights.

The desk clerk finished his call. He turned back to me with his false smile again and told me that the bellhop would show us to our room. Bambi gave my arm a squeeze. When Winston Harris had called earlier to tell me that he had a room available, I wondered for a few seconds how he had gotten my cell number and then realized that Bambi must've taken it upon herself to call him. So far she hadn't let on to that, acting as if this was all a big surprise to her. She can put on a hell of an act when she wants to, just like her look of utter skepticism from a few minutes earlier. Or maybe that look was real. Maybe she couldn't believe I was actually going through with it. Anyway, I decided what the hell. What harm would one night of luxury do, especially after she'd had to put up with my spartan Brooklyn apartment all these months? I still didn't feel right about it, though, and had a queasiness working its way into the pit of my stomach over the thought of accepting the room, but I also wasn't feeling up to incurring Bambi's wrath—and I knew she'd find out about it if I turned Harris down. I told Winston Harris that this wasn't a bribe, that he wasn't buying any future favors from me, but if he still wanted to offer me the room as an act of generosity I'd take it. He stammered out that he did. After that I called in a favor from my partner, Rich Grissini, to cover for me. We were shorthanded as it was, with Mills and Derocher calling in sick, Gifford, Coleman, and Shattleford all on disability, and Lahey on maternity leave. Normally my shift was eight to five, but with the recent manpower shortage my shift overlapped with my partner's, so for the last few weeks I'd been working eleven to eight. I knew there was little chance that Phillips would've let me take personal time on this short notice.

The bellhop appeared, and he and the desk clerk had a private conversation before he offered to show us to our room. He was a smaller pear-shaped man in his fifties. He avoided eye contact with me but couldn't keep from ogling Bambi. I couldn't much blame him on either count.

The room he took us to was on the third floor next to the elevator. I could tell Bambi wasn't happy that we were being given one of their undesirable rooms, but the tightness forming around her mouth disappeared once we were shown inside. Saying it was pretty damn nice would be an understatement. What had to be at least a fifty-inch plasma TV hung on the wall opposite the bed, and the furnishings were all very modern and chic, stuff you might expect to see in a contemporary art museum. Lots of rich woods and plush cushions.

Other than a small overnight bag that Bambi had brought, we didn't have anything for the bellhop to carry, but he still made a show of walking us around the room and showing us its features. At the end of it, I gave him ten bucks, which from his sour expression was what he had expected. After he left, Bambi plopped down on the bed with the room service menu looking like a kid in a candy store. I turned from her so I could lock my service revolver in the room safe, and while I did this Bambi read me some of the menu items and their prices, two of the more extravagant items being a three-hundred-dollar sevruga caviar and lobster omelet and a fifteen-hundred-dollar bottle of Champagne.

"All on the house," I said somewhat nervously, not quite sure that Winston Harris meant for his generosity to extend that far.

Bambi grinned, her green eyes dazzling brightly. "Maybe I'll order one of everything," she said. Her grin turned more into an impish smile as she asked, "What do you want to do first—eat or get naked?"

My cell phone rang. Without looking at the caller ID I knew it was Phillips calling.

"Green speaking," I said answering the phone, wishing I had turned the damn thing off.

"Where the fuck are you?"

"Nice talking to you too, Captain," I said.

"You didn't answer me, Green. I know you're supposed to be working now. I know that because I can see your name on the board. What I don't see is you at your desk. So where the fuck are you?"

"On a personal errand, Captain. Grissini is supposed to be covering for me—"

"Grissini got clipped crossing Seventh Avenue. Right now he's at St. Vincent's with a concussion and a broken hip. So he's not going to be doing your job for you."

"Fuck," I said.

"That's exactly what I said when a call came in for a homicide and I found one of my detectives absentee while his name is written in big bright letters on my board. Where the fuck are you?"

"Midtown."

"Get your ass over to the corner of Chambers and Church Street. I needed you there ten minutes ago. And with Grissini out of commission, starting tomorrow you're back to eight to five."

I hesitated for a moment. Bambi had shifted her position on the bed so she was now sitting rigidly with her knees pulled up to her chest. A tenseness showed on her face as she listened to my end of the conversation. "You can't find anyone else to cover for me—" I started.

Phillips hung up on me. I looked away from Bambi for a moment. When I looked back, her beautiful face had scrunched up, her eyes squinty, angry.

"You've got to be *effing* kidding me," she said, disgusted.

I shrugged. "I'm sorry. That was my boss. I have to go."

"No, you don't," she said. "Call him back and tell him you're tied up."

"I can't."

"Of course you can. If you want to badly enough, that is."

I scratched my jaw. A tired sigh eased out of me. "It's not like that," I said. "I'm on duty. I have people counting on me. I had no right doing this in the first place."

I retrieved my service revolver from the safe. While I checked to make sure it was fully loaded I could feel Bambi's eyes boring holes into my back.

"You're *effing* pathetic," she said.

I turned around to muster as apologetic a smile as possible. "Look, I'll be back when I can. In the meantime, enjoy the room, order room service, do whatever you want."

"Oh, you bet I will," she said. Her eyes flashed angrily as she stared at me, her skin smoldering. "I'll be ordering room service for two. Maybe I'll invite that desk clerk up here. He's better looking than you. A lot younger too."

I met her hard stare. "Do whatever you want," I said, and then left the room.

Chapter 3

It had been six thirty when Phillips called. While the intersection of Church and Chambers was in Tribeca and less than three miles from where I was, at that time of day the traffic was brutal all along Broadway. Hell, it's brutal any time of the day, but then in particular. Even after attaching the flashing blues to the outside of my department-issued Chevy Impala, the other drivers didn't want to give me a break and I had to nudge a few cars to pull over so I could squeeze past. What should've been a two-minute drive took fifteen, and during it all I was cursing out everyone—the other drivers, Winston Harris for ever mentioning that free room, myself for being too conscientious about leaving my cell phone on, Bambi for not being able to give me a break, and even my partner, Rich, for letting himself get clipped crossing Seventh Avenue and breaking a hip.

I had worked myself into a pretty rotten mood by the time I reached the crime scene. There was already a mob there. A dozen uniformed officers were keeping the news media at a distance, and several forensics investigators and members of the evidence collection team were examining the area.

When I saw the body all of my self-pity from before bled out of me and was replaced instead by a soul-deadening sickness over what had been done to the victim. She was a middle-aged woman who had been shot once in the face and twice in the chest, and judging by the damage done to her something with a high caliber had been used, maybe a .45. She was lying on her back like a rag doll that had been tossed to the pavement, her legs twisted unnaturally behind her, her arms askew, one positioned over her head, the other at her side. The little that was left of her face stared blindly upward, her half-opened eyes dull and not much more than glass. I sat down on my heels so I could get a closer look. From the amount of damage done to her face the injury there looked more like an exit wound from a hollow-point bullet. I lifted her head up and, sure enough, found a small hole in the back of her head. I gently lowered her back to the concrete and continued examining the damage done to her. Both earlobes were torn, and three fingers on her left hand had been cut off, one on her right. From the quality of her blood-splattered designer clothes, my guess was she had been well-off when she was among the living. I focused my attention back on the missing fingers of her left hand.

"He did it for the jewelry."

One of the forensic investigators had walked over to me. He nodded grim-faced at the mutilated left hand. "He cut off her fingers for the jewelry. I guess it was faster for him than pulling them off her fingers. Same thing with her ears. He ripped the earrings off of them. We found one of her fingers discarded twenty yards up the street from here. From the skin abrasions it was clear he pulled two rings from it."

He pointed out where the finger was found. The area had been marked.

"Which finger?"

He smiled grimly. "Third. Left hand."

"Anything else found?"

"Three .40 caliber shell casings."

"That's it? No handbag? Identification?"

He shook his head.

Fuck. With more than half her face blown off an ID was going to be a problem unless we got lucky with her fingerprints being in the system. I'd have to have forensics work on a facial reconstruction drawing, but even if they came up with an exact likeness an identification probably wouldn't happen until we received a call from a concerned relative.

"From her chest wounds and the way she fell it looks like she was shot first from the front," I said, "but the head wound makes it look like she was shot from behind."

"That's what it looks like," he agreed. "There are no powder burns on her front, but if you lift up her head you can see the residue near the entrance wound. After she was on the ground he must've lifted up her head and shot her from in back with the muzzle pressed against her skull. The blood splatter indicates that also. From the size of the entrance and exit wounds, hollow-points were used."

I didn't bother lifting her head up again. I'd seen the powder marks the first time I did.

"What was the point?" I asked. "All three shots were probably kill shots. Why shoot her three times? And why in the back of the head?"

The investigator continued to stare grim-faced at the body. "The head shot was probably done to remove her face. But who knows? Maybe it was all just sport. Fun. Maybe he was out hunting and found an easy target and went overboard." He turned from the victim to look at me. "But you're the guy who's supposed to be answering those questions."

I stood up slowly, feeling both my knees and my back creak as I straightened them. "You take pictures yet?"

He nodded.

"You guys need anything else?" I asked.

"Nope."

"How about the collection team?"

He peered over at the three members of the team who were working their way down the street.

"Maybe twenty minutes."

"All right, then, let's get the body moved to the medical examiner."

I left him and the dead woman to walk over to the spot where the severed finger had been tossed. The area had been marked with chalk. There was nothing special about it. The perp must've pulled off her rings and tossed the finger in the gutter as casually as someone else would have tossed away a gum wrapper. I squeezed my eyes tight for a moment and rubbed a hand across them. This was not good. A wealthy woman who we might not be able to identify, at least not without someone coming forward, shot dead and her body mutilated in this type of neighborhood. *Fuck*. While not the West Village, and with nowhere near that type of foot traffic, this was supposed to be a safe area for tourists. It was only several blocks from City Hall and another few from the WTC Memorial. The street itself was not that far removed from the Village, with the same type of offbeat stores littering it. This type of shit wasn't supposed to happen here. It wasn't supposed to happen anywhere in Manhattan anymore. The Bronx, maybe, but not here.

I thought about the finger that had been left. The third finger on her left hand would be where she'd been wearing an engagement ring and wedding band. Did the perp leave it so we'd suspect she was married, or was it just a random act? I didn't have a feel one way or the other. All I knew was my head was starting to hurt thinking about the shitstorm that was going to come down because of this murder, especially given the savagery of the crime.

If she was married, statistically the husband would be the best bet for her killing, but given the brutality of what had been done to the body, there would have to be a tremendous amount of hatred involved, even if it was all done purposely to look like a robbery. There was a deep stench of a pure psychopathic personality behind this. It could be a hit man, but why so violent, why such overkill? Using this type of firepower? A .40 caliber is a military weapon, not something usually used for street crimes. I called my department and talked with Thomas Jones, our computer research specialist, and gave him what I had—the caliber used, a description of the victim, what was done to her, the time and area of the shooting. He promised he'd make this killing a priority and get back to me with any profile matches.

One of the uniformed officers wandered over to me and introduced himself as Patrolman Dave Stevens from the Ninth. "You took your sweet time coming here," he complained. He gestured toward a crowd of TV cameramen and reporters that had gathered up the street, all of whom were being kept back by a line of uniformed cops. "This has turned into a zoo."

I peered up ahead. "The hyena exhibit."

That cracked a razor-thin smile from him. "You got that right."

"Who called this in?"

He consulted a notepad and read me the name on it. "James Longo. He owns Longo Books over there." Stevens nodded towards a quaint bookstore two doors over from where the killing occurred. "Called it in at six fourteen. Thought he heard gunshots. Claims that by the time he looked outside all he saw was the dead body."

"How long did it take between hearing shots and looking outside?"

Stevens shrugged, rolled his eyes. "Claims a couple of minutes. He said he'd hang around until we told him otherwise. He looked shaken up by the murder."

That got my pulse racing a bit. "Does he know the victim?"

"Claims he doesn't."

"Any witnesses?"

"None yet. We've gone door to door. Some people heard the gunshots but didn't make the connection to what they were. No one yet is ready to say they looked outside and saw anything. What about the media? You want to talk to them?"

"Not me. I'll get someone from media relations for that. Anything else you can tell me?"

He shook his head, his lips pushing into a bitter smile. "I can't believe this shit going down here and in broad daylight. You see what that animal did to that poor lady?"

"Yeah."

Both of us turned to watch the dead woman carried into the back of an ambulance. I told him we'd probably need the block closed for another twenty minutes. He nodded and left to join the other patrolmen keeping the media at bay. I then called for a media relations officer to be sent to the scene, giving the dispatcher a rundown on what we had. After that I made my way up and down the block talking with tenants of each store. No one saw anything. As Stevens had told me, some of the tenants admitted hearing noises but claimed they hadn't made the connection that they were gunshots. In a vintage clothing store I noticed a security camera that was angled to capture the front of the store. Giving it a closer look, I wondered if it would also pick up part of the front sidewalk. I asked the girl working there if the system was active. She told me she'd check and left to go to a backroom. When she came back she was holding a videotape, her eyes wide under a circle of black mascara and her chalk-white face even paler than before.

"This is what's been recorded so far today," she said, handing me the tape.

I thanked her, finished checking the rest of the businesses on that side of the street, then worked my way down the other side until I reached the bookstore. By this time the media relations officer had shown up and was giving a briefing. Lieutenant Irving Stone. I knew Irv from my old Brooklyn neighborhood. He was Mike's age, and back in the day he could hit a baseball a mile. We all thought he'd end up in pro ball. His joining the force was what got me thinking about doing the same.

Irv must've sensed me watching him because he turned from the crowd he was addressing and gave me a pained grimace once he recognized me. Yeah, I was sure he was having fun stonewalling their questions about a violent killing none of us had any knowledge about yet. I nodded toward him, and his grimace deepened before he turned back to his audience. I think at that point I was grimacing too as I made my way up the steps to the bookstore.

The owner sat in an overstuffed leather chair that was situated near the children's book section and faced the front of the store, his eyes jerking to the door as I walked in. Longo was maybe in his mid-forties and was a large man with stooped shoulders. He had long, reddish hair and thick sideburns, and this gave him a shaggy appearance. His face was long and lean, his cheeks hollowed, and his nose angled sharply like an eagle's beak. He wore a tweed jacket complete with leather patches and a pair of rumpled corduroy trousers as if he was trying hard to play the part of a college professor. I introduced myself. He was nearly out of breath telling me in a stilted voice how he'd been waiting for someone from the police to show up. When he tried to explain how stunned he was when he heard the gunshots, he had to stop for a moment to drink some water before he was able to find his voice again.

"I was in the back room working on next month's newsletter when the shots were fired," he said. "It was maybe two minutes after that before I was able to get up and look outside."

"You knew they were gunshots right away?"

He nodded. "Yes, certainly. When I heard those shots I went numb. I wish I hadn't, but I did. By the time I looked outside whoever killed that woman was gone."

"Did you see anyone else?"

"Only her." He looked away and shook his head. "Simply awful what was done to her. Barbaric."

"Please describe the shots."

"What do you mean?"

"Were they fired close together or was there some time between each shot?"

He looked away from me, a constipated look pinching his face as if he were trying to replay the event in his head. Half a minute later his eyes shifted back to meet mine.

"The first two shots were bang-bang, no time between them," he said. "The third came about ten seconds later."

"What time were the first shots?"

"Six ten."

"Did you hear anything else?"

He shook his head.

"No one yelling anything beforehand or afterwards?"

"No."

This was consistent with what I had already been told in the other stores along the street. Two loud noises close together—the shots that were fired into her chest, then ten to fifteen seconds later for a third shot that was fired into the back of her head. Nothing else distinguishable heard before or afterward.

"Was anyone else in the store?"

An apologetic smile. "We close at five-thirty on Wednesdays unless I have a signing scheduled. The store was already locked up when the shootings happened. I was ten minutes away from leaving when I heard them."

"You didn't answer me. Anyone else in the store at the time?"

"Just myself. Normally my wife would've been with me. She manages the children's book section, but she left early today for an errand. Thank God."

"How about when you closed up?"

"I had three employees leave then. No customers at that time. Why?"

"I'll need their names," I said. "They might've seen someone suspicious loitering outside."

He accepted that and told me he'd get that for me. While he was copying his employee information onto a sheet of paper I asked him if he knew the victim.

He gave me a confused look. "No. Why would I know her?"

"I thought maybe she might've been a customer. The officer you talked to felt you were shaken up pretty badly."

His lips pressed into a harsh thin line, his color not much better than what the dead woman's had been. "Of course it shook me up," he said. "A woman was shot to death right outside my store. I was the one who checked to see if she was still breathing. I saw up close what was done to her. But no, I didn't recognize her. Even with what was done to her face I think if I had known her I would've recognized her."

He handed me a sheet of paper with his employees' names and phone numbers while I handed him a card with my contact information. I asked him to call me if he remembered anything or if he or his employees saw anyone suspicious hanging around. I gave a quick glance towards the aisle of mystery books that I stood next to and, before leaving, suggested that maybe someday he'd be selling a book based on this murder. He made a face as if he just tasted something unpleasant.

"Maybe," he said. "But to be honest I never much cared for police procedurals."

Once back outside I was swarmed by news reporters and cameramen and had to wait until I was safely back in my car before I could call my department. Phillips had left for the day and I got Captain Joe Ramirez instead. I filled him in on what I had so far. "I'd like to get back to the station and see if there's anything on the surveillance tape. Maybe we'll get lucky. In the meantime we need to expand the canvass outward at least four blocks and see if we can find any of the other missing fingers. Also we need to talk to workers and transit police over at the Chambers Street and City Hall subway stations. Maybe one of them saw someone suspicious pass through."

"What about your partner, Grissini?"

"He's at St. Vincent's with a broken hip."

"You're kidding! I didn't hear about that."

"I don't know the story yet either, but that's what Phillips told me. What about it, Joe? I could use some help."

He started to grumble about how thin they were, especially with game two of the Yankees-Sox playoffs that night. I interrupted him to let him know that I was missing the game also, and more than that, but I didn't elaborate on the extra that I was missing.

"Yeah, I know." He hesitated for a moment before telling me he'd send out a canine team and also a couple of detectives to canvass the neighboring subway stops. "What do we got here?" he asked.

"Hell if I know. It's too early. We don't even have an ID on the victim yet."

"Yeah, but come on. Your gut. Is this a spouse trying to make it look like a psycho, or do we have the real deal?"

"My gut? We've got a psycho. Someone who's just starting. My gut's telling me it's going to get a lot worse if we don't get lucky. But that's just my gut. What the fuck does it know?"

"I had to ask," Joe said.

He hung up on his end, and I headed back to the station, surveillance tape in hand.

Chapter 4

I got lucky with the surveillance tape. Not slam-dunk lucky, not by any means, but the tape had a time track running in its lower-right corner, and according to that clock a man walked into view at six ten and twenty-three seconds. He had been heading in the direction of the murder and, while still in view of the surveillance camera, stopped, almost as if he were frozen in his tracks. He stood like that for forty-seven seconds, then slowly started to lift up his hands as if he were surrendering. His hands were halfway up when he flinched and stumbled backward, his hands frantically patting at his chest while he stared down at his open palms in disbelief. After several seconds of that, he looked back up and stared straight ahead for several more seconds before turning and running in the direction he had come from, his head lowered as if he were trying to protect it. He wasn't the killer, that much was clear, but he had to have witnessed the murder. From his reaction, the killer must've also turned the gun on him and made him think that he had been shot in the chest. I played the tape a couple of dozen times and nothing else made sense.

When I was satisfied with my interpretation of what I had seen, I printed out a dozen different frames from the tape, then had those blown up so they focused on my witness. He was in his late twenties, maybe early thirties, and was beanpole thin with this gawkiness and nervousness about him that gave you the impression that he'd have trouble making eye contact with anyone. He wore a windbreaker and light-colored slacks, and his hair was long and unruly, as if it hadn't been cut in years, at least not professionally. He was also gaunt and unhealthy looking, but that might've been exaggerated given how scared he was in that videotape. Fear can do that to someone.

I scanned the blown-up photos of the witness into my computer and emailed the images to Thomas Jones, then called him to let him know they'd been sent. I asked if he could try matching our witness against driver license photos in the DMV database. He told me he would, and also that so far he'd had no luck finding any profile matches to our killer.

"I've gone back three years and haven't found anyone cutting off fingers for souvenirs or expediency," he said. "Same with using a .40 caliber for street shootings. The only perps I found favoring that caliber were using it for bank jobs, and they're all currently in the system, two in Attica, another at Southport."

I suggested that maybe we'd have better luck identifying the witness, and asked him how much longer he was going to be on the job. Jones told me he was already on his third hour of overtime and was hoping to be out by ten so he could catch the rest of the game, and asked what I would need him for later. I explained how forensics was going to be dropping off a facial reconstruction drawing of the victim, but for him not to worry about it and to enjoy what he could catch of the game, that we could do an DMV database search on it tomorrow.

"There's a good chance someone will call in identifying her after we get the drawing out over the airways," I added.

"Yeah, well, I wouldn't bet on it," Jones said. "I have a feeling the only luck we're going to have tonight is the Yankees laying waste to Boston. Sox have Pedro Martinez pitching and we've owned his ass the last two years. Yankees' his daddy, right? I'm predicting a sweep."

"A sweep, huh? Wishful thinking. Last year they took us to seven games."

"And they blew it by leaving Martinez in too long," Jones said. "They'll find a way to blow it this year too. It's in their nature. You wait and see."

I told him I hoped he was right, and I got off the phone so he could get started searching for my witness. As I sat at my desk my stomach rumbled. It was already past nine and I hadn't eaten anything since noon. I bought a couple of hot dogs from the vending machine, nuked them, and brought them back to my desk. Other than the mustard I slathered on them, they were tasteless.

I thought about calling Bambi, but I had no idea when I'd be heading back to the hotel. I wanted to get a name for the victim that night if possible. If she was married and her spouse was behind her murder, it would make all the difference talking to him before he had a chance to calm himself down and fine-tune his story. If I called Bambi without being able to give her a definitive time of when I was leaving, I knew she'd put me through the wringer. I wasn't up for her games right then.

I was pouring myself a cup of what had to be New York's worst brewed coffee—something my station house specialized in—when Joe Ramirez came by to let me know that the canine team found the other three fingers in a sewer grate off of Church Street not too far from Chambers. Joe was a few years older than me and he looked about as tired as I felt, his eyes puffy and bloodshot, his suit appearing as if it had been slept in. I knew he hated this late shift, especially having to deal with the type of crimes that come at night. Early on before his promotion we were partnered together for a few years. I liked the guy.

I asked, "Did he pull jewelry off them, or was he just fucking with us?"

Joe made a face at that. "Forensics found skin abrasions consistent with something tight like rings being pulled off of them. Same as with the first finger found. How about you, anything show up on your videotape?"

"Yeah, I found myself a witness."

He raised an eyebrow at that. I brought him back to my desk and played him the videotape, then showed him the blown-up photos I had printed out. His eyes narrowed as he studied them.

"Any idea who he is yet?" he asked.

"Jones is running a match against the DMV database. We'll see what he finds."

"Send these to the FBI," Joe said. "They might have him in their system. And let's get this out over the news."

"I'd like to wait on that," I said. "How about giving me some time to find him on my own? Maybe the killer didn't get a good look at him."

"How wouldn't he have? He pointed a gun right at him!"

"Maybe. We're guessing that from the videotape. But I'd just as soon not let our perp know we're looking for this guy, or give him a better idea of what the guy looks like. I don't want to turn this into a race. I want to find our witness in one piece."

Joe gave me a look as if I was nuts, but he told me he'd give me twenty-four hours. "If you don't know who he is by then we'll have to get him on the news tomorrow night. You going to be hanging around any longer tonight?"

I shrugged, told him I was going to have to. "I want to ID the victim if I can," I said. "Forensics is working on a drawing of what she would've looked like if she still had her face intact. Game plan is to get the drawing on the news and see what happens. I'm also keeping my fingers crossed that we get something from expanding the canvass."

"Might as well uncross them. Martin called in a half hour ago. He and Schaefer found nothing at the subway stations. I've already reassigned them."

"Fuck."

"That was a long shot at best," he said.

"Yeah, I know, but you can't blame a guy for hoping. I'm still going to be hanging around, though, as long as you sign off on the overtime. I want to see what happens with the drawing forensics comes up with. Who knows, maybe our witness calls in the meantime. Or maybe someone else. When I get that drawing out over the news, how about some help chasing down leads?"

Joe shook his head, his thick eyelids half-closed. "Sorry, Stan, I'm squeezed tight as it is tonight. You're on your own with this. No problem as far as the overtime goes. Maybe you can get Phillips to assign you some help tomorrow."

We both knew there was little chance of that unless our perp slaughtered more people—or our victim turned out to be someone with a high enough profile. Until then I was going to be pretty much on my own.

After Joe left I received a call from the medical examiner's office. Cause of death was either of the two bullet wounds to the chest. The gunshot to the back of the head was done post-mortem. I asked her what was used to cut off the fingers.

"A serrated blade," she said. "Something very sharp. The fingers were sliced off cleanly. Right now I'm guessing something military, but we'll be narrowing it down to a make and model, if possible."

The rest of what she told me was what I had already guessed—that the victim was initially shot from in front and had landed on her back; that death had been instantaneous with one hollow-point rupturing her heart, the other obliterating nearly both her lungs; that she appeared to be in her early fifties; and that no blood, hair samples, or skin other than from the victim was found. She told me she'd call back when she identified the type of knife that was used.

A half hour later Thomas Jones called to tell me he was

having no luck matching my witness against anyone in the DMV database and that he was calling it quits for the night. During the next hour while I waited for the facial reconstruction drawing I followed the Yankees game over the Internet and thought about giving Mike a call. I knew he'd be sitting alone in his empty studio apartment watching the game, and the thought of that bothered me, but I didn't call him. By the time Albert Milanaski from forensics delivered me the drawing the good guys were up two to zip.

The drawing was of an attractive woman with a slender face and almond-shaped eyes. Her nose, which had been almost completely missing from the corpse, was narrow and somewhat longish, and her mouth, which also had been blown off the corpse, was drawn as wide and full. The drawing reminded me of Helen Mirren from the British series *Prime Suspect*. The drawing also included the height and weight of the victim: five foot three inches and a hundred and seven pounds. As small as she was, when I had seen her body lying torn and bloodied on the sidewalk I'd had the impression of her being even smaller. Death has a way of diminishing a person.

I faxed the drawing to the local stations and then got on the phone with each of their news directors and was told they'd be using it as well as displaying the tip number that had been set up. That number ended up generating twenty-seven calls—God knows how many we would've gotten if most of New York hadn't been tuned in to the baseball game. I was left by myself to check them out. It took me more than two hours and none of them led anywhere. By the time I was done it was one thirty, and the only thing positive from the night was that the Yankees had won three to one and were up two games to none in the series.

It was one forty-six by the time I got back to my hotel room. An empty bottle of champagne had been left on the carpet, and the remains of a beef tenderloin dinner and what looked like an untouched platter of caviar were on a small table that had been rolled in and set up with a silk cloth and a single red rose in a crystal vase. I picked up the Champagne bottle, rolled the table out of the room, and left it all in the hallway. Bambi was out of it as she lay curled up in bed. I got in and joined her. The bed was about as comfortable as any you could ever imagine and I was tired as hell, but my mind was racing too much for me to get much sleep. I kept playing back that videotape and the look of absolute horror that formed over my witness's face as he stopped dead in his tracks. I also kept seeing the victim lying crumpled on the sidewalk. And I kept wondering when more bodies were going to be found, because I knew our guy wasn't done, not by a long shot. Maybe I ended up getting a total of a half hour's sleep, maybe less. By six o'clock next morning I was both exhausted and wide awake. I was also antsy to get back on the job. Bambi was groggy and still mostly out of it. I took a quick shower and instead of trying one of the hotel's three-hundred-dollar omelets, I grabbed a bagel and cream cheese on the way to the precinct.

Chapter 5

Dozens more calls about the dead woman had come in overnight and it took me until eleven to track them down, but none of them led anywhere. After I finished up with that I went through the list of bookstore employees that I was given, but none of them saw anything, at least that's what they were telling me. Bambi called once to tell me I was an asshole and that she was at that moment enjoying a five-hundred-dollar breakfast and I could go fuck myself for not being there with her. Before I could say a word she hung up on me. I thought about heading back to the hotel but I wasn't up to the icy welcome that she would've had waiting for me, and at the time I still had more leads to look into. Later that morning the ME's office called to tell me they were able to identify the make and model of the knife that was used. It probably would be of little help in tracking down the killer since according to the woman I was talking to it was a popular brand with probably thousands sold over the Internet, and more sold at stores and pawnshops, but when we found our guy and he still had the knife on him it would help with a conviction. I called Phillips to give him the information. He didn't seem too optimistic about it.

I took my lunch break at noon and visited Rich Grissini at St. Vincent's, bringing him an Italian sausage hero slathered in onions and peppers from his favorite takeout place, guessing that at this point he'd be sick of hospital food and badly in need of some unhealthy grease in his system. He looked in pretty rough shape lying in bed in his hospital gown, both eyes blackened as if he'd been in a brawl, his skin tinged a sickly yellow and sagging loosely around his jowls. He peered at me through thin slits, the whites of his eyes bloody. He tried to grin but it was a feeble attempt.

"Hey, look who the cat dragged in," he said in a thin voice, his lips moving about as much as a bad ventriloquist's. "You ain't lookin' so hot. Whatsa matter, you didn't sleep so good last night?"

"How could I, worried about you?"

That got a weak chuckle out of him. I pulled a white plastic hospital chair up next to his bed and unwrapped his sandwich. He licked his lips and asked whether it was from Toscone's.

"What do you think?"

"Fuck, I can't eat it, Stan," he croaked, disappointment settling over his features. "I can't eat nothin'. They got me under the knife at seven. My right hip's fractured in three places and they're going to try to repair it. I'm just hoping I don't need an artificial one, not at my age. You eat the sandwich. It would break my heart for a Toscone sausage hero to go to waste."

My stomach was making noise again. It had been almost five hours since that bagel and cream cheese, and that had been all I'd eaten that day. I took a halfhearted bite out of the hero and chewed it slowly. Rich was six feet and two hundred and ten pounds, but I couldn't believe how shrunken he looked lying there. I couldn't believe how much older he looked either. Christ, he was only five years older than me, but right then you'd never have been able to guess that.

"It hurts pretty bad, huh?" I asked.

He shook his head from side to side an inch or so. "They got me so pumped up with morphine that it ain't so bad. My head hurts more than anything. Fucking concussion. Anyone call in the *sumabitch* who hit me?"

"Not since I checked. You don't remember make and model, huh?"

"I never even saw the *sumabitch* coming. Damn bastard

nailed me out of nowhere." He shifted his eyes away from me for a moment. "Last I remember I was chasin' some purse snatcher across Seventh when bam, lights out. Then I woke up here."

We both knew he was lying. Even if I didn't know him well enough to know what that hard smirk twisting up his lips meant, I'd been partnered with him long enough to know that his favorite pastry shop was on the same block on Seventh where he had been hit. At that time of day he would've been heading over there for a cannoli and an espresso.

"Sorry I couldn't cover for you," he said, his smirk fading and his mouth dropping loosely open. His eyes shifted back to me. "Phillips chase you down yesterday?"

I nodded and went over the Chambers Street shooting, giving him everything I had.

"Sounds like the first of many until you catch the asshole," Rich said. "Fuck, though, at least you got a witness. What do you think happened? Perp shoot at him and miss?"

"Hell if I know. We only found three shell casings at the scene, which is how many bullets the victim took. I guess it's possible he picked up one of the casings to try to keep us from knowing there was another shot fired, but everyone I talked to only heard three shots."

His eyes glazed as he thought about that. "Whole thing sounds so savage," he said. "Cutting off her fingers . . . ripping earrings off her ears . . . blowing her face off . . . I don't know . . ." His voice trailed off. Then his eyes focused back on me, a glum smile showing. "Stan, you should put in for another partner. Even if my surgery goes well, I'm going to be bedridden for months, and I don't think I'm going to be coming back. Right now I'm thinking about putting in for disability and calling it a career."

I put a hand on his shoulder. "We'll talk about this again after you're on your feet again, okay?"

He shrugged and seemed to sink deeper into his bed. "I'm kind of tired, Stan. But before you go at least finish that sandwich. Let me get some pleasure from it."

I was hungry so I ate the rest of the sausage hero. I told him I'd check up on him later, and I was three steps out of St. Vincent's when Phillips called. He had an ID for the dead woman. Her name was Gail Laurent. She was fifty-two, had a home address in Princeton, New Jersey, and was widowed. Her husband had worked as a financial analyst in one of the Twin Towers and died on 9-11 with three thousand other New Yorkers. A daughter of Laurent's, also from Jersey, became concerned when she couldn't get a hold of her mother this morning and contacted the Princeton police, who were on the ball enough to check Laurent's driver's license against the drawing we had put out. Phillips told me the daughter was on her way to the precinct, and it would be best if I got my ass back there pronto, although he didn't say it quite that politely.

Rachel Laurent physically resembled her mother. Petite, with a slender athletic build, and blond hair that was pulled back into a ponytail. Her facial features were similar enough to the drawing to leave no doubt that she was related to the victim. Under normal circumstances she would've been very attractive, but as I talked to her she was a wreck, her eyes puffy and her skin blotchy and raw.

She thought her mother had gone to Manhattan for a day of shopping. She claimed her mother had no enemies and that there was no reason anyone would want to hurt her, and also that her mother had not dated since her father died. She was adamant that her mother was not romantically involved with anyone—that she was close with her mother and would've known if she was. That morning they were supposed to meet for breakfast, and she knew something was wrong when her mother didn't show and she couldn't reach her by cell phone.

I had her give me her mother's cell phone number and tried to get a description of the jewelry her mother might've been wearing. Earlier I had put in a call for a social worker. When she showed up, I had her accompany us while I brought Rachel to the morgue to identify her mother's body. She didn't take it well when she saw the body. I watched helplessly as she broke down, wishing there was something I could do other than promise I'd find the person who had done this, but that was all I could do. I don't think she heard me. She was sobbing too hard.

At four o'clock I was back in Tribeca looking for my witness. I started on Chambers Street and worked my way toward City Hall, showing photos from the videotape to every market, drugstore, coffee shop, and restaurant that I came across. It was at a small grocery store on Murray Street when I found someone who recognized the guy in the photo. The cashier—a girl in her early twenties with piercings all over her face, tattoos wrapping around her neck, and long black hair that reached halfway down her back—told me with a sly smile that the man in the photo was Lisa's boyfriend. She pointed out a small woman in her mid-twenties working behind the sandwich counter.

"What do you mean her boyfriend?" I asked.

"Well, not really," she said, her smile stretching a bit over her private joke. "He comes in like every week and just like stands and gawks at Lisa. And she's the only one he lets wait on him. I tried talking to him once and he like couldn't look at me. Why, what did Mr. Freakazoid do?"

"Mr. Freakazoid? Is that his name?"

She rolled her eyes at me as if I was dense. "That's just my nickname for him. So like come on, what did he do?"

"Nothing. I need to talk to him is all."

I left the cashier to talk to Lisa. At first glance she wasn't much to look at: a short, square body and an equally square-shaped face, as well as reddish-brown hair that was thinning badly and a dead-fish paleness to her complexion. But she had soft eyes, and as soon as she noticed me approaching she showed one of the nicest smiles I had ever seen. Seeing that smile instantly lifted my mood and even made me feel a little weak in the knees. I could see the attraction then. I identified myself, handed her one of the photos, and asked if she knew the man in it.

"That's Zachary," she said in a soft voice that matched her smile. Her forehead wrinkled as a perplexed look formed over her face. "He usually comes here every Wednesday night, but he didn't come in yesterday. Is everything okay?"

"I hope so. I need to talk to him. We believe he witnessed a crime. Do you know his last name?"

Her perplexed look intensified.

"It's funny," she said. "Zachary's been coming here every Wednesday night for over three years. I know he told me his last name once, but I only think of him as Zachary . . ."

"Maybe he used a credit card?"

She shook her head. All at once the skin smoothed out across her forehead and her smile flashed back on. "Lynch, that's his last name. I'm sure of it. Lynch."

"Any idea where he lives?"

"I'm sorry, I don't." Her smile faded and a sadness showed in her eyes. "I don't know much about him except that when he comes here he would like to talk more with me than he does, but I also know I'd make him too uncomfortable if I pressed him. I was worried when he didn't show up last night and I almost called the police, but I was hoping he would show up tonight. Thursdays are usually my night off. Would you please call me when you find Zachary? I would like to know that he's okay. I would ask you to have him call me but I know the idea of that would terrify him."

"Sure."

She wrote down a number on a slip of paper and handed it to me. The smile she gave me damn near broke my heart. She asked if I could be gentle in my dealings with Zachary, that he had a delicate soul. I found myself unable to refuse her and promised that I would within reason. Yeah, I could see the attraction, and it was pretty clear it went both ways.

I called my precinct and waited while they looked up Zachary Lynch's address. There was only one listed in Manhattan and it was a Tribeca address a few blocks from Chambers Street. Lynch must've been on his way to see Lisa when he stumbled upon Gail Laurent's murder.

It was already past six and my stomach was rumbling again. I picked up a couple of slices of cheese pizza and ate them as I walked what I hoped would be the same path Zachary Lynch would take if he was out again walking to the grocery store. I didn't want to miss him if he was.

Chapter 6

Zachary Lynch's address was a one-bedroom walk-up in an early-1900s building off of West Broadway. I knocked on his door, announced myself, and, after several minutes of no one answering, began debating whether to look for his landlord or try for a search warrant. A voice from inside interrupted me by asking if I could slide some identification under the door.

"Open your door a crack and I'll show you my badge and police ID," I said.

"I–I don't have a chain lock," he said.

"For Chrissakes, if you did I'd be able to kick the chain in if I wanted to. Just open the door."

He opened the door enough for me to show him my badge and ID, then he opened the door to let me in. In person he was the same stick he was in the video but was even taller than I had thought—at least six and a half feet. He had the look of someone who was perpetually crouching for fear of cracking his head against a doorway. He was also as nervous and jittery as he appeared on the tape, and when he looked at me he jerked his head away as if he'd been slapped and stumbled back a step. His reaction surprised me enough to ask him what was wrong.

"Nothing," he muttered, averting his eyes from me.

I stared at him for a long moment. He was a mess of discomfort and nervous twitches. I showed him one of the photos from the surveillance tape and he looked it over and nodded, tugging uneasily at his lower lip.

"I guess you'd like to talk to me about that," he said.

He wasn't looking at me so it wouldn't have done much good to nod.

"Yeah, I'd say so," I said, not bothering to hide my sarcasm. Then I remembered the promise I had made a half hour earlier to be gentle. I didn't like that he hadn't bothered to come in on his own after witnessing a woman being butchered, but a promise was a promise. I took a deep breath to calm myself.

"A woman was murdered on Chambers Street yesterday evening, and we're hoping you can help us identify the person who killed her," I continued, my tone softer and as non-threatening as I could make it under the circumstances. "I need to talk with you."

He nodded, still looking away from me, still tugging uneasily on his lower lip. He led the way into a small cramped room that would normally have been a living room but was being used as a workspace. A computer bench with a laptop, printer, and other equipment was pushed against one wall, while books and magazines were stacked all along the floor and against the other walls. He removed a stack of papers from a battered cloth recliner and left that for me to sit on while he took a chair next to the computer. The room had a stale, unhealthy smell to it, as if it badly needed to be aired out. It also needed more light.

Lynch, still unable to look directly at me, gave me a helpless shrug. "I'm not going to be able to help you, officer," he said.

"Detective Green," I said. "And let's talk and decide later how much help you'll be able to give us."

I noticed he had adjusted his computer's webcam so it was pointed at me. While he appeared to be fumbling through some papers he snuck several glances at my image on his computer monitor before bumping the webcam with his elbow so it pointed elsewhere. The whole thing struck me as a peculiar thing to do, but I ignored it. I explained to him what was captured on the surveillance tape.

"At ten minutes past six you were seen on that tape. At the same time a fifty-two-year-old woman named Gail Laurent was being brutally murdered less than a hundred feet away from where you stood. You witnessed her murder."

His nodded dully, more to himself than to me. "I can't help you," he said.

"Why can't you help me?"

"Because I can't tell you what the murderer looks like."

"What do you mean?"

"I don't know what he looks like, so I can't tell you what he looks like. I don't even know the murderer's sex, to be completely honest about it. I can only guess that the murderer was a man."

I stared at him for several minutes while he continued to look down at the floor, a sick smile pulling at his lips. Neither of us said a word. The room made me think of a tomb the way it was so damn stuffy and quiet.

"He tried to shoot you," I said.

He nodded, still smiling sickly. "I think so. At least I think he tried to. I'm not sure what happened. Either his gun jammed or he was out of bullets, but yes, I'm pretty sure he wanted to shoot me."

"Let me get this straight. He's facing you from less than a hundred feet away. Not just facing you, but pointing a gun at you. At six ten yesterday it would still be light out. You're trying to tell me you were unable to get a good look at him?"

He seemed stuck. The sickly smile frozen on his face had morphed into something hopeless. Finally he made up his mind and nodded weakly.

"I had an accident some years ago," he said, his voice flat and barely above a whisper. "It left me changed. Damaged, I guess, at least according to the doctors. They believe it left lesions in the occipital lobe of my brain, so now when I look at people I don't see them as they really are but instead as hallucinations. At least that's their explanation for what happened to me." He looked up at me for a second before flinching and averting his eyes from me. "If I was able to describe the person who did this I would've contacted the police."

"What do you mean you see hallucinations?"

"That's what the doctors tell me I see." He shook his head as if something were fogging it up and he were trying to clear away the cobwebs. "If I told you what I saw it wouldn't help you except to make you think that I was insane."

"Try me."

His eyes were still staring hard at the floor. They had a vacant, distant look, his face wooden.

"I'll tell you what I can," he said. "But I'm sure it's no more than what you already know. I was walking down Chambers Street a little after six, as you already know. I was looking down toward the ground as I usually do when I'm outside my apartment when I heard what must've been two gunshots. They startled me, and by reflex I looked up. That's when I saw someone bent over a woman's body. I guess he was lifting up her head. It was hard to tell exactly with his back to me. I heard another gunshot, this one more muffled than the other two, and saw what must've been pieces of her face flying off of her. After that he was bent over her doing something to her . . . I'm not sure exactly what except he was using a knife . . . maybe cutting off pieces of her?"

"He cut off several of her fingers," I said.

His face ashen, he nodded, again more to himself than to me.

"He noticed me then," Lynch said. "He stood up and pointed his gun at me. I think he tried to fire it. I'm pretty sure he did, but for some reason it didn't go off. I'm pretty sure he tried to shoot me."

"Did he say anything to you?"

Lynch shook his head.

"He didn't say anything when he saw you? Not for you to lift your hands or anything?"

"No. I lifted my hands because he pointed a gun at me. He didn't order me to."

"Describe him to me."

"It wouldn't do you any good."

"Look, I don't care if you're convinced you saw a hallucination. Just describe him as best you can."

I waited for him to answer me. When he didn't I asked him what the guy was wearing. His eyes shifted to a different part of the room as he thought about it.

"A New York Mets sweatshirt. Black, hooded, with 'New York Mets' spelled out in blue letters. Faded blue dungarees. Sneakers, also, but I didn't see the brand, just that they were gray. They looked old."

"You can tell me all that but you can't tell me what he looked like?"

"My perception and cognitive processing with objects is normal. It's with people that it's different . . . I don't see them the way other people do . . . everything's different . . . their size, shape, color, physical characteristics. There's nothing else that I can tell you about this person that could help you."

I didn't know what to make of him. He seemed sincere enough—maybe he even believed the bullshit he was telling me. I mean, fuck, if he was determined to keep from being a witness he could've told me any number of stories that would've been easier to sell: that he was too afraid to look directly at the killer, that he suffered some sort of temporary blindness or, better yet, amnesia, or the old standby, that he was too traumatized to remember anything. Hell, I'd heard them all from my years of being a cop. This was different. He even had me wondering about it.

"What color are my eyes?" I asked.

Without looking at me: "Gray."

"My hair?"

"Brown."

"Is it short or long?"

"About average."

"How come you're able to tell me all that?"

He smiled. It was the defeated smile of someone who knew he was in a losing battle. "Because I saw your picture from your ID," he said. "I also caught you on my webcam so I could verify that you're the same person as your ID."

"So you can see pictures okay?"

He nodded. "It's only when I look at someone in the flesh that I see them . . . differently."

He almost told me then what he thinks he sees, and it was clear it wasn't hallucinations, at least not in his mind. A coolness whispered through my head as I stared at him. "What color are my eyes when you look at me directly?"

His mouth crumbled for a second before he told me that I didn't have eyes, just dark holes.

"What else do you see when you look at me?" I asked, my voice odd, almost as if it were echoing from someplace off in the distance.

"You don't want to know," he said.

"Humor me."

He closed his mouth. He wasn't going to tell me.

The coolness in my head left me light-headed. I stood up shaking my head trying to clear it. Taking him to the station was risky. He was obviously cracked, and if his statement about what the killer was wearing turned out to be on target we wouldn't be able to use it in court with what a defense attorney would do to him on the stand. But if I tried to sell Phillips on the information coming from an anonymous source, he'd rip me a new one. As bizarre as Zachary Lynch seemed, something might click when he looked at the mug shots. It was all I had.

"You're going to have to come with me," I told him.

It was almost as if he'd been punched in the gut the way he reacted to that. His eyes glazed over as he stared at the floor, his mouth hanging loosely open. I considered him for a long moment. I wished there was another way, but there wasn't.

"Detective Green," he said, his voice cracking. "Please. You know I had nothing to do with that woman's death."

"It doesn't matter. I need to bring you in to look at mug shots. If I don't my Captain would look to bust me down a grade, and he'd be sending me right back out to bring you in."

That wasn't exactly true. Knowing Phillips he'd send another detective for Lynch. Me, I'd be too busy being ordered to take a psych evaluation.

"This doesn't make sense," Lynch implored. "What if I was blind? Would I have to come in then?"

"Yeah, well, you're not blind. You were able to give me a full description of what the perp was wearing. I'm sorry, I have no choice in this. I'll try to get you in and out of the station as fast as I can."

"What if I refused to go?"

"Then I'd have to arrest you as a material witness. You'd end up spending the night in lockup before you'd have a chance to see a judge about bail. It wouldn't be pleasant."

He squeezed his eyes shut at the thought of that. He stood up slowly, his legs wobbly, and nearly fell back into his chair before he was able to regain his balance. Perspiration gleamed off of his forehead and neck. As we walked out of his apartment, he suggested that I keep our police sketch artists away from him. That it wouldn't help his credibility as a witness if he was forced to give his recollection of the killer.

"They'd think I was insane if that happened," he said hopelessly.

"Yeah, well, we'll see."

"You realize this isn't going to help you."

I didn't answer him. The idea of going to the station scared the hell out of him, that much was obvious, and I couldn't help feeling lousy about it. It made me feel almost as if I were pulling wings off a fly. We walked in silence.

When we approached my car I tried making small talk, asking him if he was following the Yankees-Sox series. As if to answer me, a gurgling noise came out of him. He had stopped dead in his tracks, his face drained of color and his mouth screwed open as if he were trying to scream. My first thought was that he was having a heart attack, but then I realized his eyes were transfixed on a man walking in front of us. What I thought was a heart attack was raw terror. My heart started racing. The man up ahead didn't have on a Mets sweatshirt; he was dressed more like a lawyer, wearing a bluish-gray pinstriped suit, but there was a reason why Lynch reacted so violently at the sight of him. I reached inside my jacket for my holstered service revolver and took hold of it.

"Is that who you saw yesterday?" I asked in a whisper.

Lynch shook his head.

"What then?"

"Nothing," he said breathlessly.

I looked from Lynch to the man walking down the street and back to Lynch. There was no question that the man terrified him.

"What is it about him? And don't tell me nothing!"

The man had turned the corner and was out of sight. I let my hand slip off my service revolver. Lynch wasn't saying anything, and wasn't going to say anything. Whatever it was that terrified him was locked up tight. I reminded myself that he was an even crazier sonofabitch than I was so far giving him credit for. Christ, I almost chased a man down in the street because of the delusions of an obviously disturbed mind. I wondered briefly how this guy functioned in the world.

Lynch had been holding his breath and finally let it out so that he was now breathing raggedly. When he could he told me he had never seen the person before, and for me not to mind him.

I stood there wondering what I was doing. Lynch was drenched in sweat and his eyes and mouth twitched the way a meth head's would. I almost took him back to his apartment. How could I trust anything coming from him? But as I said before he was all I had. If I didn't get lucky with him I knew my next break in the case wouldn't come until another body was found. And I knew there would be another body. There was too much bloodlust with the last killing.

I asked Lynch if he needed to see a doctor. He told me he didn't. I recited the warning signs of a heart attack and asked if he had any of them. Again, he told me he didn't. Some color had come back to his face and he was breathing more normally.

Neither of us said a word as I drove to the precinct. Once we got there, I led him through the station house and to an interrogation room on the second floor, and the whole way Lynch kept his eyes shielded so he wouldn't have to look at anyone. I sat him down and brought him first a black coffee and a couple of doughnuts, then a stack of mug shot books. He mumbled out a thanks for the coffee and with resigned futility picked up the first of the mug shot books. I left him alone, stood on the other side of a one-way glass partition, and watched as he listlessly studied the photos in the book.

If anything his expression had become more grim. Any hope of one of those photos clicking something inside him was a pipe dream at best.

Phillips had left for the day. He wanted to be updated on any new developments, so I called him at home and told him I found our witness and that we had a description of what the perp was wearing that night. I also let him know that our witness at that moment was at the precinct looking through mug shot books. I left out the part about Zachary Lynch's mental stability, or his claim about seeing hallucinations. Phillips remained quiet while I filled him in. When I was done he commented about how I had to start cutting back on my overtime hours, the implication being that I needed to start working harder during my shift. Not a word about Rich Grissini or how his operation had gone. I thanked him for his encouragement and got off the phone. After that I found Joe Ramirez and filled him in, giving him the whole story, hallucinations and all. He raised a skeptical eyebrow and asked me what I thought.

"What do you mean?"

"Is this an act or is he genuine?"

"I'm pretty sure he's genuine. If he wanted to get out of being a witness there'd be easier ways than faking these hallucinations. Although, who knows, maybe this is all tied to a disability claim from the accident he says he had years ago."

Joe thought that over. "That would be a kick in the pants, wouldn't it? If he'd been faking all these years and can't come clean now because of a claim he's still trying to milk. What do you think, you saw his performance out on the street, how good was it?"

"Pretty damn good. But then again, kind of a funny coincidence for him to go nearly catatonic over the first person we come across."

Joe scowled considering this. Rubbing a thick hand across his eyes, he let loose with a weary sigh and told me that I needed to look into Lynch's background. "Find out if he's even on disability," he said. "Check into this so-called accident. We need to know if he's legit how much of what he's telling us we can trust. If he's really seeing these hallucinations, maybe they're exaggerations of what he's really seeing and we can still get something useful out of him."

"Yeah, I bet that's all it is. Exaggerations. And I've got dark holes instead of eyes."

Joe gave me a deadpan stare.

"You said it, not me." He pushed his chair away from his desk and stood up, straightening his back slowly and grimacing with each vertebra that cracked. "I'll go talk to this guy and see what I think."

I followed Ramirez out of his office. While I walked with him I asked whether any more bodies had turned up with missing fingers and perforations from .40 caliber slugs.

"Not yet," he said. "But give it time."

He disappeared into the interrogation room. I watched through the glass partition as he introduced himself to Lynch. I couldn't help feeling insulted by the way Lynch was able to look at Joe straight on, and at how comfortable he seemed with him. I watched them talk for a few minutes and then headed back to my desk.

Chapter 7

Thursday's one of the nights when I get to call my kids. After our divorce, Cheryl remarried and moved a hundred and ninety miles away to Cumberland, Rhode Island. My lawyer told me I had little chance of joint custody with the hours I worked and the nature of my job, so I didn't fight her on moving our kids out of state, and because of that, she pretty much agreed to what I asked in return. Still, it wasn't as amiable as it might sound. There were a lot of hard feelings between of us—she had her long laundry list of issues, and me, I felt blindsided by the divorce. I guess I shouldn't have. I knew there were problems. The last year or so together I could feel the frost building up, but I was just too damn tired from the job to figure out what was eating at her, and according to Cheryl that was the final straw, the one thing she couldn't forgive me for. I think she was full of shit about that part of it. If she were completely honest about it she'd admit that her biggest issue with me was that she ended up a stay-at-home mom instead of a big-time Hollywood actress like one of her cousins. She always felt as if there were bigger things in store for her and that it was my fault that none of those bigger things ever happened.

I called her at home and her new husband answered, which annoyed me as it always did. They had caller ID and there was no reason why Cheryl couldn't have picked up, but as usual she didn't, and I was stuck trading small talk with the new hubby until he called Cheryl to the phone. When she got on I could feel the frost before she even breathed a word.

"It's past nine o'clock," she said, her voice mostly flat

but with that unmistakable edge she had when she was aching for a fight. "Your visitation order requires you to call by eight."

"I've been on the job. This is the first break I've had in hours."

"If it was important enough to you you would've found the time."

I found myself tensing. The same tired old argument. I took a deep breath and released it slowly, trying to keep from taking the bait.

"Cheryl, not tonight, okay? It's been a long day. How about letting me talk to my kids?"

"Emma's already in bed. I'm not waking her." She hesitated for a long moment before telling me she'd see whether Stevie wanted to talk to me. After a few minutes my son came on. His voice sounded hurt as he mumbled out a hello.

"I guess you're mad at me, huh?" I said. "Here I am over an hour late calling you. I feel bad about it but this is the first chance I've had all night to call."

"Why, what have you been doing?"

"Looking for someone who did a pretty bad thing."

"I'm not a kid. You don't have to talk to me like I'm a kid!"

He was only eleven. He was still a kid as far as I was concerned, but I guess eleven today isn't the same as when I was his age.

"Okay, fair enough. The guy I was out looking for murdered someone."

"Did you find him?"

"Not yet. I found a witness, but I don't think he's going to be able to help me. He doesn't see things the way you and I do. He sees things differently."

"How?"

"I don't know," I said. I took a sip of my coffee and made

a face at the bitterness of it. "I think he sees stuff distorted, kind of as if they're nightmares. Probably the way your Red Sox are seeing things right now after the beating they took last night."

"It was a close game last night. Just wait. They'll bounce back when they come home to Boston."

"Sure they will," I said. "Everyone here's talking sweep."

"Yankees suck," Stevie said.

"Hey, fresh mouth for an eleven-year-old."

"Well, they do," my son argued stubbornly.

"Sweep," I said.

"Dad, I don't want to go to New York for Thanksgiving."

"Why don't you want to come?"

"Because."

"That's not good enough."

He hemmed and hawed for a while, then told me it was because he wanted to hang around with his friends.

"Stevie, I've put in to take time off, and I've got things planned for us. Knicks tickets, Radio City Music Hall—"

"I don't like your girlfriend. That's the reason, okay? I don't want to be there with her."

I squeezed my eyes shut and pushed a hand through my hair. I wasn't up to this either. I couldn't have just one easy conversation with my kid.

"There's nothing wrong with her—"

He snorted, interrupting me. "Yeah, right. *Bambi*. Mom says that's a stripper's name."

"Your mom shouldn't be saying stuff like that, and you and Emma are going to come here for Thanksgiving."

I thought I heard him mutter, "We'll see," but while I was still trying to decipher what it was he had said he told me he had to go and hung up before I had a chance to ask him to tell Emma that I loved her. I thought about calling back, but

I didn't. I was afraid of what I might end up saying to Cheryl and I didn't know what to say to Stevie. Instead I sat and thought about the distance that had developed between my kids and me. It was there with Emma and it was getting worse with my son. Even him becoming a Red Sox fan was part of it. He was five when I took him to his first Yankees game and by the time he was eight he was a diehard fan. His favorite player was Derek Jeter, and like Jeter he wanted to play shortstop and was always trying to copy the way his hero played. And then there was his Yankees jersey: number two, Jeter's number. That used to be his most prized possession. After Cheryl divorced me he threw his jersey away, and all of a sudden he hated the Yankees and loved the Red Sox. I guess in his mind it was a way of striking back at me. The logic of a nine-year-old. For the last year he'd argue with me until he was nearly hoarse that Jeter stunk and Nomar Garciaparra was the best shortstop in baseball. I tried to handle it good-naturedly and with humor, especially after the Red Sox traded Garciaparra late this season, and that just frustrated him all the more. I was at a loss as to how to deal with his obvious resentment toward me.

I sensed someone standing close by and saw Joe Ramirez frowning at me.

"Deep in thought?" he asked.

"Yeah, you could say so."

He handed me a folder. Inside was a police report from six years ago for a convenience store robbery up in Harlem where the cashier was killed and a bystander was shot in the chest. As I read the report more carefully I saw that the bystander was Zachary Lynch, and that he had been clinically dead for six minutes before being revived. The report didn't mention anything about hallucinations afterward or any other lingering mental illness. The case was still open. Lynch had been unable to remember anything about the shooter and there were no other witnesses. Joe had written a name on the front of the folder.

"That's the neurologist who treated him at Mount Sinai," Joe said, referring to the name he had written. "Lynch was a first-year med student at Columbia when he was shot. Since then he taught himself computer programming and works in his apartment doing contract jobs. He's never been on disability. Another thing, his hallucinations are consistent. If we find the perp, he claims he'll be able to identify him. We wouldn't be able to use him in court, but at least we'd know we had the right guy."

"You believe him?"

Joe shrugged. "About how reliable he'd be, I don't know. That's why you need to find out more about his condition. But yeah, I believe he thinks he sees hallucinations."

I tossed the folder onto my desk. "Good work, captain," I said. "You got a lot out of the guy, but then again, he felt comfortable with you and was willing to open up. Me, I've got these dark holes for eyes."

Joe gave me a funny look. "You okay, Stan?"

"It's been a long day, that's all."

"Why don't you call it a day, then? Christ, you've pulled a double shift as it is. It's not going to do any good having Lynch look through mug shot books or having him talk to a sketch artist. I'll have a uniform run him back to his apartment. Why don't you go home."

"Nope," I said. "It was traumatic enough for him having me bring him here, God knows what one of our uncouth uniforms would do to the guy. I'll take him back. Besides, it's on the way to Brooklyn."

Joe told me to try to get some rest, that I looked like I needed it. I could've said the same to him—with the way his eyes looked he could've had soot rubbed underneath them—but I just wished him a quiet night and got up to retrieve

Zachary Lynch. When I walked into the interrogation room, Lynch caught a peek at me and flinched the same as before. I couldn't help feeling pissed off about it, especially after the way he had reacted earlier with Joe. Again, it had been a long day.

"Put the book down," I told him. "We're done. I'm taking you home."

"I'm sorry I couldn't help," he said.

I didn't bother responding. Like before, he shielded his eyes while I led him through the station. Neither of us said a word to each other until we were a few blocks from his apartment. When we were stopped at a red light I asked him what he saw when he looked at me.

He showed a sad reluctant smile. "What difference does it make, detective?"

"None," I said. The hell with this. The hell with sitting with this guy any longer than I had to. I stuck a pair of flashing reds on my roof, then hit the accelerator and sped through the traffic light. A few tires squealed as cars braked to keep from hitting me. The hell with them also. After I let Lynch out in front of his apartment I drove over to St. Vincent's to check on my partner. He was still in surgery. His wife, Mary, and their three kids were holed up in the waiting room. Mary told me it could be several more hours before they knew anything and that I should go home and she'd call me later. She didn't look like she was holding up too well and neither did her kids. I sat and waited with them. At twelve thirty a surgeon came out to tell us that Rich was in post-op and that the surgery had gone well. Something about his manner seemed off to me, like he was holding something back. Maybe he was just tired. Anyway, he was only allowing immediate family to go in to see Rich. I offered Mary to wait for them so I could drive them back to Queens, but she told me that wasn't necessary, that she and the kids were going to be spending the night with a cousin of Rich's who lived a few blocks from the hospital. I left then, and it was one o'clock before I was crossing the Brooklyn Bridge and heading back to my apartment in Flatbush.

A note was taped on the outside of my door from Bambi reiterating that I should go fuck myself. I took it down and went inside. It was about what I was expecting, which was the reason I didn't call her back during the day. I didn't bother checking whether her clothes and other stuff were still in the apartment. I knew it would all be gone. I went to the fridge, took out a couple of Miller Lites, and brought them to the living room. I sat on the sofa, cracked one of the Millers open, and drank it slowly.

It was funny. With Bambi gone it was as if she'd never been there. Almost as if I had never known her. It was a coin toss whether I'd see her again or whether this was simply a dramatic statement on her part, but at that moment I didn't much care either way. I finished the first beer and started on the second. It was hard at that moment to believe that she had lived in my apartment the past nine months. Same was true with Cheryl and my two kids. Even though I had pictures of them scattered about, none of it seemed real. It was as if they were ghosts, really nothing more than whispers, and it was hard to believe that any of them had ever lived there. Same wasn't true with my parents or Mike. I could feel their presence. It had been my parents' apartment for more than forty years, and after Pop died I stayed to take care of Mom. When her mind started to go and we needed to move her to a nursing home where she could be better taken care of, I took over the apartment. It was under rent control and I could afford it, but that was only part of the reason. Even though Cheryl always complained about the place being too small and old-fashioned, and even though Bambi wanted us to move to Manhattan, I wasn't going to give up the apartment. I felt a connection that was too important for me to give up.

As I drank my second beer, I looked around the room. Most of the furniture in the apartment had been my parents'. The bookcases, the dining room table and chairs, the china cabinet, the dresser bureaus. The sofa I was sitting on had been reupholstered several times by my parents and once by me, as had the loveseat. There was just too much of my life in all of that furniture to give any of it up. Too many memories.

I finished my second beer, and thought about calling Mike. I wanted badly to talk to him, but it was late and he had enough problems of his own. Sitting there I felt more numb than tired. After a while I closed my eyes.

Chapter 8

Friday, October 15, 2004

It was raining the next morning, kind of a cold wet unpleasant October day. They were supposed to play the third game of the playoffs in Boston that night, but if the weather was anything like this they were going to have to cancel it.

I had a late start that morning. Before heading to the station I stopped off to visit Rich. He was in plaster from his chest to his knees, and he looked miserable lying there. He had dropped even more weight since the day before, and the way the skin sagged along his face I couldn't help thinking of a tire that had been deflated. I tried joking around with him and he halfheartedly tried giving it back, but he was too tired and too doped up on pain medication to keep his eyes open, and after a short while he dozed off. I couldn't shake this feeling that something more was wrong with him than recovering from a surgery. Mary came in as I was leaving, and from the look she gave me she must've picked up that same vibe. I didn't know what else to say to her other than lying about how Rich seemed to be in good spirits earlier.

I had turned my cell phone off before visiting Rich. After getting back in my car I turned it on and saw that I had a message from Phillips. He wanted to know why there wasn't an artist sketch from our witness. I turned my phone off again and sat quietly in my car for several minutes wondering what the fuck I was doing. In the end I called Phillips back and explained that Lynch wasn't a reliable witness and there was no point in trying to get a description from him. From the stone-cold silence I received back from Phillips I knew that Joe Ramirez had already filled him in on that.

"It's ten thirty," Phillips said at last, breaking his silence. "Where are you?"

"I've been visiting Rich. He had surgery last night in case you weren't aware."

"Your shift starts at eight," Phillips said.

"Poor guy's not looking too good, but thanks for asking."

"Did you hear what I said?"

"Yeah, I heard what you said. The last two days I've put in thirty hours. You can cut me some slack here."

"Thirty hours, huh? And where are you with the case?"

I almost hung up on him. He knew damn well where I was with the case. I had left him a detailed report the night before, and he had Joe's also. I took a deep breath and let it out slowly, trying to quiet the noise rattling in my head. I wasn't going to play his game.

"I found a witness," I said. "The guy turned out to be mostly no good, but how was I supposed to know that?"

"You seen the papers the last two days?"

"Yeah, I've seen them."

"How about you quit your excuses and get somewhere with this case!"

"Here's a novel idea," I said. "Why don't you assign me some help so I'm not working a major crime by myself?"

"You have a partner. You want a new one, put in a request. And from now on I want you here at the start of your shift. No more excuses. You don't like it and want to work elsewhere, put in for a transfer. I'll be glad to sign it."

Phillips hung up on me. I called him back. I'd had it with his bullshit.

"You want this case solved before more bodies start piling up, then put more manpower on it," I said. "You can either do it now or when you're forced to put a task team together."

"You don't know there are going to be more bodies," he stated as if he actually meant it. We both knew that Gail Laurent wasn't going to be the last person our perp killed, and we both knew she wasn't the first either.

"There already are more bodies," I said. "You know as well as I do we just haven't found them yet. Our perp was out of bullets when he tried to shoot our witness. A .40 caliber is going to hold between ten and fifteen rounds in a clip. So what happened to the other rounds?"

"The gun could've jammed," Phillips tried arguing. "Or maybe he did some target practice first."

The gun jamming was unlikely. It happens but not often, especially with newer model automatics. As far as our perp firing off some practice rounds, yeah, probably, but you're not going out hunting without reloading first, and our perp was out hunting that day. I didn't bother mentioning any of that to Phillips—he knew it as well as I did. I just sat and waited for him to say something and after half a minute of silence he reluctantly asked what I needed. I gave him a list, the top item being sending officers out canvassing the area for anyone seeing a guy in a black hooded Mets sweatshirt, faded jeans, and gray sneakers.

"I thought the witness was unreliable," Phillips complained.

"He mostly is, but this is worth checking out. At least Captain Joe Ramirez thought so."

I hadn't discussed that with Joe, but I knew he'd back me up. I also knew Phillips would hate putting resources on this type of canvass. This was two days old already, and a man in jeans and a hooded Mets sweatshirt would've blended unseen into the area. If anyone was going to remember seeing him we would've known already because they also would've had to have seen something else to have made an impression, something like a bloody knife or an automatic sticking out of his pants. But there were video cameras in the subways stops, and maybe other store surveillance cameras in the area that could've picked him up. While it was a long shot, something could come of it. He had me tell him what I planned to do while he wasted manpower on this. After I did he told me I had my canvass and hung up abruptly.

The night before I had called Mount Sinai to confirm that Dr. Wallace Brennan still worked there and to get his hours. Six years earlier he had been Lynch's neurologist. I called back and was able to get him on the phone. He told me he wouldn't be able to discuss a patient without a signed consent form, but that he'd have the hospital fax a form to my station. We agreed on a time when he'd be available to talk with me, assuming I had Lynch's consent.

I drove back to the station to pick up the form, and while I was there I called Lynch. He told me he'd sign whatever I needed him to but I was wasting my time—that Dr. Brennan would tell me the same that he had been telling me. After I got off the phone with Lynch I called Rachel Laurent to make arrangements to meet her at her mother's house.

Zachary Lynch was right, at least about Dr. Wallace Brennan giving me the same story.

"His brain was deprived of oxygen for over six minutes," Brennan said in explaining the damage that had occurred. "He was fortunate that he didn't end up brain dead from the incident." Brennan frowned, adding, "At least in a way. I'd have to think the damage Mr. Lynch suffered provides more than its share of challenges. Imagine living out your life in a horror movie, seeing everyday people as demons and monsters."

I consulted a notepad. I had done some research and

knew that the occipital lobe was responsible for the visual processing within the brain. I asked Brennan whether he confirmed that Lynch had suffered lesions there.

Brennan's frown deepened. "That type of damage wouldn't be detectable by an MRI. We couldn't be absolutely sure of the existence of those lesions without the benefit of an autopsy, but they would explain his altered perceptions."

"I don't get it," I said. "How come this only happens when he looks directly at someone and not a photograph? And why does he only distort people and not objects?"

Brennan shrugged. "It's peculiar but it's explainable. We performed enough tests on Mr. Lynch to verify that this is what is happening. And it's not distortions. The way his brain visually processes people isn't as some twisted or misshapen representation of them, but as something completely unique. He may look at two people, both six feet tall, and see one of them as under two feet in height, the other as a nine-foot monster."

"And these hallucinations—"

"Visual interpretations," Brennan corrected me.

"They're consistent? He sees the same person the same way every time?"

"That's correct."

"And you say he sees people as demons and monsters . . ."

"Not everybody," Brennan said, smiling patiently, "but a high enough percentage of people to make life a challenge for him."

"And what about the other people, the people he doesn't see as demons and monsters—does he see them normally?"

"No. He has an equally altered visual interpretation of them."

"What about hypnosis?" I asked. "Would that help in getting him to remember what someone really looked like?"

"Not at all. It's not a matter of a memory locked away in

his unconscious. These visual interpretations of his are as real to him as how you're seeing me right now."

"How about his account of what a person is wearing? Can we trust that?"

Brennan smiled weakly. "As much as you could from any other witness."

I was going to leave it at that. Brennan couldn't tell me anything that contradicted what Zachary Lynch had said, but there was something I was curious about. I asked Brennan how Lynch would see identical twins.

"That's an interesting idea." Brennan chewed absent-mindedly on a thumbnail as he thought about it. "I don't have the answer to that and I don't see how it would help you if I did, but it would be interesting to know that. Yes, very much so."

I could see the wheels spinning behind Brennan's eyes, probably as he was trying to figure out how to convince Lynch to agree to this type of test. He was right—knowing that wouldn't help as far as Lynch as a potential witness went—but for some reason I wanted to know the answer to that also. It was twelve thirty. I had arranged to meet Rachel Laurent at her mother's house at two, and I had an hour and a half to drive to Princeton. I thanked Brennan for his time and left him pondering how a man with a damaged occipital lobe might perceive identical twins.

Chapter 9

Rachel Laurent followed me as I went through her mother's house. At one point she asked whether I'd like some coffee, and the effort in that seemed to sap the strength out of her. While I searched her mother's bedroom she sat in a corner, somberness masking her features. I found a closet full of men's clothing, but she looked it over and told me it was her father's.

"I guess my mom couldn't give up that piece of my dad," she said, her mouth weakening and wetness showing around her eyes.

Other than that clothing and a shaving kit in the bathroom, which Rachel also told me had been her dad's, there was nothing to indicate a man had been spending time there. Nothing to indicate Gail Laurent had been involved in a romantic relationship or had problems with anyone. Rachel gave me permission to turn on her mother's computer, and there was nothing suspicious from her email or from the websites she had bookmarked. I now had little doubt that Gail Laurent's murder was the random act of a serial killer. It had been too brutal to have been a simple robbery, and unless it turned out to be contract killing made to look like something else it seemed the work of a psychopathic mind. So far it appeared that the only person who would benefit financially from Laurent's death was her daughter, Rachel, and I had a hard time believing she could be responsible. Her father's death on 9-11 resulted in a large financial settlement, which Rachel told me her mother insisted on sharing equally with her. She was an only child, and while she was going to be inheriting a large sum from her mother—the house alone, a stately four-bedroom brick colonial in an upper-class neighborhood, was probably worth at least a million—I just couldn't see it. She'd have to be putting on an amazing act and be one ice-cold sociopath otherwise. Still, I was going to have to look into it and check her phone records and finances.

When I was done with my search I told Rachel that I would have that coffee she offered earlier if it were still available and if she were willing to join me.

We went downstairs to the kitchen. She found some French roast to brew, and while we waited for the coffee she joined me at a small glass table. She looked so worn out emotionally that I hated asking her how much she was going to be inheriting from her mother's estate. She gave me a puzzled look and told me she wasn't going to be inheriting anything.

"I thought you were an only child?" I asked.

"That's right." From her blank expression it hadn't dawned on her yet why I was asking about the money, or maybe it had and she was just too exhausted to care. "I was only willing to take money from my dad's settlement if my mom agreed to leave her money to the types of charities my dad would've wanted to support. I couldn't stand the idea of becoming rich off my parents' deaths. I also didn't want to think about losing my mom, and that seemed the best way to distance myself from the idea of it. So we worked out her will together. I did the same with my own will."

"That includes the house?"

"That includes everything my mom owned."

"Anyone at these charities know money was being left to them?"

She gave me a puzzled look and shook her head.

The coffee had finished brewing. I got up and poured two cups and brought them back to the table. She just didn't seem to have the energy left to do that.

"I'd like to see a copy of the will," I said. "Also your phone and bank records. It will help move things along."

She nodded. "I'll call our lawyer and arrange for him to send you a copy of whatever you need. I'll get my records together also and send copies to your precinct."

We drank our coffee quietly for several minutes. I broke the silence by asking whether she had a date yet for the funeral. She told me it was that Sunday.

"I don't have much family left," she said, struggling to keep her tears held back. "My grandparents are gone, and I only have an uncle on my father's side. There won't be many people attending. Just Uncle Robert and friends."

"I'll have to be there," I said.

She gave me a questioning look.

"In case anyone shows up who you don't know . . ."

I didn't spell out that her mother's killer was the person I was concerned about showing up at the funeral, but she got the idea and her mouth started to tremble. She put a hand to her face as tears leaked from her eyes. I sat frozen, wanting to comfort her but not sure how to do that, not even sure if it was possible. In the end, I sat silently drinking my coffee and feeling like a fraud and a coward. Eventually she fought back her grief and composed herself. When she could talk she gave me the time and place of her mother's funeral. I left her then.

While walking to my car I held my jacket collar closed and lowered my head against the rain. It was a miserable day, and it pretty much matched my mood. While on I-95 North heading back to Manhattan I almost called Cheryl to let her know how much I appreciated her poisoning my kids against me and Bambi, but I had just enough wits about me to realize what a mistake that would be. Instead I fumbled with my notepad until I found Zachary Lynch's number, then called him. First time I got his answering machine. I left a message that I knew he was home and for him to pick up to save me a trip to his apartment. I called again afterward, and this time he picked up.

"Detective Green?" he asked, an uneasiness in his voice.

"Yep," I said. "I wanted to ask you again about your being able to identify the killer if you saw him in the flesh. You're sure you could do that?"

He hesitated before telling me that he thought he'd be able to. "Why . . . have you found someone?"

"Not yet. The woman who was murdered, her funeral is this Sunday. I'd like you to accompany me. It's possible the killer might show up. Sometimes they like to do that."

"I don't know . . . I'm not sure I could . . . That would mean I would have to look at everyone . . . You don't know how hard that would be for me, detective . . . I'm not sure I'm up to doing that."

"It could be our best chance to catch this guy before he kills someone else. I'm sure you'd like to do everything you can to help us."

"I would, detective, but what you're asking of me . . . I don't know."

According to the odometer my speed had edged past ninety. I didn't trust these New Jersey staties to pay any special attention to my NYPD badge. The way my day was going they'd write me up just the same as the next guy. I eased my foot off the gas.

"Lisa told me you were a good guy," I said.

"Lisa?"

"Yeah, from Strombolli's. Where you go food shopping every Wednesday night. So what do you say, Zach? Will you help us?"

"What . . . what else did Lisa say?"

"I'll tell you Sunday. Okay?"

He cleared his throat and in a hoarse whisper told me he

would go with me. I let him know what time I'd be picking him up and suggested he wear a suit and tie. After getting off the phone with Lynch I called Phillips. So far the canvass had turned up nothing of interest. They had collected several dozen videotapes and gone through half of them.

"Anything from the daughter?" Phillips asked.

"Nothing."

"Is she involved?"

"I don't think so, but I'm checking her out."

"Anyone else benefit from Laurent's death?"

"Not that I can see."

He grunted. "So if you're right, this killing was random."

If I was right. Sonofabitch had to stick that in there.

"Yeah. Look, it's already four thirty and I'm still stuck on 95 North trying to get out of Jersey. As you mentioned to me the other day, I've already put in enough overtime this week. I'm calling it a day."

"We've still got videotapes to look through," he complained sourly.

"Good thing you've got other resources on this, huh? I'll be in tomorrow at eight."

I hung up before he could say anything else, and for good measure I turned off my phone.

With the rain beating down and the start of rush hour, traffic back to New York was brutal, and it wasn't until eight that I was able to pick up a pizza and get back to my apartment in Flatbush. There were no messages from Bambi, not that I expected any. I took a couple of beers from the fridge, turned on the set, and saw that the Yankees game was being rescheduled for Saturday—that the weather in Boston had been just as lousy as it had been in New York.

I left the set on but barely paid attention to it as I ate the pie and drank my beer. I guess I wanted the background noise and wasn't really up to being left alone with my thoughts.

After a long while I turned off the TV. In the quiet of my apartment my thoughts started drifting to the murdered woman and the other bodies that were sure to be coming; to my partner, Rich, lying in his hospital bed encased in plaster but having something more wrong with him than just that; to Bambi and her discontentment; and finally to my failed marriage and my kids. The quiet became too much for me. I picked up the phone and called this guy I knew, Earl Buntz, who for the right price could get his hands on anything.

"Three tickets for tomorrow night's game in Boston," I said. "How much?"

"Ah, jeez," he moaned. "Stan, that's a tall order. It was a bitch of a game to get tickets for in the first place, but fuck, with tonight's game rained out it's going to be near impossible. Tickets have all been snatched up already, you know?"

"Find some."

Earl sighed and told me he'd see what he could do. Ten minutes later he called back. He found three primo lower-box seats along the third base line.

"How much?"

"A future favor, that's all. Enjoy the game."

"I'm not doing that. How much?"

He let out a low painful moan, sort of as if he were having his teeth worked on. "Stan, if you want to pay cash I guess that's your business, but it's not going to be cheap."

"How much."

"A thousand bucks apiece. Three grand. And I won't be making a dime off this. My good deed for the year. So you want them?"

Fuck. Three grand. My share of the cost of taking care of Mom as well as my child support payments had been bleeding me pretty dry. I wasn't sure how I was going to come up with three grand, but I told him to get me the tickets.

"You sure you don't want to owe me a favor instead?"

"Yeah, I'm sure. It might be a few days before I can get you the money, but I'm good for it."

"Seeing how you're Mike's little brother, I can let it slide a week," Earl said. "After that it's going to have to be five points. You okay with that? You're sure you'd rather not just watch the game on TV?"

I told him I was sure. He gave me another heavy sigh and told me he'd have the tickets run over to my apartment by ten the following morning. Before hanging up he told me to say hello to Mike the next chance I had. After I got off the phone with him I called Cheryl. This time she picked up first instead of making me go through her new hubby.

"I don't know why Stevie said that the other day. I haven't been saying anything about your girlfriend's name—"

"Forget it," I said. "She's out of the picture now anyway. I want to take Stevie and Emma to the game tomorrow night."

"What game?"

"The baseball game. Yankees, Red Sox."

There was dead silence on her end while she digested that. When she finally spoke I could picture the tightness pinching her mouth as she said it was going to be around forty degrees out tomorrow night, and she didn't feel the ballpark would be a good environment for a seven-year-old.

"Emma will be fine," I said. "Just bundle her up. There will be younger kids than her there. And it will be a memory she'll never forget."

Another hesitation. Then her voice even more pinched she asked, "Do you already have tickets?"

"Yeah. Lower-box seats along the third base line. They're supposed to be good seats."

"How can you afford them?"

"That's my business," I said. "I've never been late with my child support, have I?"

"I've never said you have. I'm just asking, that's all. If you want to do something for Stevie and Emma there are better ways to be spending your money."

"Not for me. Not right now, anyway. Look, I'll be picking them up at three so I can take them out to dinner before the game."

I could almost hear the thoughts running through her head while I waited for her to answer me. When she finally did her voice sounded brittle and with that edge to it that I knew so well.

"I don't want to get their hopes up," she said. "I don't want to tell them about this only to have you cancel at the last second."

"I'm not going to be canceling."

"You better not. You have this one last chance, Stan. Not just with me but with them. If you let them down on this—"

"Chrissakes, give me a break, okay?" I told her, and then got off the phone before she could raise my blood pressure any higher than she already had. The only times in the past I had ever disappointed my kids by not showing up to something was when I was on the job and had no choice about it. She knew that as well as I did, and I was sick of her throwing it in my face.

I was too worked up to hang around my empty apartment. I got in my car and drove back to Manhattan. Joe Ramirez seemed surprised to see me when I walked into his office.

"You can't keep away, can you, Stan?" Joe said, shaking his head, a thin smile showing.

"Not tonight anyway." I filled him in on what I learned from Lynch's neurologist and my gut take on Rachel Laurent. He nodded, only half paying attention to what I told him since Phillips must've included all of that in his day report.

"We've still got a stack of videotapes," Joe said. "If you want to help out I'll sign off on the overtime."

"Nothing yet, huh?"

"Nothing." Joe shrugged and gave me a tired look. "Assuming that Lynch is right about what our perp was wearing, we're still wasting our time. Odds are our guy ditched his Mets sweatshirt after he was spotted. We've been checking trash receptacles in the area, and nothing yet, but city trash collection in that area was last night so we're pretty much fucked there. Checking those tapes is about as useful as sitting around holding our dicks, but I guess right now that's the best we got."

I thought he was being overly pessimistic, but given the mood he was in I wasn't going to argue with him. There was a chance we'd catch the sonofabitch on tape.

"I'm surprised we haven't found any more bodies yet," I said.

"Yeah, so am I."

I told Joe that since the tapes were my idea I'd help out with them. I turned to head toward the video room, then asked him without much hope whether there'd been any luck tracking down sales for the make and model of the knife that the perp had used. Joe's expression turned more dour as he told me that our Crime Center was still trying to track down Internet sites selling that model, but we both knew it wouldn't help much even if we were able to get all those sites to hand over their customer lists. We'd still have all the pawnshop and back alley sales that we would never find out about, and that would be the vast majority of sales. It would be an amazingly lucky break if we found our guy this way—about the same as drawing four aces from a pair—but sometimes you do get lucky.

What we used as a video room had been the smallest of our interrogation rooms when I started with the department fifteen years ago. Now it had four TV monitors and video players, as well as computer equipment for printing images from the video and for transferring the images to a format the computer could deal with. Matt Chase and Allen Wang were in there going through videotapes. Wang worked the same day shift I did. He gave me a bleary-eyed look and nodded to me before turning back to his monitor. He had a kid in college and could use the overtime. Chase appeared even more pissed off than his usual self as he stared at his screen. "What a way to waste a night," he complained bitterly. "I heard this was your idea, Green. Thanks a lot, pal. I could be out there doing some good instead of this shit."

"Anytime," I told him. "By the way, Yankees game was rained out."

"Yeah, I heard."

"No Mets fans yet, huh?"

Chase didn't bother answering me. Wang shook his head.

There was still a large stack of tapes to go through. I picked up three of them and took them to one of the open stations. Since, as Joe had pointed out, there was a good chance our perp had ditched his sweatshirt after the killing, the protocol we were using was to search through the tapes from two hours before the murder to a half hour afterward. It was tedious work. Even with fast-forwarding through the tapes, I still had to pause every time someone came into view wearing a dark jacket, sweater, or sweatshirt to make sure it wasn't a guy wearing a black hooded Mets sweatshirt. It ended up taking four hours to get through those three tapes, and when I was done I was feeling as bleary-eyed as Wang looked. At that point it was one o'clock. Joe had brought in pizza and I ended up hanging around another hour and a half to help finish off the remaining tapes.

"Fucking waste of a night," Chase muttered as he turned off his monitor. I couldn't disagree with him, although given the mood I was in spending the night occupied with busy work was better than the alternative, namely sitting alone in my apartment and feeling like a failure. Anyway, at least I had a clean conscience that all current leads for the case had been explored, at least to the extent I was capable of doing. That would help when I saw Rachel Laurent at her mother's funeral. The six hours of overtime would also help to make a dent toward paying off those baseball tickets—after deductions a smaller dent than I'd wish, but at least it'd help somewhat.

I left the station and was back in my Flatbush apartment by three, and in bed ten minutes later. As exhausted as I felt I was again too wired to sleep and had too many thoughts running through my mind. I couldn't shake this uneasiness inside me. It had been two months since I had seen my kids, and the thought of seeing them the next day mostly scared the shit out of me, especially thinking about the indifference I'd been hearing in their voices lately. I couldn't help feeling as if Cheryl was right, that this was my one last shot with them, that if I waited until Thanksgiving it would be too late.

At some point I must've dozed off for a couple hours. The last thing I remembered before the alarm woke me at nine was looking over at the clock and seeing it was past seven and thinking how I was going to be dead on my feet later. All the two hours of sleep did was leave me feeling drugged. I stumbled out of bed. I had a busy day ahead of me.

Chapter 10

Saturday, October 16, 2004

The tickets were delivered as promised, and by ten fifteen I was in my car trying to navigate out of Brooklyn and toward Rhode Island. It took me nearly an hour to drive the nineteen miles to get to I-95 North, but after that I was cruising along at a good clip. I felt nervous but also excited. I still hadn't figured out how I was going to raise three grand, but I decided to worry about that later. At eleven thirty Phillips called me on my cell. I didn't want to answer his call. Fuck, I knew it was a mistake, but I couldn't help myself. I knew what it would be. Another body had been found. This time it was a man in his early to mid-thirties. He had been shot three times in the chest and both his ring and pinky fingers on his left hand were cut off. As with Gail Laurent, hollow-points were used and a good chunk of his face was blown off by a single shot fired at close range to the back of his head. Given the powder burns the muzzle was pushed up against his skull. In this case the body had been left in a dumpster behind a luxury apartment building at an Upper West Side address. The medical examiner was still working to narrow down the time of death, but it appeared the man had been dead for several days.

"How long had the body been in the dumpster?" I asked.

"Forensics is still working on that."

"Okay, keep me informed," I said. "I'll be back in the city tomorrow. I've got Gail Laurent's funeral in the afternoon, but I can spend some time on this tomorrow morning, at least as long as you're okay with signing off on the overtime."

In the background I could hear Phillips's fingers drumming hard along his desk.

"Uh-uh," he said, "I need you back here now. I'm putting together a task force, and I need you here for the debriefing."

I almost hung up on him. I thought about claiming the cell signal had broken up and I couldn't hear what he was saying. I wanted to. Fuck, did I want to. Instead I heard myself in a strained voice telling him I had plans that I couldn't change.

"If you want to keep working for the department you better find a way to change them."

"Are you serious?"

"What do you think."

Phillips didn't utter the latter as a question. There was no misunderstanding the intent in his voice. Then again, we'd had an uneasy relationship from the beginning. There are some guys you just don't like on sight, and for whatever reason that was the way it was with both of us, him maybe more than me, although not by much.

"You don't need me for this," I said. "You know everything I do."

"You've been working the case full-time," Phillips said, making no attempt to hide the exasperation in his voice. "You're going to be here for the debriefing. Three o'clock. Understood?"

For a long moment I thought about telling him to go fuck himself, but I knew he was serious about drumming me out of the force if I didn't show up, and the thought of not being a cop anymore hit me hard. What would I do? Private security, cab driver, office work? The idea of any of that left me in a cold sweat. Instead, I calculated out how much time I needed to drive to Cheryl's, and then from there to Boston.

If I kept a heavy foot on the gas and gave my best impersonation of Jeff Gordon I could make the drive from New York to Cumberland, Rhode Island, in two and a half hours. From there to Boston would be another hour, plus a half hour to park and get the kids into their seats. Things could still work out as long as I left Manhattan by four; it would just mean I'd have to buy the kids hot dogs at the game instead of taking them out to dinner first.

"Can you move the time up?" I asked.

"No. The time's set. I've got FBI agents coming at three."

Phillips hung up on me. I drove on for another ten miles trying to decide what to do, but every time I seriously considered leaving the force I began to panic, my heart pounding away in my chest like crazy. I called Cheryl and told her that I had to change plans and wouldn't be there until six thirty.

"About what I was expecting," she said, her voice oddly flat.

"What's that supposed to mean?"

"Nothing, except that I was expecting this call, just like I'm expecting another one from you at six thirty."

"Yeah, well, sorry to disappoint you but I'm going to be there at six thirty like I'm saying I'm going to be."

"Sure you will."

I almost threw the phone out the window. Instead I gritted my teeth and flipped it shut. I pulled off at the next exit and headed back to the city.

A .40 caliber with hollow-point bullets had been used on the latest victim and the lab guys were still working on determining whether the same gun was used in both shootings. The medical examiner's office was able to narrow the time of death to between one and four AM Wednesday morning, and they also were able to figure out that the body had been lying in the dumpster for at least forty-eight hours, untouched during that time except for being chewed up a bit by rats. Trash pickup for the apartment building wasn't until Tuesday, and the body wouldn't have been discovered until then if it hadn't started to get ripe. Nothing smells quite as bad as a decomposing body.

So far that was all we knew: the caliber of the gun used, roughly when the killing happened, and how long the body had been sitting in the dumpster. That was it. There was no identification left on the body and the victim's remaining fingerprints weren't in the system, nor was there enough of his face left for us to do much without a forensic reconstruction drawing. No one had been found in the apartment building who saw or heard anything. There was no forensic evidence that the body had been killed at the site, and no idea where the victim's missing fingers were. A canine team was brought to the area but found nothing related to the murder. All we really knew was that our killer had had a busy Wednesday.

Three rounds were used on Gail Laurent, four rounds on our new victim. I was still expecting another body to be found, maybe two, depending on whether the clip for our killer's .40-caliber automatic held ten or fifteen rounds. And it would be far worse if our killer had two or more fully loaded magazines.

After being briefed on the second killing I sat at my desk, my leg bouncing up and down nervously as I kept glancing at the time waiting for three o'clock to come. The one thing this other killing showed was that the fingers weren't cut off for expediency. If he was spending time moving a body to a dumpster, he wasn't cutting off fingers because he was too rushed to pull jewelry off of them. He was doing it because he enjoyed it. This was his thing, his signature: cut off some fingers and blow away a good chunk of the victim's face. There was no question anymore that we were dealing with someone who got off on what he was doing. The one saving grace was that he had been spotted. He didn't know that we couldn't identify him and maybe that would keep him holed up, afraid that we were out there after him. Maybe it would buy us enough time to catch him before he worked up enough nerve to go out hunting again.

Joe Ramirez wandered over to my desk with a decent cup of coffee for me that he had brought in from outside. I was surprised to see him. His shift ended at six AM and he should've been in bed getting some sleep, but it made sense with his knowledge of the case for Phillips to have included him on the task force. I grunted out some thanks for the coffee, and while I sipped it I told him my theory about how this pretty much left us with a serial killer.

"Maybe," he said. "Then again, maybe not. We could have some joker trying to cover up a murder with a second one."

I drank more of the coffee and shook my head. I noticed Joe peering at my leg bouncing up and down and I forced myself to sit still.

"I don't think so," I said. "Gail Laurent was murdered out in the open. Hers was probably the riskier of the two, and we would have had him if we caught any sort of break with our witness. So far I haven't seen any reason why someone would want to hurt her. If he was trying to cover up this new murder, he would've been more careful with whoever he selected afterward. My gut's telling me the first murder was experimental, with him seeing how easy it was and how much he enjoyed it. With Gail Laurent he was more emboldened and more reckless."

Joe Ramirez shrugged, not convinced. "Maybe," he said, giving me a long hard look. "So what's the deal? How come you can't sit still?"

"Because I can't be here," I said. I looked away from him. "I've got tickets to the Yankees game in Boston tonight.

I'm planning to take Stevie and Emma to the game."

I didn't tell him the rest, that I was afraid I was losing my kids and that this damn baseball game could very well be the last shot I had with them. He seemed to sense what I was thinking, though. He'd gone through his own divorce a few years ago, which was the main reason he agreed to take the graveyard shift. Working the hours he did was better than sitting alone in his apartment at night staring at the walls. Knowing Joe the way I did, if he'd been doing the latter, he probably would've swallowed a bullet by now.

Joe said, "You don't need to be here. I can handle the debriefing. If you like I'll talk to Phillips."

I shook my head. "Wouldn't do any good."

My eyes stayed glued on my hands folded in front of me. I could feel Joe staring at me.

"Stan," he said. "The hours suck, but if you ever want to move under my command I'll see what I can do. I'd be glad to have you."

"Thanks," I said, forcing a smile. "I appreciate it, but you're right, the hours do suck and I'm not quite sure yet where things stand with my girlfriend. It might be over already, but if it isn't taking the graveyard shift would be the final nail. And things aren't that bad between me and Phillips. Besides, I can understand his point in wanting me here."

"I didn't hear things were rocky with your girlfriend. Nice-looking girl. Brandi, right?"

"Bambi. It just happened."

"Sorry to hear that, Stan." Joe placed a hand on my shoulder. "I'm sure your kids will understand if you miss an inning or two of the game."

I nodded and waited until he walked away before shifting my gaze upward. Time dragged painfully as I waited for the debriefing. Not much new came out of forensics other than that they had determined from the way the blood had smeared along the victim's clothing that he had been wrapped in something, probably plastic, before being moved to the dumpster.

Once three o'clock came we sat around the meeting room and waited another forty minutes for the FBI agents to show up. Phillips had brought in six other detectives from the unit for the task force, and the FBI sent two field agents and a profiler. After the agents showed up and got settled with coffee and doughnuts and introductions were made, Phillips started the debriefing by going over what we had for the second killing. Time dragged as I kept mentally calculating how much time I needed to get my kids to the baseball game in Boston. Each time I went through my calculations I'd slice more time off to make it doable.

It was a quarter past four by the time Phillips finished up and started taking questions, and that chewed up another eighteen minutes. I was brought up next to give my dog and pony show, and as I looked at the faces of the detectives and FBI agents watching me, I once more tried to figure out how I was going to get my kids to the game without missing too much of it. Two of the younger detectives sat at attention while I gave a rundown on the basic facts of the case and my take on Rachel Laurent. The other detectives from the department made no attempt to hide their boredom. The FBI agents looked mostly uninterested. For a short while I thought I was actually going to be able to get through it quickly, but that changed once I got to Zachary Lynch. I could see them all paying attention then as I explained about Lynch and his condition. Jack Hennison, who had been on the force over twenty years and had seen it all, was having a hard time sitting still.

"Bullshit!" Hennison exploded at last, his ears tinted a bright crimson. "What are you telling us? This guy's brain damaged so he can't see what people look like but he can tell you what they're wearing?"

"That's what he says. That's what his neurologist claims also."

"And you believed that crap?" Hennison demanded, his face having turned the same beet red as his ears under his military-style buzz cut. He stared around the room to see how many others were buying what I was saying.

Before I could comment the FBI profiler interrupted, asking for clarification on something I had said. This was the first time she had spoken since entering the room and it was almost like the old EF Hutton commercial the way all eyes turned to her. You couldn't blame anyone. She was an exceptionally attractive woman in her thirties with piercing green eyes and blond hair pulled back, and she reminded me of Helen Hunt from the TV show *Mad About You* except her features were harsher and more angular.

"Mr. Lynch is able to process photographs of a person normally?" she asked, her face screwed up into a quizzical expression.

"That's right."

"But if he were brought to this same person, he would see something entirely different?"

"That's what I'm being told."

"Really?" She rubbed her forefinger lightly across her lips while she considered this. The time she was taking for her next question was maddening. Finally she asked, "How did he describe the assailant?"

"He refused to. His neurologist claimed it wouldn't help us, so I didn't push him."

That brought a loud snort from Hennison. From the corner of my eye I could see Phillips's jaw locked into a bulldog expression as he stared bullets my way. The FBI profiler turned to an FBI colleague sitting to her right—a thick-shouldered college linebacker type wearing a suit jacket that was too tight across his chest—and told him that they should try hypnosis on the witness, that maybe they'd be able to unlock something from his unconscious.

"I brought that up with Dr. Brennan," I said. "He claimed it wouldn't do any good. The way he explained it is that Lynch's problem isn't caused by any psychological or emotional issue, but by the way his brain processes visual inputs, so hypnosis wouldn't do us any good since there wouldn't be any memories to unlock."

"According to one of your reports, there's no actual documentation of this so-called scarring of Mr. Lynch's occipital lobe."

"Yeah, well, that type of documentation would have to wait until he's dead so they could do an autopsy on him. Give it fifty years or so and they'll be able to tell us for sure."

That brought a laugh from Joe Ramirez and a slight smile from her.

"Detective Green," she said, "my background was in psychiatry before joining the Bureau. Perceiving someone differently in photographs than in person wouldn't be something that could be explained by occipital lobe scarring. There has to be an emotional or psychological component to this. Not all doctors are infallible. Some have been known to make mistakes, even noted neurologists. We'll try hypnosis, assuming Mr. Lynch has no objections."

I almost told her fat chance since I could guess how Zachary Lynch would respond to that type of request, but I kept my mouth shut. I just wanted to get on with this. A quick glance at my watch showed it was five ten, and I was anxious to wrap things up so I could get out of there. I asked if there were any more questions, hoping to hell there weren't. The FBI profiler's smile became more amused as she asked for my take on the killer.

"I don't know," I said. Another glance at my watch showed that one more minute had ticked off. I looked back at her and tried hard to ignore the tightening in my stomach. "I don't have enough information yet. My gut's telling me these were random killings and that our boy was out there having fun. He's probably holed up now, worried that we have a description of him. Once he realizes that we don't, he'll be out hunting again. That's my take on it. Anything else?"

She showed me more of her amused Cheshire Cat–type smile and asked me why I thought our killer was shooting his victims in the back of the head post-mortem. Christ. This could go on all day if I let it. I told her I didn't want to offer any further conjectures, just facts, and besides, she was the trained profiler, not me. Without looking at Phillips, I could just about feel his glare burning a hole through me. I started shuffling my notes together to let the room know I was done. A few more questions came from Hennison and the other detectives from the precinct. Then the linebacker FBI agent had to pipe up and ask why I was the only detective assigned to the first murder.

"Is that usual procedure here?" he continued. "This was an exceptionally brutal murder done in broad daylight. I would've thought there would be more detectives working this."

"I'll leave that for Captain Phillips to answer. If there's nothing else, I have another engagement."

With my head bowed I nearly sprinted toward the door, raising up my hand at the last moment to flick a wave to the room. Phillips, who had been sitting stunned at my quick departure, barked out that he wanted me there for the rest of the debriefing. Joe Ramirez, bless his heart, spoke over him, announcing that I had already briefed him and that he'd be able to fill in for me for the rest of the meeting. I could sense some of my fellow detectives were annoyed that I was leaving early, but I got out of there before any of them could voice their displeasure.

I couldn't help feeling an uneasiness in the pit of my stomach as I made my way out of the room and through the building, kind of like I was a kid who was caught playing hooky from school and was going to catch hell later. By the time I reached my car I was sweating hard. I was filled with so many mixed emotions, worrying about both getting to my kids on time and the way I had walked out of that room—and I couldn't help feeling as though I had let down my fellow officers. I also didn't trust Phillips. A lot of heat was going to be coming down on this case, especially once the papers realized the two murders were connected, and now he had his scapegoat. I was the lead detective on the case who couldn't show enough dedication to sit through a debriefing meeting.

I sat paralyzed in my car, wanting to drive away from there but also feeling pulled back to the meeting. When I looked at my watch I was stunned to see it was already a quarter to six. I decided to quit playing the games I'd been playing and be realistic about the situation. If I left now, I just didn't see how I could get to the ballpark any earlier than ten o'clock. By then Emma would be cranky as hell and Stevie would be hating me for missing half the game.

My cell phone rang. Caller ID showed it was Phillips. I didn't answer it. Instead I sat for a long time with my head in my hands trying to figure out what the fuck to do. I felt so damned tired right then, and when I had got up enough energy to look up again another twenty minutes was gone. I had no choice. As much as I hated doing it I called Cheryl.

"I'm so sorry," I started. "An emergency came up at work—"

She hung up on me. I started to get out of my car to head back to the meeting. Instead I got back behind the wheel and drove uptown. I was able to park on West 67th, and from there I entered Central Park. It was becoming dusk out. Most of the tourists and locals were gone. I walked for a while before sitting on a bench. I turned my cell phone off. The last thing I wanted right then was to get another call from Phillips—or, worse, from Cheryl reading me the riot act.

My thoughts kept fading in and out on me while I sat there. At some point I started thinking about a conversation I'd had with Mike over a year ago when I had first found out that Cheryl was moving to Rhode Island. We were having some beers at a dive bar on Flatbush Avenue, and Mike kept asking me what I was going to do. I didn't have an answer for him. I had been dating Bambi for several months and Cheryl's news of moving out of the city took me completely by surprise. Mike tilted back his longneck until he had the bottle drained, then signaled the bartender to bring us another round. After the bartender dropped off a couple of fresh Buds, Mike asked me again what I was going to do.

"What can I do? According to my lawyer I can't keep her from moving, and I've got little to no chance for joint custody. So you tell me, what can I do?"

Mike, his eyes half-closed, took a long pull on his beer and wiped his mouth with the back of his hand.

"Providence is near Cumberland, right?" he asked.

"I don't know. Maybe. So?"

"It's a city," he said. "They've got crime, corruption, violence, all the stuff you live for. They must need cops."

"It's not that easy," I said. I looked away from my brother. The place was mostly empty, just a few hardcore drinkers scattered about. I took a long drink of my Bud to keep up with my brother and settled my gaze back on him.

"You can't walk into a department and get a job just like that," I said, snapping my fingers for emphasis. The noise caught the attention of several customers in the room who turned our way for a moment before huddling back over their drinks. "It doesn't work that way," I continued, keeping my voice low. "Even if I could get a job in a department near where Cheryl's moving I'd be throwing away fourteen years toward a pension. I've got obligations, for Mom and child support payments for my kids. Mike, it's not worth discussing."

"I think it is," my brother argued stubbornly.

"Chrissakes, Mike," I said, still keeping my voice low, not wanting to share my life story with any of the alkies sitting nearby. "I've lived my whole life in Brooklyn. What do you want me to do, chase after Cheryl to some podunk town in the middle of nowhere? Even if I was able to get on the force there, knowing her she'd just pack up and move somewhere farther away." I shook my head, trying to end the discussion. "Besides, Bambi and I are starting to get more serious. She's moving in with me next month. I'm not going anywhere."

"We're talking about your kids, Stan. About whether you're going to be in their lives."

"I'll be in their lives. Don't worry about that. I'll be calling them four times a week and driving up whenever I can. And three weeks a year I'll have them back in New York."

"I'm not the one who has to worry about this." Mike's jaw fell slack as he stared at me. "You'll be two hundred miles away. It won't work, Stan. You'll lose them."

I shook my head and looked away from my brother, staring instead at my hands as I rolled a beer bottle between them.

"There's nothing else I can do," I said, shrugging.

Neither of us spoke for several minutes. Mike broke the quiet by telling me it came down to which was more important to me, my kids or being a cop. I said something again about it not being that simple, and that I'd make sure I wouldn't lose my kids. We spent the next hour drinking in silence before calling it a night.

* * *

It had started getting dark. Off in the distance I spotted what had to be someone selling drugs. From his appearance and that of his customers, I was guessing he was dealing either meth or ecstasy. I got up and walked over to him. The kid was in his early twenties, with long greasy hair and that cranked-out meth addict look about him. He tried staring me down, knowing full well I wasn't one of his people. The last thing I wanted right then was to have to spend the night booking anyone, so I showed him my badge and scared him into handing over his product and beating it. It turned out it was meth. I found a place to dump it and then ground it into the dirt with my heel. After that I gazed off into the dusky haze searching for something—I'm not sure exactly what. Whatever it was I didn't see it. I then headed back out of the park.

Chapter 11

I drove back to Flatbush and ended up in a sports bar a few blocks from my apartment. The place was filled with Yankee fans, and there was a lot of excitement over the game—the Yankees were absolutely killing Boston. Every few minutes there'd be a roar in the place, and I'd look and watch the Yankees scoring more runs. I could barely concentrate on the game, though. My mind just kept drifting on me. Mostly I sat slowly drinking one beer after the next. At one point I took out the tickets I had gone three thousand dollars in debt for and placed them on the bar in front of me. I smiled bitterly at them and at the thought of spending all that money I didn't have only to disappoint my kids more than I already had. The guy on the bar stool to my right noticed the tickets and asked if they were genuine. My voice catching in my throat, I told him they were.

"Fuck, man," he said, a big grin breaking over his face. "You could've been at the game giving all those *chowdaheads* shit over the beating they're taking? What the fuck's wrong with you?"

"Hell if I know," I answered back.

Something about my tone warned him he'd better drop the subject. Out of the corner of my eye I saw him elbowing his buddy on the other side of him, and then heard him as he told his buddy about me having those tickets. I felt my hands clenching into fists, but he was smart enough to avoid any further direct conversation with me, and his buddy sensed that he'd better keep his mouth shut also.

* * *

The game ended up being a nineteen-to-eight slaughter. While the rest of the bar whooped it up and celebrated, I sank deeper into my thoughts. I tried to justify how things had turned out by telling myself that it would've been worse with Stevie if I had taken him to the game—that with his team taking the beating that they did, he would've ended up resenting me all the more, and that Emma would've only gotten bored and cold being up that late at a baseball game. Of course I knew I was full of shit, but I tried convincing myself of it anyway.

It was three thirty in the morning before I worked up the strength to head back to my apartment. When I opened my apartment door and walked in I nearly fell over a suitcase of Bambi's that she'd left in front of the doorway. After simultaneously cursing her out and regaining my footing, I stood still until I could hear her tossing around in the bedroom, then stood even stiller until I heard her snoring and knew that she was asleep.

I turned on the lights to see that there were two more of her suitcases in the living room, as well as a small wall of boxes left stacked up next to the TV. An empty highball glass also lay on the floor alongside the sofa. From the sound of her breathing I knew there'd be a mess in the kitchen. I picked up the glass and brought it into the kitchen. A tequila bottle that was one third empty sat open on the countertop, as well as a bottle of grenadine. I screwed the tops on both of them and put them away, then tossed what was left of some limes down the disposal and washed out the glass. After I was done wiping off the countertop I turned off the lights and went back into the living room.

As tired as I felt I knew I'd only be tossing and turning all night with the thoughts that were buzzing through my mind. This was going to make three straight nights with little or no sleep, but that was the way it was going to be. You can't squeeze blood from a stone, right? I made my way over to my recliner, deciding it was best to just let Bambi sleep alone in the bed. I just didn't have the strength to deal with her right then.

I sat in the dark and thought about all the wrong turns I'd made over the last few years. Cheryl hadn't made things any easier by moving to Rhode Island, and I wasn't kidding Mike when I had told him how she'd probably move again if I followed her there—I knew her well enough to know there was a good chance that's what she would've done. Still, though, this was on me. That night after I left Mike I had promised myself I would visit my kids every weekend, and how had that worked out? Over the last seven months, I'd driven up to Cumberland five times. With each visit I only felt the distance between me and my kids growing. It killed me during my last drive up to see how close my kids had gotten to Cheryl's new husband, Carl, and it took every bit of resolve I had not to punch his lights out when he gave me that look of pity and disappointment over how Stevie and Emma were so standoffish with me.

For a while I sat and wondered how much damage had already been done and whether it was at all salvageable. I couldn't help laughing as I thought about how the night had gone—how I had spent three thousand dollars only to end up jeopardizing my job and at the same time ruining any chance of a relationship I might still've had with my kids. After a while I just felt too damn tired to do much of anything other than close my eyes, my mind shutting down on me.

Sunday, October 17, 2004

An early morning sunlight filtered in through the windows, leaving the room a murky gray. I stared bleary-eyed at my watch until I could make out that it was a quarter past five. I decided I had enough self-pity for one night. It was about time to do something constructive, or at least try to, anyway.

I forced myself to focus back on the case and the two murders, about what the sequence of events must've been. Of course, I didn't even know if I was still on the case. After walking out of the meeting the way I did, it wouldn't surprise me if Phillips reassigned me to something else—a low-level B&E, or maybe a mugging, or something that would feel like a slap in the face. And that would only be if he wasn't filing insubordination charges and trying to get me bounced from the department. I didn't think he'd get anywhere if he tried, not with Joe Ramirez covering my back, but I wouldn't put it past him to put me through the ordeal.

I waited until six o'clock to get a change of clothing out of the bedroom. Bambi was still dead to the world and making the same labored breathing sounds she always made after having one too many the night before. I took a quick shower, dressed in a suit and tie that would be appropriate for a funeral, and left the apartment without waking Bambi.

Chapter 12

First thing, I investigated the Upper West Side address where the second body was found. An alley ran behind the apartment building making it easy for someone to park as close as thirty feet from the building's dumpsters. If the body was wrapped in plastic, one person would've been able to drag it over easily enough.

The dumpster that the body had been left in was closest to the alley, and was four feet high, opening at the top. According to the initial medical examiner's report, the victim was five foot eight inches tall and a hundred and sixty-four pounds. Two men would be able to get the body inside that dumpster fast and easy; one person would be able to do it if he could lift the body high enough so it leaned over the edge of the dumpster. Then it would just be a matter of lifting the body up until it fell in. Forensics wasn't able to find any of the victim's blood on the outside of the dumpster, so the perp either washed down the container walls with chemicals or, more likely, kept the victim wrapped in plastic until he had it in the dumpster, then went in after it to remove the plastic wrapping and cover the body with enough garbage to hide it from sight.

I walked back to the part of the alley where the perp had most likely parked and, while timing it, played out in my mind how the disposal of the body would've taken place. One person could've managed it in less than three minutes, and if it was done between one and four in the morning, that would explain why he wasn't spotted. The perp must've known about the dumpster and the easy access to it before the killing. Maybe he lived here once, or had a friend or relative who did, or maybe he spent time searching out locations. Hell, he could even have worked for the waste disposal company that serviced the building. These murders weren't spur of the moment. The killer spent time planning them, both the sequence of the murders and the signature he left us. He orchestrated Gail Laurent's murder to leave us wondering whether it was a brutal street killing or something else, knowing that once we found the second body we'd have our answer that we were dealing with something more ominous.

I walked through the alley slowly as I searched it, then circled around the building trying to get a sense of anything that could help us. I came up empty. After that I talked with the doorman. His shift ran from midnight to eight, so he would've been working when the body was dumped. A detective from the precinct had already interviewed him—from the doorman's description it must've been Jack Hennison. He hadn't seen or heard anything that night, and didn't remember anyone suspicious hanging around the building beforehand. There were security cameras on both sides of the building, but they wouldn't have captured the dumpster, and even if they did, the tapes were rotated after twenty-four hours so Wednesday's tapes were already history.

The doorman took a sip of the coffee I had brought him, then to lighten the mood asked, "How about that game the other night? Nineteen to eight, *damn*. Those Yankees are something else, huh? Steamrolling right over those Red *Sux*."

I wasn't in any mood to trade small talk about the game. I nodded and walked away, probably leaving him thinking I was one of the legion of masochistic Red Sox fans.

I turned my cell phone on to listen to Phillips's message from the other day. It was about what I expected: him warning me to get my ass back up there or face disciplinary actions. There were other messages waiting for me also. Agent Jill Chandler—the FBI profiler who had reminded me so much of Helen Hunt—had called two hours after Phillips. She wanted to talk with me on Sunday if possible to pick my brains on any thoughts or feelings I might have about the case. Bambi also left several messages. She called first at seven thirty to tell me that she was back at the apartment and wanted to know when I'd be there. She sounded timid in her message, maybe even a bit vulnerable, and told me she was going to be making us tequila sunrises. After that she left another message at nine, and a third one an hour later. I guess she had gotten tired of waiting because with each successive call her voice showed more of the effects of the tequila. The last message waiting for me was from Cheryl. She had called after midnight. Her voice was so strained I could barely hear her. She wanted to let me know how sick she was of how I was treating our kids, and how she was going to see her lawyer about changing our agreement—that as far as she was concerned all I was doing was damaging both Emma and Stevie, and that I deserved no further contact with them.

I replayed that last message several times and stood motionless as I listened to it. A slow simmer of anger burned inside, and I could feel the heat of it rising up my neck. Some of my anger was at her; most of it, though, was directed at myself. For several minutes I didn't trust myself to move. When I did I decided to take my anger out on Phillips. He was going to threaten me with a disciplinary hearing for wanting to see my kids on my day off? Fuck him. My hands shook as I called his home number. It was a quarter past seven on a Sunday morning. I knew he'd be asleep, and when he answered the phone I could hear the grogginess in his voice. I could also hear his wife next to him complaining about being woken up.

"Who's this?" he croaked.

"Detective Green."

"Wha—? Chrissakes, what are you calling for this early on a Sunday morning?"

"I got your message from yesterday," I said, my teeth clenched to the point where my jaw ached. "I want to know if you're planning to file disciplinary charges against me."

"Are you out of your fucking mind? You're waking me up on a Sunday morning to ask me that?"

"That's right. I'm working on the case right now, and I've got Jill Chandler at the FBI wanting to meet with me, and Gail Laurent's funeral later this afternoon. If I've got my shift captain trying to put me out on the street, then I don't see much point in doing any of that, especially on my day off."

I stood listening to Phillips's ragged breathing over the phone. He told me in a tight, barely controlled voice that he wasn't going to be putting me up for disciplinary actions, that Joe Ramirez explained the situation to him later.

"Hennison's been made lead detective for these murders," he added. "You're still assigned to the case, and I still want your best effort on it. I also don't want you ever calling me again this early on a Sunday morning for something like this. Understood?"

"Captain, if you're going to leave that type of message on my cell, you should expect me calling to clarify the situation."

He hung up on me.

The call helped. I could breathe easier, some of the pressure building up in my chest having been released. I found a diner near Union Square and had a breakfast of bacon and eggs and pancakes, and after lingering a bit over the coffee I headed to St. Vincent's to visit Rich. He looked more shriveled than he had even the other day and there was something not quite right about his eyes, and he also kept pressing a button to increase his morphine dosage. We traded a few good-natured cracks about each other's appearance, but it seemed forced on both our parts. I told him about the second murder and that interested him until the morphine took effect and he drifted off. I waited for him to wake up, but when he did he was too drowsy to do much more than keep his eyes half-opened. I promised him I'd bring a Toscone sausage sandwich next time I saw him, and that barely sparked a smile from him.

After leaving St. Vincent's I went to the precinct. Jack Hennison was there, which surprised me since he usually made Sundays off-limits. He looked like he hadn't slept much the night before with thick grayish bags under his eyes and an unhealthy pallor to his skin. Of course, he was probably noticing the same about me. He pulled a chair up to my desk and, after perching on it like a hawk, told me about him being made the lead for the case. I could tell he was trying to gauge my reaction to that, and I told him it didn't much matter to me, which was mostly true. Hennison was a solid detective, and I doubted he'd do anything to get in the way of the investigation.

He had brought a file with him and, while consulting it, filled me in on what they had discovered since the meeting the other day. The victim had been identified as Paul Burke. He was thirty-one, lived alone in a co-op apartment in the West Village, and worked as a financial analyst for one of the Wall Street firms. The last anyone saw of him was midnight when he left his office. They were concerned about him at work when he didn't show up Wednesday morning, and his boss had called the police then and again on Thursday and Friday, convinced that something must've happened to him, that only death or a serious injury would've kept him out of the office. Hennison showed me a photo of the victim taken recently at a company event. He was a good-looking man—athletic, strong chin, with dimples showing in his cheeks as he smiled for the camera. It would have been near impossible to match that photo with what had been left in the dumpster. So far no connection had been found between the two victims.

"Gail Laurent's husband was a financial analyst," I said.

Hennison's eyes glazed as he stared at me. "Yeah, so?" he said. "So are probably fifty thousand other people who work in New York. They worked for different firms. The daughter didn't recognize Burke's name. There's no connection."

"I was just pointing it out," I said. "Did you find where he was killed?"

"We're still looking."

"You search his apartment yet?"

Hennison made a face at that question, not bothering to mention the obvious, that not only had they searched it but had found nothing helpful. After waiting for him to answer me and getting annoyed that he wasn't going to, I asked whether there was any chance Burke was murdered there.

He scowled at the idea. "None. They have a doorman, and the guy didn't see Burke come home Tuesday night. Forensics went over his apartment and found nothing, no blood traces, no gunpowder residue, no recent heavy cleaning. Zero footprints that a shooting could've happened there."

"You check whether his mail was picked up?"

"Yeah, it hasn't been since last Monday. I'm telling you, the guy never made it home Tuesday night."

"You've been busy."

"You're fucking right I've been."

An obvious thought stopped me. "Burke didn't have a girlfriend, did he?" I asked.

Hennison understood the ramification of that—because

if the guy did, why didn't she get worried about him being missing and call us. He shook his head. "No sign of one from his apartment. According to his buddies at work he was straight but too much of a workaholic to get involved in a relationship. Instead, he was into hookups. Quick, easy sex. Supposedly he was pretty active." A thin smile replaced the scowl on Hennison's face, and it tightened to the point where it looked etched on. "It's going to be a pain in the ass tracking down all his partners. His buddies gave us some club names, but that's all we've got right now until the FBI can crack into his laptop. The guy had to password-protect the damn thing up the wazoo."

My gut was still that both murders were the random work of a psychopath, and I told Hennison that. "It's not going to help knowing who Burke's been in bed with. He worked on Wall Street, lived in the Village. What's going to help is knowing why his body was dumped where it was on the Upper West Side."

"Ramirez told me your theory," Hennison said. "I don't know if I buy it yet. If this guy was hopping around from bed to bed as much as it sounds like, we've got a lot of potential boyfriends and exes we're going to have to look at. Laurent's murder could've been done for no other reason than to confuse us about this one."

"Jack, take another look at Gail Laurent's crime scene photos. Tell me this guy wasn't getting off on what he did."

"I've seen them," he said. "And I'm not convinced of that." He gave me a cautious look. "Ramirez told me you were planning to go to Laurent's funeral today. You still doing that?"

"Why wouldn't I?"

"Just asking."

"You don't have to worry about me, Jack. I'm happy you're the lead on this. I don't need the headache right now.

And yes, I'm going to the funeral and I'll be bringing Zachary Lynch with me. He claims if the killer shows up he'll be able to recognize him."

"Fuck," Hennison said, his face reddening at the thought of Lynch. "If this guy wasn't loony tunes, we'd *be* somewhere right now instead of wandering around with our heads up our asses. I'm putting together lists of people we need interviewed. When you're done with the funeral, if you want more overtime today see me. I'll be living here until we get somewhere with these murders."

I told him I'd probably take him up on that. He gave me a tired nod, his expression softening.

"I'm glad you're taking this the right way," he said. "I had nothing to do with me being made lead. Phillips has his reasons, whatever the fuck they are, but you know I wouldn't screw over a fellow Brooklyn guy."

I couldn't help smiling over that comment. Yeah, we were both from Brooklyn, but he grew up in the Williamsburg area, which was a different world as far as Flatbush went. As a kid growing up, the only thing I remembered about kids from Williamsburg was that whenever I ran into one I would always seem to end up in a fist fight—usually the other kid's decision, not mine. I doubted any of them would lose sleep from screwing over a guy from Flatbush.

My cell phone rang. Hennison used that as an excuse to get back to making his lists. I waited until he was out of sight before answering my phone and hearing Bambi on the other end. She wanted to know why I didn't wake her the other night.

"I know you came home," she told me. "I saw that you cleaned up in the kitchen. Thanks for that by the way."

"I thought you needed the sleep," I said.

"You could've woken me," she said, and from her tone I could picture her exaggerating her pout. "I stayed up until two last night waiting for you. I guess I dozed off. Where were you?"

"At Pinstripes watching the game. I hung around afterward. I don't know, I guess I just didn't feel like going home to an empty apartment. I got back sometime after three thirty."

"Oh, okay." She hesitated, then "Stan, why'd you have your cell phone off?"

"Phillips had been calling me to give me shit. I didn't feel like taking any more of his calls last night."

"Really?" A bit of a chill entered her voice. I knew that she wanted to say something about how I had no problem turning off my cell phone last night but had to keep it on during our big night out last Wednesday. She held it back though and instead asked me how my night was.

"The Yankees won big," I said, as if that answered what she was asking. "Look, I've got a call I need to make. We'll talk later."

"Don't you want to know where I was the last two nights?"

"That's your business."

"I was with my friend Angela." Her normally tough bluster was gone. I heard her exhale a lungful of air, then add, "I was just so mad at you for leaving me alone in that hotel. I know, I know, you couldn't do anything about it, but I needed a chance to cool off. Maybe I was trying to get you to miss me a little also. But I wasn't sleeping with anyone if that's what you were thinking. You can call Angela and ask her if you'd like. And I'm sorry about that crack I made about that desk clerk."

I hated hearing that vulnerability in her voice. The suggestion to call her friend was childish—as was the idea that her friend wouldn't just repeat whatever Bambi wanted her to. Still, my gut feeling was that Bambi was telling me the truth. I decided if she wasn't it didn't really matter.

"I'm sorry too," I said.

"Will you be home later?"

"By seven o'clock. I promise." I hesitated for a moment, then added, "You went through a lot trouble. Packing up those boxes and carting them out, only to bring them all back two days later."

"I know," she agreed. "I guess I was trying to get your attention. I'll see you at seven."

She hung up. I sat for a moment, losing my train of thought. The little sleep I'd had over the last three days left me with both a headache and this fuzziness in my brain. I got up and poured myself a cup of the mud that we have masquerading as coffee at the precinct. After several sips of that, I called the number Jill Chandler had left. She answered on the first ring and insisted she'd been up since six going over reports on both murders, so there was no chance that I had woken her. Her apartment was on East Houston, only ten minutes away. We arranged to meet at my desk in a half hour.

Jill Chandler showed up on time, carrying a bag from Katz's Deli. She looked softer than she had the other day. Instead of pulling her hair back tightly she had let it down, and instead of the dark blue suit and sensible shoes that marked her as FBI, she wore a thick white cotton sweater, jeans, and tennis sneakers. Maybe it was also the way the late morning light hit her, or maybe it was the sleep-deprived fuzziness clouding up my head, but I didn't see any of the harsh angles to her that I thought I'd seen the other day. When she took two bagels with cream cheese and lox out of the Katz's Deli bag and handed me one, I began to think I might like her. Any lingering doubt was removed when she also took out two black coffees. Thick slices of Bermuda onion and tomato had been wrapped separately, and I added them to my sandwich and took a healthy bite of it. It had been a while since I'd visited Katz's. We ate in silence, with Jill Chandler putting her sandwich down first.

"That was quite an exit you made yesterday," she said after wiping a small smudge of cream cheese from the side of her mouth, an amused smile twisting her lips. "I don't think your boss was too happy about it."

"He wasn't," I agreed.

"I'm guessing from the brevity of your comments at yesterday's meeting that you had somewhere else you badly needed to be."

From the way she looked at me I could tell she was curious to know my story. For some reason I didn't want her to think of me as someone who would let down on the job, but I also didn't want to get into my divorce, my relationship with my kids, or how damn impotent I ended up being the other night, so I just shrugged and told her that, yeah, I had someplace else I needed to be. I knew that she wanted to probe the subject further—probably her years of profiling had left her hating open questions—but she left it alone.

"I'd like to hear your thoughts on these murders," she said. "You've been the closest to them, at least Gail Laurent's, and I'd like to know what you think we're dealing with."

"Pretty much what I said yesterday. Our guy's having fun. He's cutting off fingers and blowing off his victims' faces partly as a signature to us, and partly because he's enjoying what he's doing. And there are more than just those two bodies."

"Why do you say that?" she asked, her lips pursed.

"I'm guessing you've seen the videotape of our witness stumbling onto Gail Laurent's murder?"

She nodded. "It was shown after you left."

"Then you know that our guy tried to shoot Lynch and the only reason he didn't was he was out of bullets. So far seven rounds have been accounted for. Our guy's carrying a .40 caliber, which is going to hold either ten or fifteen rounds, and double that if he's got two magazines. Odds are he was fully loaded before he went out hunting last Wednesday. So what happened to the rounds we haven't accounted for yet?"

"Zachary Lynch didn't fit the profile of the other two victims," she said, confidently. "They were both well-off, and dressed in a way to indicate that. Mr. Lynch, to put it politely, looked like he could've been living out on the streets. More likely, our killer was only trying to scare him away."

"I don't think so. Our perp would've thought that Lynch would be able to identify him."

"Not if he was in disguise. He could've even been waiting for a witness to come along."

Jill Chandler was looking pleased with herself over that idea. I didn't buy it. That our guy would be waiting for a witness or disguising himself smelled wrong to me. If I could trust Lynch and his claims that he saw objects normally, just not people, then he would've noticed if our killer had been wearing a mask. No, it was just dumb blind luck on both their parts: Lynch, that he wasn't shot, and our killer, that Lynch couldn't identify him.

I picked up what was left of my sandwich and chewed it slowly, all the while Jill Chandler smiling to let me know how very pleased she was with herself. When I was done I asked her why she really wanted to meet me because I knew it wasn't to get my "thoughts" on the killer. From the way she blushed, it occurred to me that her agenda might've been of a more personal nature, or at least partially so. She lowered her eyes for a moment and nodded.

"Very good," she said. "You caught me."

"Yeah, well, I might not have a degree in psychiatry or be a trained profiler, but you learn something after fifteen years on the job. So what do you really want?"

"I asked Mr. Lynch yesterday about hypnosis and he was strongly against the idea. I could try scaring him by threatening a court order, but from his reaction I doubt that would work, and I also doubt we'd be able to find a judge who would support us. You've already established a relationship with him. I'd like you to talk to him for us."

"It won't do any good," I said. "There's nothing I could say to him that would change his mind. He doesn't want anyone else knowing what he sees."

She smiled at that. "Why would he be so private about his hallucinations?"

I scratched my jaw as I thought about it. "He doesn't believe they're hallucinations. I'm not sure what he thinks they are, but whatever it is he's not sharing."

Her smile dulled enough to show she didn't believe that. "You will talk to him for us?" she asked.

I told her I would, for all the good I thought it would do. It was getting about time for me to head out for Gail Laurent's funeral, and I asked Jill if she had anything else she'd like to discuss. There was a slight hitch to her mouth as she told me there wasn't, at least not at that moment. It was clear there was something else on her mind, but she was going to keep it to herself. I thanked her for the bagel and watched as she gathered up her stuff and left.

Chapter 13

Once again Zachary Lynch flinched when he accidentally caught a glimpse of me, and once again he made sure to keep his eyes averted afterward. Anyone else, I would've been offended, but by now I was used to it.

The suit he wore was several sizes too big, and he looked so damn uncomfortable in it. His tie was also knotted improperly—kind of the way you'd tie a shoelace—and although I could tell he hated doing so, he stood still so I could tie him a Windsor knot. While we drove I tried making small talk, asking him if he caught any of the Yankees-Sox series. He seemed distracted and was mostly just squirming in his seat. He said something under his breath about not having any interest in sports, and that he watched little TV.

"I'm sorry that FBI agent bothered you," I said.

"There's nothing in my subconscious that hypnosis could unlock," he said under his breath, his discomfort palpable. "I'm not subjecting myself to it."

"I know. I talked with Dr. Brennan. I believe him, I believe you. Still, it would get them off your back. The FBI can be damned persistent. It might be worth just doing it. After all, what harm could it do?"

Lynch's expression turned wooden as he stared straight ahead. "No," he insisted. "Under no circumstances."

My lack of sleep must've left me more slow-witted than I had imagined, because it hit me then why Lynch was being so antsy and it wasn't because of the FBI descending upon him like I had first assumed. I'm sure that was part of it, but there was something else eating at him, and I couldn't help smiling as I realized what it was. Lynch seemed to sense this. He glanced in my direction but hurriedly looked away, his skin color paling to an even unhealthier shade.

I said, "I promised to tell you about your friend from Strombolli's."

"Lisa," he whispered softly.

"She was worried about you Wednesday when you didn't show up. You like her, don't you?"

It was barely noticeable, but I caught him nodding.

"I think the feeling's mutual," I said. "She hinted as much. You should ask her out."

A bare trace of a smile cracked his face, and then just as quickly it was gone.

"That would be hilarious," he said, more to himself than to me. "Asking her on a date with me being the way I am."

I could tell he was mulling it over, though. I couldn't help myself and I asked him what he saw when he looked at her. He didn't answer me, not directly anyway, but that crack of a smile came back, and this time it lasted for several seconds.

We drove in silence after that. He was more relaxed, though, most of his uneasiness from before gone. After we crossed into Jersey I asked him about his life before the convenience store robbery in Harlem when he was a medical student at Columbia. He told me how being a doctor was all he wanted growing up but the way he was left after being shot made it impossible to continue at school. Since he couldn't be around people anymore, at least most people, he taught himself computer programming and was able to get short-term assignments where he wouldn't have to leave his apartment. The only time he ventured outside was during his weekly excursions to Strombolli's. Telling me all that exhausted him, but also seemed to be a good release for him. I had the idea that this was the longest personal conversation he'd had with someone in person since that night in Harlem six years ago.

The funeral service was being held at the grave site, and I arrived there twenty minutes before the service was scheduled to start. Around forty chairs had been set up for the bereaved. Lynch and I left the car and walked until we reached a spot far enough to the side of the chairs that we'd be able to see people clearly but still remain mostly unobtrusive. Rachel Laurent sat stoically in the front row flanked by an older man in his sixties who I assumed was her uncle and a young woman her age who was probably a close friend. A few other people were scattered about, some the victim's age, some Rachel's. Rachel sensed I was standing there and turned to look at me before facing front again. Zachary Lynch's eyes held steady on her, his features relaxed.

"She's drowning," he said under his breath, a soft sigh escaping from him.

"What?"

He looked startled for a moment, as if he hadn't expected me to hear him. "In her sorrow," he explained. "She's drowning in it."

I wanted to ask him how the fuck he could see something like that when everything was supposed to be clouded by hallucinations, but I bit my tongue. More people arrived as we waited for the service to start. Lynch sucked in his breath as he looked at each newcomer. He flinched at the sight of a few of them, though most generated little reaction. With all he shook his head in a short, jerky motion to indicate they weren't the killer.

The service started on time, and more people showed up as it went on. About two thirds of the seats ended up being taken. Rachel almost made it through with her stoic front intact, but near the end she lost it and wept uncontrollably. Some moisture showed in Lynch's eyes as he watched her, and he clenched his teeth to keep a stiff upper lip himself. I stood as I always did at these funerals: impassive, business-like, but wanting more than ever to catch the piece of human waste responsible.

After the service ended and people began to disperse, I signaled Lynch to walk with me so it looked as though we were attending one of the other grave sites.

"If our guy shows up over there, you'll be able to see him, right?"

"Yes, I think so, but I don't understand," Lynch said. "The funeral is over. Why are we still here?"

"Sometimes these psychos like to show up afterward. Just keep your eyes peeled."

We stood fifty yards from Gail Laurent's grave, hidden mostly from sight by an elm tree. I watched as the workers filled in the grave. No stragglers came by. Once the workers were done and gone, the cemetery was empty. We moved a few times over the course of an hour, but nobody showed up other than a man in his fifties walking an overstuffed English bulldog. Lynch shook his head as the man passed us, just as he had earlier with everyone else. I checked my watch. It wasn't worth spending any more time there. Our killer wasn't showing up. I told Lynch we would be heading back. As we drove out of the cemetery I asked him if he had eaten anything yet that day.

"Not since breakfast."

"Let's get you something then."

"That's okay," he said, his eyes squinting badly against the late afternoon sun. "This took a lot out of me. Please, I'd like to just go home."

I gave him a quick look and figured the real issue was he wasn't up to being around any more people. At the first fast food drive-thru place we came to, I pulled in and asked him what he wanted. He admitted he wouldn't mind having a cheeseburger and fries. I ordered him two of both, as well as a chocolate shake, and the same for myself. While he nibbled on a French fry he told me this was the first time he'd had any fast food since the incident six years ago.

"I used to live on this stuff when I was at Columbia," he told me, his lips twisting crookedly into what must've been a sheepish smile. "You'd think us med students would know better."

"There are some fast food joints closer to your apartment than Strombolli's. Why not go to one of those for a change of pace?"

He shuddered at the idea of it. "Too many people in them," he said. "Besides, going to Strombolli's once a week is about all the excitement I can take."

His crooked off-balance smile flashed for a moment to indicate that it was a joke. We ate in silence, and after we were done and I was driving us back to New York, he fell into a deep sleep. He was breathing so shallowly that I studied him for a moment to convince myself that he really was just sleeping and hadn't passed out or dropped dead on me. Once I convinced myself of that, I turned on WCBS and listened to some of the pregame talk for the upcoming Yankees game. The general consensus was that Boston was toast and this was going to be a four-game sweep. It sure seemed that way with El Duque taking the mound. I couldn't think of a single time when the Red Sox had been able to beat him. El Duque always seemed to have their number and find ways to keep them off balance.

When I arrived back at Lynch's apartment building, he was still out of it, his head bent so that his chin rested against his chest. I shook him gently at first, then a little more roughly until his eyes fluttered open. He was disoriented and clearly had no recollection of where he was, and as he pulled himself forward and turned to face me, he shuddered and his skin blanched a sickly white. For a moment I thought he was going to scream. He didn't scream, though. Instead, he blinked wildly and jerked his head away, rubbing a hand across his mouth. His eyes locked onto the front entranceway of his apartment building. I had a strong impulse to grab his head and force him to look at me until he was willing to tell me what it was he saw.

"Detective Green," he forced out in a breathless voice. "I'm sorry, I must've dozed off."

"No need to apologize for that," I said, my voice sounding stiff and unnatural to me. "I appreciate your help today."

"Anything I can do." His crooked smile showed briefly. "Short of hypnosis, that is."

I watched as he left the car and walked with an awkward gait to his building, all the while keeping his eyes shielded so he wouldn't accidentally look at anyone walking by. Once he was inside and out of sight, I headed to Toscone's to pick up a sausage, pepper, and onion hero. I still had time to visit Rich before meeting Bambi back at the apartment at seven as promised. Traffic was light to Toscone's, and then afterward to St. Vincent's. Mary was keeping Rich company, and when she saw me she announced that she was going to stretch her legs for a bit so that the two of us could talk shop in private. Rich looked as shriveled as he had this morning—at least the parts of him that weren't encased in plaster—and had that same off look in his eyes, but he was more alert and, as he spotted the paper sack in my hand, started sniffing in the air.

"Toscone's," he said with a thin smile.

I handed him the sausage sandwich. He started on it but it seemed a joyless activity, and after only a few bites he put it down.

"My stomach must've shrunk since coming here," he said, a dejected frown creasing his face.

"Hospital food will do that to you."

"Yeah, that must be it," he said. As he lay on his hospital bed, he seemed to shrink into it, looking so much smaller than anyone his size had any right to look. Maybe it was an optical illusion caused by the white plaster cast blending in with the hospital sheets, but whatever it was, I couldn't shake this sense of him being diminished. His eyes slid toward me, a glimmer showing in them. "You know the key to solving these murders?" he said. "Figure out why your perp chose that address on the Upper West Side to dump that body. Let's say he killed this guy somewhere between Wall Street and the Village, why'd he cart that body all the way up to the Upper West Side?"

"Yeah, well, I agree with you, but Hennison doesn't think it's all that important. He's assuming our perp spent time scouting for locations."

"Fuck that," Rich said, more light flickering in his eyes as he showed a tight bare-fanged smile, and for the first time looking more like his old self. "There are a lot of places you can dump a body that'd be safer than some high-end luxury building uptown, and I don't care if it was four in the morning. Your perp was putting himself at risk doing that. There has to be a connection to that building, some type of message your perp was trying to send."

Rich stopped himself. His head tilted slightly to the side as he gave me a slow look, his eyes narrowing. "What the fuck difference does it make what Hennison thinks?" he asked.

"Phillips made him lead for these murders."

"You're kidding me!"

"Nope."

Rich sunk deeper into his bed as he digested that. Finally he shrugged and told me it was just as well. "You don't need the headache," he said. "This is going to get a lot worse. Fucking Phillips, though."

I nodded. It was getting late, and if I wanted to keep my promise to Bambi I had to get going. I lied to Rich and told him he was looking better, and I think I was able to do it with mostly a straight face. He gave me a look as though I was full of shit and told me that I wasn't looking so hot myself.

"Get out of here," he said. "Go home and get some sleep. Christ, no wonder I lost my appetite looking at you and your bloodshot eyes. I've seen bullet wounds more appealing. And don't worry, if I come up with any more ideas how to crack this case, you'll be the first guy I call, not Hennison."

I had to smile at seeing more of my old partner breaking through. I told him if I saw Mary, I'd send her back up. He told me not to bother, that he could use a break from her also. I gave him a short wave so long and headed out.

With Yankee fans hunkering down for what should be the last game of a four-game sweep, traffic back to Brooklyn was lighter than usual for a Sunday evening. I got back to the apartment ten minutes earlier than promised. Bambi had her suitcases put away and the boxes that had been stacked up earlier were gone. She also had the dining room table set with my parents' old lace tablecloth and silver candleholders with long white candles burning in both. When Bambi heard me, she came out of the kitchen wearing an apron over her clothes and a tenuous smile across her face. In the year or so that we'd been living together this was the first time she'd gone to this kind of effort to make us dinner. It made me reconsider her earlier claim that she had spent the two days with her friend Angela and not shacked up with some guy where it ended fast and disastrously, but again I decided if that was case it didn't matter.

"I'm making leg of lamb," Bambi announced. Her smile had turned more tentative as she watched for my reaction. "Dinner should be ready in twenty minutes."

"It smells great," I said. "But I was planning on taking you to Lucia's so we could celebrate properly us being back together."

She hesitated as she thought about that. Lucia's was her favorite restaurant. Somewhat reluctantly she told me it would be a waste to throw dinner away. I didn't argue with her. The exhaustion from the last three days finally caught up to me, and it hit me hard.

"We'll do it later this week," I said.

Her eyes lowered as she nodded, but she mostly did a good job of hiding her disappointment. She came over to me, and we embraced and kissed, and again I didn't argue with her when she suggested that I sit in my recliner and that she would bring me a drink. While I waited I must've dozed off because next thing I knew she was shaking me awake. I felt drugged as I forced my eyes open. She handed me a glass filled with ice and a brownish-orange liquid.

"I thought I'd make the tequila sunrises that I was going to make last night," she said.

She went back to the kitchen, and I sipped my drink while trying to keep my eyes from closing. Somehow I managed to, and a few minutes later I heard the clatter of dishes as Bambi set the table and brought food out. Bless her, she had carved the leg of lamb. I don't think I would've had the strength to. Along with the lamb, she made roasted potatoes and string beans, and had bought some red wine. Normally I'm not a wine drinker and would grab a beer instead, but this time I didn't make a fuss. The food was pretty good, which surprised me. When I didn't cook we usually either ate out, had takeout, or microwaved. I had no idea Bambi had it in her.

We didn't talk much during dinner. I guess neither of us wanted to risk what felt like a fragile peace. I was going to have to tell her about the three thousand dollars I was in debt for, but now was not the time. After we were done, Bambi made coffee and brought out a plate of tiramisu she had prepared herself. I was surprised at how good the dessert was—

she had never let on before that she could cook anything much more than hamburgers and hot dogs. While we were slowly eating it and drinking the coffee, Bambi commented how I was probably going to want to watch the game. I shook my head, and suggested instead that when we were done we clean up the dishes and go straight to bed. When I said that the tentativeness in her smile disappeared, and for the first time that night the real thing showed through.

Bambi had one more surprise for me. She insisted that I relax while she took care of the dishes. I didn't fight her on that either, and while it was a struggle, I managed to keep my eyes from closing while I waited for her. Later, when we went to bed, I stayed awake until we were done, and then I was out like a light.

I woke up in the dark feeling an uneasiness inside. Squinting at the alarm clock I saw it was one twenty-two in the morning. Bambi was on her stomach sound asleep. I pulled myself out of bed and made my way to the living room. I turned on the TV to see that David Ortiz for the Red Sox had just hit a two-run homerun in the twelfth inning to win the game for Boston. I sat down and watched them recap more of the game. Mariano Rivera had given up the tying run in the ninth thanks to a walk, a stolen base, and a single. After a while I turned the set off and joined Bambi back in bed.

Chapter 14

Monday, October 18, 2004

I got up early to make Bambi and me a breakfast of French toast and sausage and still made it to the station by seven thirty. Hennison was already there. He looked disheveled with several days of stubble on his face and his suit rumpled as if it had been slept in, which it probably had. His attitude toward me had cooled. I knew he wasn't happy that I hadn't taken him up on his offer of more overtime after the funeral. He barely acknowledged my presence as he tossed a paper onto my desk. As I looked it over he told me it was a list of tenants at the Upper West Side apartment building that he wanted me to interview.

"What about the knife?" I asked.

He gave me a cold stare. "What about it?"

"I'd have to think with the FBI involved, we should have a list by now of Internet purchases for that make and model."

"How's that your business?"

"Because I'd like to conduct the interviews," I said.

He kept his cold stare going while he considered some smartass crack back at me, but I guess he decided it would be better to just get the work off his desk and have one less thing to worry about. He nodded to me. "Yeah, we've got a list," he said. "You want it, you can have it, but I still want those tenants interviewed."

"How about a list of owners licensing .40 caliber pistols?"

"I've got that covered," Hennison said. From the way he

looked at me I could pretty much tell that he had spent the day Sunday and a good part of the night calling those gun owners and getting them to agree to provide ballistic samples. I could also tell he was resenting me for him being made lead for these murders. There was no question he was feeling the pressure. The papers still hadn't connected the two murders—we kept enough out of our news briefings so they wouldn't be able to connect them—but Hennison had to know he only had a few days before the brass felt compelled to connect the dots for them or, worse, before some enterprising reporter did it himself. Once that happened and the city realized we had a serial killer out there, the heat was going to be scorching.

I collected the list of knife purchases from Hennison and took it back to my desk. Unless our killer was the dumbest fuck alive on the planet, there was little chance that he'd allow a knife to be tracked back to him or, for that matter, that he'd have any registered .40 caliber in his possession. While you're not expecting a Mensa candidate, these types of killers usually possess an animal caginess that makes this routine tracking of leads mostly pointless. Unless you get lucky with forensics, more often than not these types of cases break because a witness or informant drops in your lap. Still, until you find either hard evidence or a witness more reliable than, say, Zachary Lynch, all you're left with is tracking down leads and hoping you catch a break.

I felt more clearheaded than I had over the past few days, but I also had that same uneasiness that I had woken up with the other night. I couldn't shake this feeling that something was more wrong than simply Mariano Rivera blowing a playoff game for the Yankees. As I was scanning the list of knife purchasers the FBI had come up with, I received a call from a detective out in Queens who I grew up with in Flatbush. It had been a few years since we spoke, and we spent some time catching up. He had been an usher at my wedding, and at one time dated Cheryl's sister, and he gave his condolences when he heard about my divorce.

"My brother, Andy, is going through it now," he said. "The whole custody business is killing him."

"Shit, I'm sorry to hear that."

"Yeah, I know. Listen, Stan, that woman shot with a .40 caliber in Tribeca. You're the lead for that right?"

"Not anymore."

He hesitated. "Should I be talking to you or someone else?"

"I don't know. What's up?"

"Some dogs were found shot up. I talked with the patrolman who investigated the area, and he told me heavy firepower was used. Made me think it might be a .40 caliber."

"Who's the officer?"

"Juan Fullijo."

I thanked him for the call and then spent the next twenty minutes on the phone before I was able to reach Fullijo. I asked him about the dogs.

"There were three of them," he said. "We found them under the Steinway Street overpass in Astoria."

"What was done to them?"

"They were shot, you know, several times each. Big holes blown out of them. From the way they looked, maybe they were there for several days, maybe a week. Hollow-points might've been used."

I felt my heart skip a beat. ".40 caliber?"

"We didn't do ballistic testing," he said, sounding confused. "These were dogs, right? Why the interest?"

"We've had a couple shootings here in Manhattan where a .40 caliber was used. Were these dogs shot point-blank in the back of the skull?"

"One of them was, yeah. Blew the little guy's face right off."

I couldn't help smiling bitterly at that. Same goddamn sonofabitch. Maybe this time we'd find a witness—at least one who saw more than hallucinations.

"We're going to need autopsies on these dogs," I said. "And we need the area marked off as a crime scene."

"I think the carcasses are being disposed of," Fullijo said, distracted. "I'm sorry, detective, but shit, these were dogs. It's not procedure to do autopsies."

"You did fine, officer," I said, and I got off the phone with him so I could track down the carcasses before they were lost. I got lucky. They were minutes away from being cremated when I found them and arranged for them to be sent to Manhattan for examination. I then filled Hennison in. He maintained a good poker face throughout, only a glint of light in his eyes betraying his excitement.

"You don't know yet if a .40 caliber was used," he said.

"Not yet."

"You send forensics there?" he asked.

"I figured I'd let you do it."

His poker face finally cracked and he shook his head grimacing. "The fucking psycho had to shoot dogs," he said.

He made a call to send forensics to the scene. After that, the two of us headed over to Queens together.

Chapter 15

The dogs' bodies were left under the Steinway Street overpass in an area of overgrown grass and weeds between the Brooklyn-Queens Expressway and the Grand Central Parkway. Hennison and I stood off to the side watching while forensics combed the area. Officer Fullijo had shown up to point out where the dogs were found, although that wasn't needed since all three of those spots were marked by dried blood. Fullijo looked annoyed as he talked to us, probably thinking he was going to be blamed for not securing what turned out to be a crime scene and allowing the dog carcasses to be moved. Of course, it could've just been all the noise from traffic making it hard to talk, let alone think. After Fullijo repeated to Hennison everything he told me, he left.

Hennison tried saying something to me, but I didn't hear because of a driver on the Parkway blasting his horn. The overpass amplified the road noise around us—and there was plenty of it with the north and south sides of Astoria Boulevard flanking both the Expressway and Parkway, as well as Steinway Street running overhead. Hennison looked as annoyed as Fullijo had when he repeated his comment to me about how the dogs must've been dumped there.

"Someone would've seen the shootings otherwise," he said. "We would've had to've gotten a call from a witness if they were shot here. Besides, it doesn't make sense. You've got Saint Michael's Cemetery a few miles away. Why wouldn't our perp take them there where he'd have some privacy?"

I shrugged noncommittally, watching as a member of the

forensics team picked something out of the weeds and bagged it. Hennison watched him also.

"You're not seriously thinking they could've been shot here?" Hennison asked.

"I don't know. Maybe they could've been. Late at night it would be dark enough that someone driving by would only see the flashes from the gunfire. Maybe not even that. You'd think someone would've heard shots, but with LaGuardia nearby, he could've timed his shooting with planes taking off. Maybe the road noise covered it. Or maybe the drivers passing by just didn't know what they were hearing."

From Hennison's blank expression he must've only heard part of what I said over the traffic noise, but he didn't care enough to ask me to repeat it. We stood watching as forensics continued their examination of the area. When they were done, one of the team members—a thin dark-haired woman in her twenties—came over to fill us in. We all walked farther away from the overpass and toward the center of the median area so we'd have a better shot at hearing each other. The forensics team member told us the shootings occurred at the site.

"How do you know they weren't dumped here?" Hennison demanded.

"From the blood splatter and bone fragments found," she said. "And we dug four bullets out of the ground."

".40 caliber?" I asked.

"Possibly. I'll be able to tell you definitively later. But they were hollow-points."

"Shell casings?"

She shook her head. "They must've been picked up afterward."

"Any idea when the shootings happened?" I asked.

"Sorry, no. The ME's going to have to tell you that. But the fact that we weren't able to pull any tire tracks makes me think it happened at least a week ago."

"Anything connecting us to the shooter?"

She smiled anemically at the question. "The whole area is pretty well contaminated by garbage being tossed from the overpass. I counted enough used condoms to make me think that vice should be watching the area. We did find a large amount of dried blood on the edge of the grass on the Expressway side. This wasn't where we were told the dogs were found, so maybe it came from the shooter. We've collected all of it, and we'll see what we come up with."

I thanked her for the information. I could tell she wanted to ask if this was related to the killings we had in Manhattan, but instead she gave me a tired smile and walked back to join her team. Anyway, she'd know the answer to that before I would from the ballistics testing.

Hennison had driven us to the site and had left his car in the left lane of the Expressway that had been cordoned off for the police. Once we got back in his car, he proceeded to navigate so we could cross the Queensboro Bridge and get back to Manhattan. At first he seemed too preoccupied to notice much more than the traffic, but after a while he called Central over his two-way to ask whether any calls were placed over the last week about gunfire near the Steinway Street overpass. The dispatcher put him on hold for several minutes to check before coming back to tell him there hadn't been.

"I can't believe no one heard those gunshots," Hennison muttered to himself. "A .40 caliber is going to sound like a fucking cannon." His eyes shifted sideways toward me. I think up to that point he had forgotten I was in the car next to him.

"It's the same guy," he said.

"Yeah, I'd bet that also. But we'll see what ballistics comes up with."

He nodded, his lips pressed into tight bloodless lines and

his eyes hard marbles as he stared ahead. "What do you think this fucker did? Round up three strays just to bring them there and shoot them? Christ, that would be a tough act. You'd think after the first shot, the other two dogs would be hightailing it away."

"Maybe he drugged them first," I said. "Or put some stakes in the ground so he could tie them down."

Hennison shook his head angrily. "Goddamned psycho," he spat out. "I hope that is his blood and one of those dogs bit his fucking balls off."

"It would make our life a hell of a lot easier if that's what happened."

"Fuck yeah, it would. I still can't believe no one called us on the shooting. Someone must've seen or heard something. Goddamn it, what was the point of shooting these dogs?"

I didn't bother answering. We both knew it could've been for any number of reasons. Most likely, though, our killer was testing out his gun and wanted to see firsthand how much damage a .40 caliber hollow-point would do. Even if I had answered, I don't think Hennison would've noticed. He was too distracted to pay much attention to anything I said. As we got onto the Queensboro Bridge, his eyes showed a glint of life. Smiling grimly, he said, "What I'm thinking is after the ME gives us a time of death for these dogs, we see if we can get the story played up big by the news stations. Maybe it will flush out a witness."

"It's worth a shot," I said. "As long as Phillips goes along with it."

"He'll go along with it," Hennison insisted under his breath, but we both knew that wasn't necessarily true. The problem with playing up the story would be that a reporter might end up connecting it to Gail Laurent or Paul Burke or, worse, to both. Hennison again fell deep into his own thoughts. When he pulled onto the next street, he started chuckling to himself.

"What theory do you think our FBI profiler comes up with to explain our perp shooting off only one of these dogs' faces?" He was laughing harder now and had to wipe a few tears from his eyes. "I bet she claims deep down he's a dog lover, and was too traumatized after seeing what he did to do the same to the other two dogs."

"How much you want to bet?"

He peered at me sideways, a shit-eating grin stretching across his face. "Fifty bucks," he said.

"You're on."

We shook hands.

"You just lost yourself fifty bucks, pal," he said. "The broad's a flake, although a damn nice-looking one. I'd let her profile me anytime she wants."

I was about to give him some shit, pretending I didn't catch his intended meaning of *profile*, and instead outline all of the borderline antisocial tendencies a psychological profile of him would disclose. A thought stopped me. Why *did* our perp only shoot one of those dogs in the back of the skull? You would've expected him to have shot all three of them that way. I started wondering if maybe he had been interrupted. Maybe someone heard the gunfire and stopped to investigate. An adrenaline rush hit me as I mulled that over because it made so much sense, especially explaining the blood that was found where it wasn't expected. If a passerby had stopped, we'd have another body somewhere else. I told Hennison my idea.

"Fuck," he swore after he digested what I said. He got on his two-way again to Central, this time asking if any abandoned vehicles had been found near the Steinway Street overpass area. If our perp shot and killed someone stopping because of the gunfire, and he was intent on hiding this from us, he'd have to dump the person's vehicle in a neighborhood close enough so he'd be able to walk back and retrieve his own car.

"You're wasting the dispatcher's time," I told Hennison while we waited for Central to get back to him. "Any vehicle abandoned in that area would be gone within an hour."

Hennison didn't bother responding.

"You want to pay me the fifty bucks now?" I asked.

"I'll wait," he said. "I still have faith in our profiler."

My cell phone rang. The caller ID showed a White Plains phone number I didn't recognize. The moment I heard Mary Grissini's voice I knew what had happened. I sat quietly as she told me how Rich had died early that morning. Without her mentioning it, I knew what time it had happened, that that was why I had woken up early with that uneasiness.

When my dad died it hit me hard, and it took a long time for me to come to terms with it. After that, as more people I knew passed away, I seemed to grow more callous with each successive death. None of these people were close friends or immediate family, but still, these were uncles and aunts that I'd see at family gatherings, guys I grew up with in the neighborhood, and fellow officers who had gone with me to the academy. Over the last few years these deaths barely made an impact, and it left me wondering how much the job and all the death I was constantly around had changed me, and how much of myself had been lost. Hearing about Rich hit me harder than I would've imagined. I started choking up but fought back the tears. I'd be damned if I would start sobbing in front of Hennison. I heard a hitch in my voice as I asked Mary if she'd like me to come over.

"No, that's not necessary," she said. "I've brought the boys to my parents. We'll all be staying with them for the next few days. The wake is this Wednesday and the funeral is Friday. I thought you could pass it on to the department."

She gave me the time and place for both. I sat and listened numbly. It took a long moment before I could talk again, and when I could I told her how sorry I was.

"I know," she said. "Rich always thought of you more as a brother than a partner. Stan, I hope you know that."

Fuck. More than anything I didn't want to break down right then, but it was a struggle. I could hear the hitch again in my voice as I told her how I'd felt the same about Rich and if there was anything I could do for her to call me.

"I know that," she said.

After she got off the phone, I just sat numb. I barely noticed when Central called back to tell us that no abandoned vehicles were reported near the area Hennison had asked about. At that moment not much seemed to matter.

"Was that about your partner, Grissini?" Hennison asked.

I nodded, not trusting myself to talk.

"He just had surgery, right? How's he doing?"

I couldn't answer him, at least not then, and he didn't press me. Later, when we were pulling up to the precinct, I told him Rich's wake would be this Wednesday.

Chapter 16

I met with Phillips to relay to him the information concerning Rich's wake and funeral. He stared at me stone-faced while I told him this, and then told me that he'd make sure to pass it on to the department. After that I sat at my desk and waited for the ballistics and medical examiner's reports. Word spread quickly about Rich, and detectives in the department came over to offer their condolences and ask about what happened. I wasn't much in the mood to talk. Right then I needed more than anything to focus on the job if I was going to make it through the day, so I kept it short, mostly just telling them when the wake and funeral were, and then turning back to whatever piece of paper I was trying to make sense of.

The ballistics information came first. The bullets were .40 caliber hollow-points, and they were from the same gun used in the other two shootings. Not that that was much of a surprise. The medical examiner's office called shortly after ballistics. The dogs were all fed barbiturate-laced meat before being killed. As far as when they were shot, the best they could come up with was that the animals had been dead five to seven days. A total of eight bullet wounds were located on them. The bigger news was that the blood found on the edge of the grass was human, and it didn't match the earlier victim, Paul Burke.

"Any of these dogs bite someone?" I asked.

"Impossible to tell with one of them, but the other two, no."

"What breed were they?"

"I think one was a pitbull mix; the other two, I don't

know. I'll have a veterinarian take a look at them and get back to you."

"How about sending photos?"

"Sure, I'll send you what I have, but I'm not sure how much they'll help given the condition they were left in. Scavengers and the rain the other day did a number on them."

I thanked him for the call, then relayed the information to Hennison, suggesting he have the FBI try to match the blood against the DNA samples in their CODIS system. He told me he'd bring that up at a briefing meeting he'd scheduled for two o'clock to bring the other members of the team up to speed with the recent developments. "I'm going to need someone calling hospitals about dog bite victims," he complained. The odds were the human blood left at the scene wasn't from a dog bite to the perp but from a third party wandering onto the scene and being greeted by one or more .40 caliber slugs. Still, the former possibility was going to have to be checked into, and God knows how many dog bites New York City had in any given week.

While I waited for the two o'clock meeting, I started on the list of knife purchases. I was mostly on automatic pilot as I called people and tried to verify their whereabouts at the time Gail Laurent was murdered. Those that were able to give me something definitive, I would try later to verify their alibis, those that gave me something too vague to check, I arranged for them to come to the precinct to meet with me. All of them sounded indignant at this intrusion. With some it sounded genuine; with most, though, it was forced. I was surprised at how many of them I was able to contact. I guess a lot of these guys buying military knives over the Internet didn't have day jobs.

At a quarter to two, Joe Ramirez wandered over to my

desk. By then I'd been able to get through half of the list. He put a hand on my shoulder and told me how sorry he was to hear about Rich.

"They know what happened?" he asked.

"I don't know. I didn't press Mary about it when she called, but he didn't seem right after his surgery."

"How'd she sound?"

I shrugged. "About what you'd expect."

"Christ," Joe said, shaking his head. "You don't expect to drop dead after a hip operation. Fucking world, huh? Rich was a good man, he'll be missed."

"Yeah, he will be."

Joe took a deep breath and let it out noisily through his mouth, and then we were back to business. "Those dogs that were shot . . ." he started.

"Same guy," I said. "Ballistics verified the same gun was used."

"Chrissakes," he said. "What's this guy gotta be shooting dogs for?"

"He probably shot more than just dogs at the scene. Human blood was found also. A lot of it."

"I didn't hear that." Joe's gaze lowered as he considered that piece of news. "Jesus, we can at least hope it's the perp's own," he said. "Maybe one of those dogs bit him."

"It's possible," I said. "Except they were all drugged with barbiturates, probably before he ever got them there."

"So whose blood is it?"

"Could be the perp's, could be someone else's. I guess we'll find out."

I checked my watch, saw it was a couple of minutes to two, and got out of my chair. While we headed to the meeting, Joe asked me how it went taking my kids to the baseball game. I told him I never made it, that by the time I left Friday's meeting it was too late.

"Ah, shit," he said, "I'm sorry to hear that. But it's just a baseball game. Your kids will get over it."

I nodded and told him he was probably right, not that I believed it.

Phillips wasn't attending the meeting, but the rest of the team was already waiting in the meeting room, including Jill Chandler and her fellow FBI agents. Jill had the same sharper look that she had in the first meeting, with no makeup, her hair pulled back tightly, and an unflattering blue suit and flat-heeled shoes. Her look softened, though, as our eyes momentarily met and she gave me a wisp of a smile touched with sadness. From the overall somberness in the room, word about what happened to Rich must've spread to her and the other FBI agents.

Joe and I took our seats, and Jack Hennison spoke up to go over the morning's discovery in Queens, as well as giving a rundown of what we'd gotten from the medical examiner's office. When he finished, he asked the FBI agents if they could help in matching the human blood found against the DNA samples in CODIS. Agent Thorne, the thick-shouldered linebacker type, told Hennison he'd take care of it, but that it would take forty-eight hours to get the results back.

"I'll arrange for the animal carcasses to be sent to our lab," Thorne added. "They should be able to provide us a narrower window for when the shootings happened."

Hennison looked eager to wrap up the meeting and asked if there were any questions. When there weren't, he stood up, palms flat on the table so he could lean forward and look around the room. "That's what we got," he announced, his voice raspy, not much more than a growl. "We have no idea yet whether the other blood found at the scene is our perp's or someone else's, but until another body is found, we need to assume both are equal possibilities."

"Not equal by any means," Jill Chandler said.

"Why's that?"

"Our killer is obsessed with obliterating his victims. That's why he uses a .40 caliber pistol and hollow-points, as well as shooting them post-mortem with the gun muzzle directly against the victim's skull. Something unexpected happened that made him change his plans; otherwise he wouldn't have altered his routine."

Hennison stood for a moment scratching his jaw, then shifted his gaze away from her. "Any chance he could've just been upset seeing what he did to that other dog?" he asked.

She looked at him like he was an idiot. "No," she said.

Hennison's eyes dulled, his skin color dropping a shade. He was fuming, realizing he'd lost fifty bucks to me on a stupid bet. From the look on his face, it was also clear he was trying to come up with a good crack back at her. Joe pulled the attention of the room away by asking her why our guy wanted to kill those dogs and why he chose a place as public as the grassy area between two highways.

"I first thought there might've been a socioeconomic basis for these murders," Jill told him. "But not now. I'm convinced that what we're dealing with is a full-blown narcissistic personality. What's driving him is his message. This person is working from a carefully developed script, at least in his mind, and this script is sacrosanct and can't be deviated from. This is why he didn't shoot Mr. Lynch"—she flashed me a thin smile—"and why he had to remove the body of whomever he shot from that grassy area. While he certainly enjoys killing, it's his message—his story, so to speak—that's most important to him, and for whatever twisted reason, those dogs and where he left their bodies are all part of this story that he's so intent on telling us."

"What a load of crap," Hennison muttered loud enough for the rest of the room to hear.

She turned to face him, a patient smile showing. "What is your theory, detective?" she asked.

"I don't have one," Hennison said. "I'm not a trained FBI profiler. But I'd have to think this asshole is just trying to fuck with us, see how many hoops he can make us jump through. I'd bet, though, he brought that blood with him to dump where he did. I don't care how late at night it was. If he shot someone on the edge of the West Brooklyn-Queens Expressway someone would've seen it."

Hennison was determined not to give up on our fifty dollar bet. He lowered his eyes from her and added without much enthusiasm, "I still think he stopped after the first dog only 'cause he didn't have the stomach to shoot the faces off the other two. The guy's probably deep down a dog lover."

Jill Chandler couldn't help laughing at that. It was a short burst that exploded out of her, and she covered her mouth with her hand to quiet herself. At the sound of it, Hennison eyes jerked toward her, his ears quickly glowing a bright red. The rest of his face turned just as red as he looked around the room and saw the other two FBI agents, as well as several detectives, barely able to suppress their own grins. Christ, I almost felt sorry for him. Grumbling something under his breath about the meeting being over and us needing to get our asses back to work, he left the room steaming. The rest of us followed, although at a more leisurely pace.

On the way back to my desk I stopped to pour a cup of coffee. While I was adding enough sugar to make it drinkable, Jill Chandler came up next to me. Even with my eyes fixed on my coffee, I knew it was her simply from the electric feel of her hip momentarily brushing against mine. Her hand touched my arm, and she told me how sorry she was to hear about my partner. I nodded and thanked her for that. We stood quietly for several moments. Then, as I was fumbling for another sugar packet, she asked how much I won. I turned to see her grinning at me, very pleased with herself.

"Detective Green, I'm good at what I do. From Detective

Hennison's asinine theory, and your reaction to it, you two obviously had a bet on how I would respond."

"Fifty bucks," I told her.

"That's all?" she said, disappointed. "Too bad. It would've been nice if it had cost him more money."

"It wouldn't matter. The guy's a notorious welcher. I'll probably never see a dime of that fifty. You don't like him much?"

"No strong feelings either way, although I don't appreciate the way I've caught him leering at me, or his dismissive attitude toward what I do." She hesitated, then asked, "Did you ask Mr. Lynch again about hypnosis?"

"Yeah, I asked him. He's not going to do it, and I'd like to request that the FBI not bring it up with him again. He's willing to help us out in ways he's more comfortable with, and I'm afraid if we badger him anymore about hypnosis that will change quickly."

She frowned at my statement. "I don't see how that type of request could be considered badgering."

"To him it is."

I finished stirring a fourth and final packet of sugar into the coffee and started back to my desk. Jill followed me, still frowning.

"I know if we could tap into his unconscious mind . . ." she started, but she let it drop. Instead she told me she'd leave Lynch alone for now. "Although I'm not sure how many more chances we're going to have to catch this killer," she said. "Once he finishes his *story*, that's it. I doubt we'd hear from him again."

"So what's the *story* this guy is so intent on telling us?"

"I have no idea," she said. "And I doubt it would make much sense even if I did. But in his mind, getting it out is all that matters. You have to remember, we're dealing with a full-blown narcissist. This is someone who is so caught up in his own grandiose view of himself that he believes anything concocted in his fevered mind would be considered brilliant by the rest of the world."

I nodded noncommittally and went back to my list of knife purchases. Jill left only to return minutes later to hand me fifty dollars, a big grin stretched across her face.

"I shamed him into paying up," she explained.

"Truly incredible," I said. "And who said you can't squeeze blood from a stone?"

I could tell there was something else on her mind, but she left without mentioning what it was. Later that afternoon I received photos of the dogs that were killed. The person I had spoken with was right. In the condition they were left there was nothing I'd be able to with the photos. We wouldn't be able to put them on the news, and an owner wouldn't be able to recognize a missing pet from them. The medical examiner's office called shortly afterward to make sure I'd gotten them, and also to let me know that according to the veterinarian who looked at the dogs, they appeared to be a boxer, a Doberman shepherd, and a mongrel with some Rottweiler and Staffordshire terrier in it. I took all this to Hennison. He stared blankly at the photos and made a face at my suggestion to have someone call local shelters to see if anyone had adopted the breeds of dogs that were killed.

"A waste of time," he said. "Our perp picked those dogs up off the street."

"Then see who's reporting missing pets. At least we'd know what neighborhoods he was in."

"Yeah, maybe." He turned away from me and wrinkled his nose as if he were smelling some bad cheese. "By the way, real classy move sending that FBI broad to collect your money for you."

I couldn't help laughing at that. "I didn't ask her to do squat. She figured out the bet and collected payment from you all on her own. She's pretty damn good, isn't she? I'm beginning to think there might be something to her theory about what's driving our perp. You talk to Phillips yet about playing up this dog story to the press?"

Hennison nodded. "He wants the story kept quiet," he said.

The rest of the day I continued to focus on the list of knife purchases, and was able to eliminate half the names on it. The other half, either the alibis were too vague to be corroborated or I wasn't able to track the person down. When my shift was over at five, I left. While I was sure Phillips and Hennison would've liked everyone to put in overtime until we made more headway, I wasn't going to, at least not that day.

On the way home I used a good chunk of the fifty dollars I'd gotten from Hennison to get takeout from one of Bambi's favorite Indian restaurants. Later, when I called Cheryl, several inches of frost came over the line, but she didn't hang up on me and I heard her in the background asking Stevie if he was willing to talk to me. I thought there was a chance he would after his Red Sox pulled off a minor miracle the night before and had already taken an early two-to-one lead in game five, but he refused. Emma did get on the phone for about thirty seconds to tell me how mad she was at me. At least that was something.

After dinner I asked Bambi if she wanted to go to a nightclub in the neighborhood. She seemed surprised by my suggestion and asked me if I was feeling up to it after what happened with Rich, because if I wasn't it would be totally understandable.

"Yeah, let's get out of here."

"You're sure you'd rather not stay home and watch the game?"

I told her I'd rather go out, then waited three quarters of an hour while she dolled herself up and put on a new outfit. For the last few days I'd been trying to figure out how I was going to pay Earl what I owed him. Earlier today I had made a decision and called Joel Cohen, and we had arranged to meet at his club that night.

Chapter 17

Bambi turned heads when she walked into the club wearing her stiletto heels, sheer black nylons, and a black leather miniskirt that barely covered her panties. It was only in the forties out, so she compensated by wearing a black calfskin jacket, but she had damn nice legs and she made sure everyone knew it.

The guy working the door knew me, and he nodded to let me know that Joel was in his back office waiting. It was early, only eight o'clock. Business was lighter than usual with the game underway, but there was still a good crowd. La Toya Jackson's "Just Wanna Dance" was playing over the loudspeakers, and the dance floor was already crowded with people grinding away. According to a sign out front, a local band would be coming on after ten, hopefully playing something other than disco. After setting Bambi up with a drink, I went back to talk to Joel.

A few months ago some toughs from Brighton Beach started to put the muscle on Joel and his business. These were guys straight from Russia, one or two of them ex-KGB, others pure thugs. Usually they kept their extortion racket within the Russian community, but I guess because Joel's grandparents came from St. Petersburg they felt he qualified. Or maybe this was just the first of many forays into expanding operations beyond their traditional base.

Whichever it was, Joel let me know that he'd like to hire me for security, figuring that with a member of the NYPD hanging around the club these Russians would leave him alone. At the time I told him I couldn't do it; his business was rumored to operate on the shadier side of the street, and if what I'd been hearing was true there was a chance I'd be bounced from the force if word leaked of me moonlighting for him. Joel left his offer open. When I called him today, he sounded desperate.

I knocked on the door and was told to come in. Joel sat on a red leather sofa reading a music magazine, and on looking up at me, flashed a toothy smile. With his dark shades, gold chains, and top four buttons of his shirt left unbuttoned to show off his chest, he looked like he was stuck in the movie *Saturday Night Fever*. I'd known Joel my whole life. He had grown up in the neighborhood and was only a couple of years older than Mike. When he was younger, with his dark good looks and body as lean as a knife blade, he was always a killer with the girls. Now, having gained a few pounds, his body thicker and his hairline receding, those looks had been tarnished somewhat, but he still had the same charisma.

"Stan, damn, it's good to see you!" He got off the sofa so he could lean over and take my hand with both of his, his smile near blinding. "I can't tell you how glad I was to hear from you today. What can I get you?"

"Michelob's fine."

He let go of my hand to call the bar. After that he signaled for us to both sit down.

"Joel, if I'm working security for you, any criminal activity I see I'm going to bust. Stolen property, drug deals, any of that."

He kept his smile intact, but a shadow briefly fell over his eyes. "Stan, I don't know what you've been hearing. I run a clean business, and I wouldn't expect anything less from you, but I sure as fuck could use your help right now."

He pulled a roll of bills from his shirt pocket and held it up for me. "Three thousand dollars, as we talked about earlier," he said. "But I need a commitment from you. I can't have you leaving as soon as you earn this out."

There was a knock on the door. He covered the roll with his hand while a girl from the bar came in and handed me a Michelob. After she left, I asked him what type of commitment he needed.

"Three months," he said. "Ten to midnight each night during the weeks, five-hour shifts Saturday and Sunday nights. Who knows, you might grow to like the job and want to keep it going past then."

"Doubtful. I think I'd go nuts listening to disco for more than three months."

He laughed at that. "Stan, you take this job and I'll play more rock during your shifts."

"I was serious before," I told him. "If I see any illegal shit, I'll be taking the jokers away in handcuffs, even if it's you."

"Stan, my man, again, I wouldn't expect anything else," he said, only a slight strain showing to his smile.

Three months. That was more than I wanted, but it was doable. It just meant three months of sleeping less and no overtime at work. Also, no driving up to Rhode Island, but maybe it would be for the best to let things cool down for a while. I nodded, and he handed me the three grand and we shook hands. Clapping me on the back, he told me he was glad to have me onboard. The plan was for me to start the next day. I told him about the wake I had Wednesday night, and his smile dimmed a bit, but he told me that would be fine and for me to come in afterward. We sat for a few minutes talking about the old neighborhood, and then I left him to find Bambi. I still had to tell her about the moonlighting job, and wasn't sure how'd she take it.

Bambi wasn't at the table where I had left her, nor was she at the bar. After more searching I found her on the dance floor with a stud closer to her age than I was. She spotted me and waved me over to join her. With the way my knees and back were feeling, I'd rather have just let her dance a while longer with the kid she was with, but I finished off my Michelob and went out there to join her.

We danced long enough for both of us to get hot and sweaty, all the while my knees barking up a storm. Christ, I was getting old. When we were back at our table, the waitress brought over fresh drinks and told me they were on the house. Bambi's eyes narrowed as she watched me, but she didn't say anything until the waitress was out of earshot.

"Why are the drinks on the house?" she asked. "'Cause you're a cop?"

I told her about the moonlighting job I was taking, the hours involved and the extra money I'd be making. During it all her face was inscrutable.

"Well?" I asked.

"The money sounds good," she said. "I can hang out here while you're working, and it's only going to be three months. Sure, why not. It sounds fun."

Over the next hour I nursed a couple of beers while Bambi had a few more vodka martinis. When we left she was a little unsteady, swaying enough that she needed to hold onto my arm for support. After I got her in the car and was driving the six blocks back to my apartment, I noticed her eyes scrunched as if she were deep in thought.

"Why'd you take this job all of a sudden?" she asked. "Not that I'm complaining, Stan. It sounds good and everything, but it's not like you. So what's the urgency?"

"I owe a guy three grand, and the guy who owns the club was willing to give me the money as an advance."

"Why do you owe three thousand dollars?"

"Because of my kids. Let's leave it at that."

She stared off into the distance for a long moment before nodding slowly. "Fair enough," she said.

After we got back to the apartment I started brewing some coffee, then turned on the TV to catch the final score of the game. The game had started a little after five, and it was now a quarter to eleven, and I was surprised to see it was still going on. It was the bottom of the fourteenth with Johnny Damon of the Red Sox on first and Manny Ramirez at the plate. Loaiza was pitching, which made me wonder if something had happened to "Mr. Automatic," Mariano Rivera. I watched as Ramirez walked on a full count, sending Damon to second and David Ortiz to the plate. After a long at bat where he fouled off several tough pitches, Ortiz singled to drive in the winning run. Game over. Yankees still led three games to two, and the series was coming back to the Bronx, but this gave Boston some life. I watched for a few minutes while they recapped the game and saw that Rivera had given up a sac fly in the eighth to tie up the score, making two straight blown saves.

I turned off the set. It didn't matter. Once the Yankees were back home they'd find a way to win, Boston would find a way to choke like they always did, and the universe would be back to normal. Boston beating the Yankees in a championship series in the house that Ruth built? Hell hadn't frozen over yet, at least not that I knew of. And Stevie would have these last two games to look back fondly at, so fine, let Boston win a couple.

Bambi came out of the bedroom wearing a negligee. The night's drinking showed in the paleness of her complexion. She stumbled before regaining her balance, then asked if I was coming to bed. I told her I'd join her soon, that I had something I needed to do first. She pouted and warned me not to take too long. After she stumbled back into the bedroom, I sat at the dining room table and wrote long letters to Stevie and Emma. Then I prepared packages for both of them.

When I was a kid I used to collect paperbacks. I never spent more than five dollars on any of them—which back then was still a lot of money, especially for a thirteen-year-old working off the books delivering groceries for tips. Sometimes I'd spend months scouring the used bookstores before I'd find what I was looking for. I included in my package to Stevie all of my Robert E. Howard Conan the Barbarian books, as well as my favorite Ray Bradbury paperbacks. I had no idea what books would be appropriate for a seven-year-old girl, so earlier that day during my lunch break I'd stopped off at a bookstore and gotten suggestions from a salesgirl who claimed she had bought the same books for a niece, and I included those in my package to Emma. When I was done putting the packages together and had them addressed and ready for shipping, I went into the bedroom to join Bambi. She was on her back snoring away. I decided it would be best to just let her sleep.

Tuesday, October 19, 2004

Not much happened the next day. If someone had been murdered on the edge of the Parkway, we still didn't know who it was. A body hadn't yet been found—at least none that matched the blood at the scene, and we were still waiting for the FBI results from CODIS, a database of DNA samples taken from previously convicted violent criminals and crime scenes. It was a long shot at best that we'd find a match from it, but you never know when you're going to get lucky.

We weren't going to get anywhere with the photos the medical examiner's office sent me of the dead dogs. The damage to them was just too severe for an owner to be able recognize them, and so far we'd come up empty-handed with the animal shelters we contacted. While we were on the lookout for missing pets, and had given the local reporters a story about several dead dogs being dumped off the Steinway Street overpass, none of the calls we received were a possible match. Most likely Hennison was right; the dogs were strays picked up off the street.

That afternoon Jill Chandler released her profile for the killer. She had him as a Caucasian male in his thirties, average height and weight, nondescript appearance, and college educated. His most distinguishing characteristic—at least for us—was his narcissistic personality disorder, but according to her there was little chance he was under psychiatric care or had been previously diagnosed. She also thought there was a high likelihood that he was single and still living with a parent, and employed in a job that he considered menial. While that was interesting, I didn't see how it was going to help us.

The FBI lab that the dogs were sent to was able to identify the prescription sleeping pills that were fed to them. The two FBI field agents assigned to the team, as well as Jill, were going to screen the roughly ten thousand New Yorkers who had prescriptions for that same sleeping pill, and try to come up with a manageable list of people for us to interview. Again, I didn't see how this was going to help us. I had little doubt that our perp acquired everything he was using for these killings off the grid.

I spent the morning working down the list of knife purchases, and when I was done with it I gave Zachary Lynch a call. I had eleven people whose alibis weren't good enough, and my idea was to have them come down to the station en masse to give Lynch a look at them. I still wasn't convinced about Lynch's reliability, but I figured it couldn't hurt. If he pointed someone out, I'd look closer at the guy and make sure his alibi was airtight before I gave up on him.

When I told Lynch what I was planning he wasn't too happy about making another trip to the precinct, and it took some tooth-pulling on my part before he agreed to it. I also told him that I was able to get the FBI to leave him alone, and I guess he felt he needed to show his appreciation for that. We set it up for one o'clock the following day, and then I got on the phone again with those eleven potential suspects. None of them were too happy being asked to come down to the station, but I left it as either agreeing to a voluntary trip and a short interview, or having a warrant issued with a much longer and less pleasant interrogation waiting for them.

After lunch I headed uptown and spent most of the afternoon interviewing tenants at the building where Burke's body was found. No one I spoke to saw anything the night his body was dumped, nor did anyone know Burke or Gail Laurent, and none of them gave me any reason to think they were lying. I have a pretty good radar for that, and while they were nervous, which was understandable given that they were talking with a police detective about a homicide, they seemed forthcoming.

At five o'clock I called it a day. On the way home, I stopped off to pay Earl his three grand. He didn't say anything about it, but from the way he smiled at me, I knew he knew I never made it to the game. He also knew I was working for Joel Cohen, and suggested that I be on the lookout over the next few days for some Russian-speaking muscle.

When I got home I called Cheryl, and as usual, inches of frost came over the line from her and Stevie refused to talk to me. Emma got on the phone and spent several minutes telling me how mad she was at me, but this time it didn't sound quite as heartfelt. After that I took Bambi to Lucia's for dinner and later brought her with me to the club. It was all pretty uneventful, although Bambi seemed to have a good time—especially with her drinks being comped—and she had no problem keeping herself entertained while I worked.

Right before midnight a collective moan went through the place. Asking around, I found out the Yankees had lost and the series was now tied three games apiece.

"Who's Boston got on the mound for game seven?" I asked.

"I don't know, but we've got Kevin Brown going."

For a moment I felt my stomach sink as I imagined the unimaginable. Brown had been one of the Yankees' biggest disappointments this year, and ever since they got him he was either injured or being shelled. "Boston always finds a way to choke," I said. "Why should this year be any different?"

The guy I said this to nodded, but he looked about as unsure of this as I was feeling. With my shift over, I located Bambi on the dance floor, waved her over, and we left.

When we got back to the apartment, I again wrote Stevie and Emma another pair of long letters. This was going to be my routine for the next three months and probably well beyond that—calling and writing letters everyday. Eventually I'd wear them down, or at least let them know that I cared and wasn't going to give up. When I was done with the letters I joined Bambi in bed. This time she waited up for me.

Chapter 18

Wednesday, October 20, 2004

Wednesday was more of the same with none of us accomplishing much more than spinning our wheels. I spent the morning finishing my interviews at the apartment building and could've slept in for all the good it did. No one I spoke with saw or knew anything that was going to help. We heard back from the FBI that morning, and it was the same thing with them. No DNA matches were found within CODIS, and they were unable to come up with a more specific time of death for the dogs.

At noon I left to pick up Zachary Lynch. I guess he had gotten accustomed to whatever it was he saw when he looked at me because this time when he caught a glimpse of me he didn't flinch like before. On the way over I had stopped off for a couple of sandwiches, figuring that given his near-hermit life style it would be a treat. He seemed grateful for the gesture, and we ate lunch together in his apartment before heading out. While neither of us talked while we ate, he appeared more comfortable with me and showed less of his nervous twitches.

When we were in the car and heading back to the precinct, I made an offhand comment about how he was probably going to be seeing Lisa that night. That took him by surprise.

"The girl at Strombolli's," I said. "Wednesday's when you go there, right?"

He nodded, his mouth weakening as he thought about it.

"You really think I should talk to her?" he asked under his breath, his voice barely loud enough for me to hear him.

"Yeah, you should. She'd like you to. She told me so." I paused for a moment, then asked if he was going to be heading over at six like he had the other week. He seemed startled by the question, not sure if I was just making small talk. I wasn't. While I thought there was something to Jill Chandler's theory that our killer was trying to tell a carefully scripted "story," I didn't buy that that was why he didn't shoot Lynch. I still had to think he was out of bullets. Adding the bullets that were used on those dogs, so far fifteen rounds were accounted for, and more must've been expended on whoever the unlucky person was who stopped on the Parkway. Two clips, ten rounds per clip, and it pretty much added up. Our killer could be out there looking for Lynch to tie up loose ends, and if he was he'd be looking where he'd last seen him. I didn't want to tell Lynch any of this, though.

"I think so," he said, answering my question about whether he'd be heading to Strombolli's at six. He smiled awkwardly. "Why, detective, do you think there might be a problem getting me back by then?"

I shook my head. "This shouldn't take too long. I was thinking if you'd like to get there earlier I could stop off when I drive you home."

"I appreciate the offer, but I could use the fresh air. And Lisa doesn't start work until five o'clock. During the day, she goes to college. She's studying to be a nurse."

I already knew Lisa Williams's hours and how Lynch would respond to my offer. I wanted him walking to Strombolli's, but I needed to keep the conversation appearing casual.

"So you have talked to her," I said.

He blushed, a light pink breaking up the pale grayness of his complexion. "She let it slip once," he said, embarrassed.

I commented that with him once being a medical student he'd have something in common to talk with her about, but that seemed to send him into a funk. He sat quietly after that, too caught up in his own thoughts to pay any attention to my small talk, and shortly after that I stopped bothering to ask him anything else. When we got to the precinct I situated him so he'd be able to see the suspects without them seeing him. Seven of them ended up showing up. While they waited I checked with Lynch on whether he recognized any of them. He seemed shaken up by what he saw—not as bad as when he nearly went catatonic on me that time outside his apartment building, but still, shaken up. His expression rigid, he shook his head and told me none of them shot Gail Laurent. I had a couple of the other detectives interview them about their alibis while I drove Lynch back. Neither of us bothered talking during the ride. I spent the time wondering how I was going to be able to convince a judge to issue bench warrants for the suspects who didn't show.

I pulled up to Lynch's apartment building. His skin color still wasn't right, and hard lines stood out along his mouth. I couldn't help myself. I had to ask him what it was he saw when he looked at the suspects. He shook his head and told me it wasn't anything I was looking for. He left the car, and I watched as he made his way up the stone steps of his building and disappeared inside it.

When I got back four of the suspects had been released, their alibis checking out enough. I moved from interrogation room to interrogation room, watching from behind the one-way as the other three were interrogated. While their alibis were vague, it was clear none of them were our killer. At one point Jill Chandler joined me and watched before saying the same. Shortly after that, we were satisfied enough to release them also.

At five o'clock I drove back to Zachary Lynch's apartment building. While I waited for him to leave, I called Cheryl from my cell phone. There was less frost this time, although she complained about me calling earlier than I was supposed to. Stevie still refused to talk to me, but Emma got on the phone and this time talked about more than just her being mad at me.

It was twenty minutes to six when Lynch left his building. I followed him on foot, watching as he awkwardly made his way down the street, his stare frozen downward to avoid looking at any passersby. Even though there was no chance he'd make me tailing him, nor would it've mattered much if he did, I followed at a distance and made sure to keep myself as unobtrusive as possible, the whole time ready to make a grab for my holstered service revolver. While I didn't care much if Lynch spotted me, I didn't want anyone out looking for him doing so.

Lynch made it to Strombolli's without incident. I waited across the street while he picked up a week's worth of groceries and took them to Lisa. From my vantage point, Lisa appeared nearly to be beaming while they talked. I couldn't see Lynch's face, but their conversation lasted ten minutes, so it had to've been over more than what was on his grocery list.

I followed him back to his apartment building. It was almost seven then, and after waiting for Lynch to get safely inside his building I headed off to Queens and Rich's wake. I'd spoken earlier with Bambi, and she decided she'd spend the evening with friends, which was just as well. These things tended to make you feel like an outsider if you weren't part of the fraternity.

The wake was held at a small Italian restaurant in Astoria and was supposed to start at seven thirty. I arrived a few minutes after that and the place was already crowded. It seemed well attended by our precinct, and I recognized officers from throughout the city. I talked with a few of them as I made my way to the bar. After I got a Bud, which I planned to nurse for as long as I could, I spotted Mary talking to Phillips. Her three sons stood next to her, all dressed stiffly in suits and looking about as glum as any kids I'd ever seen. Mary noticed me and gave me a brittle smile. I made my way over to her. Phillips on seeing me didn't bother hanging around.

I gave Mary a hug, then a kiss on the cheek, and the way her eyes turned liquid I knew she wasn't up to any third degree over what had happened to Rich, so I just stood quietly and held her hand. After several minutes of that, she told me that according to his doctor Rich developed some sort of post-op infection that spread quickly to his heart—too quickly for the doctors to act on it. It sounded like bullshit to me. Whatever he had, it looked like he'd had it when I first visited him after his operation, which meant he'd had it for a couple of days. Although Mary didn't say anything I suspected she thought the same. Her boys began fidgeting and she told me she was going to take them to the buffet table. Before she left I mentioned again for her to call me for anything, and she said she would.

I felt someone looking at me and turned to see Jill Chandler making her way through the crowd, holding a drink and being careful not to spill any of it. She had that softer look about her again. She parked herself next to me and commented on the turnout. I was surprised to see her. She didn't know Rich, had never met him as far as I knew, and being a member of the FBI didn't make her part of our fraternity. I asked her if she was there alone, and she rolled her eyes and made a comment about who else was she going to be there with.

"I wasn't asking if you brought a date. I meant whether the other two FBI agents on the team joined you. Thorne and Snell."

She blushed slightly at that. "No, I came alone," she said. "I thought I'd show some solidarity."

I half-turned my back on her. I don't know, it just didn't seem right for her to be there, like it was an intrusion. After several minutes I turned my head enough to see that she hadn't taken the hint and was still standing next to me. She smiled and asked me what my story was.

I stared blankly at her. "What do you mean?"

"I've read through your folder and know you're divorced," she said as if that would be a completely natural thing to tell someone. "In my head I'm always profiling people I meet, especially those I find interesting. Call it professional curiosity, but I'm wondering whether or not you're involved in a relationship."

I was taken completely aback by that. I wanted to say something other than what I did, but instead I controlled myself and asked why she'd gone through my folder.

Her smile turned more into the self-pleased variety. "Detective Green, what group tends to favor a .40 caliber handgun?"

I didn't bother saying the obvious. We both knew the answer. A .40 caliber is typically a military or police weapon, and more than a few police officers have been known to have one as a second gun.

"Don't worry, I didn't single you out, detective. The first thing I was asked to do when I was assigned to the case was go through the folders of all the team members," she said, still smiling that pleased smile of hers. "It's standard procedure but I would've done it even if I wasn't asked. I needed to eliminate the killer from being someone inside the investigation."

Standing there at a wake for my partner in a room filled with my brother officers, I was more bothered by the idea of her doing that than I should have been. It made sense for her to do what she did, and it wasn't without precedent. A cop could've been the shooter, especially if there was a motive behind the killings other than simply being the random work of a serial killer, but still, it bothered me.

"You still think a cop could be involved?" I asked.

She laughed at that. "Come on, detective, you've seen my profile of our killer. Show me a more convincing narcissist than Detective Jack Hennison."

"Nah, you've read him all wrong. It's just bluster with him. Dig deep enough under the surface and you'll find a sweetheart." I hesitated for a moment, then added, "Your question about my story. Yeah, I'm involved."

She nodded, her smile dimming. We stood quietly after that, with her sipping what looked like a gin and tonic and me nursing my Bud. A tension was developing between us. It could've been worse; at least I swallowed back a crack about how we could still be friends. Fuck, I must've been in a rotten mood. After several minutes more of this uneasiness she excused herself and slipped into the crowd. I didn't see her again that night.

The next several hours went by in a blur. I still had a two-hour shift waiting for me at the nightclub, so I nursed my beers as long as I could, which wasn't easy given all the drinks people were trying to buy me. A cop dies, you buy his partner of ten years a round. I didn't stop them from buying me them, I just passed them on to other cops. The whole night just seemed so damn surreal. Rich was gone, and for what? Because he got clipped crossing the street for a lousy cannoli? Because of some fucked up operation that a guy like Rich had no right dying from? None of it made any sense. I don't know, maybe it was just his time, maybe it was that simple, but I was having a hard time accepting it.

The wake started to lose steam around midnight. Word had spread that the Yankees got bombed badly by Boston, which only added to the weirdness of the night. It was just a baseball game—it didn't really mean shit. Inside the restaurant was reality. A good husband, a damn good father, and a hell of a friend dead for no reason that made any sense. I don't know, though. You grow up with certain absolutes, like believing in the law of gravity, and then learn at age thirty-nine that it's all bullshit. Yankees are supposed to win championships, Red Sox are supposed to find ways to lose them. Now, after blowing a three-to-nothing lead, the Yankees end up suffering what could be the worst choke job in the history of baseball, maybe in all of sports. It wasn't supposed to be that way. While Boston would have plenty of opportunities to blow the World Series, it still seemed as if the world had been flipped on its head. Maybe hell did freeze over and I just hadn't gotten the weather report.

Fuck it, it was just a game.

I got to the nightclub around twelve thirty. The place was quiet, almost like a tomb. If the Yankees had won, it would've been filled with people celebrating, but I guess as it was they were either at home in shock or drowning their sorrows. Around one o'clock, Joel came out of his office to check that I was there and to ask how the wake went. He didn't say anything about it, but he seemed on edge, as if he were expecting something to happen. While we talked, his eyes kept shifting toward the front entrance. Before he headed back to his office, he asked if I could stick around until three. I told him I would.

I used the slow night to write my letters to my kids. Whatever Joel was expecting didn't happen, at least not by three o'clock when I left.

Chapter 19

Thursday, October 21, 2004

The city was in mourning the next day. It was one thing for the Yankees to lose, but to the Red Sox? And in the way they did? Maybe it was just me and the mood I was in, maybe I was overly affected by having almost no sleep the night before, but the somberness seemed palpable, almost like a fog that had descended over the city.

No one talked much inside the precinct, at least not much more than what was needed for the job, which meant we were mostly like monks that day since not much was going on with the investigation. We had our informants out in force looking for psychos who liked military knives and .40 caliber automatics, but the leads they gave us went nowhere.

I was able to get bench warrants for the four potential suspects who didn't show up the other day, which surprised me given the thinness of my reason, but I guess the judge must've been in a rotten mood after the Yankees collapse. I rounded up the four without having to exercise the warrants. While none of them were happy about it, they all agreed to accompany me back to the station, and I was able to keep the warrants in my back pocket.

Zachary Lynch also wasn't happy about making another trip to the station, but he agreed to it and, after a quick look at the suspects, told me they weren't our shooter. I drove him back afterward, and during the ride he mentioned how much this took out of him. That while he'd like to help, he wanted me to limit his involvement to only suspects where we had strong evidence. I wasn't in much of a mood to respond to that, which just made things tense again between us. When I pulled up to his building, he got halfway out of the car before stopping to thank me for pushing him to talk with Lisa the other day.

I drove back to the station and finished interviewing the suspects, at least to where I was able to corroborate enough of their alibis to convince myself that none of them were our killer.

I left at five o'clock when my shift ended, figuring I'd already wasted enough of the taxpayers money. When I got home I called Cheryl, and this time Stevie was willing to talk with me. Mostly it was to brag about the Red Sox beating my Yankees (as if I personally had a financial stake in them), but at the end he thanked me for the package I sent. I was relieved that Cheryl hadn't censored the books I'd included. I was worried that she would take out the Robert E. Howard books, claiming they were too violent and racy for an eleven-year-old, especially given the Frank Frazetta artwork on the covers.

"The books look really cool, dad."

"Hey, those are some of my favorites."

"I'll let you know what I think." He hesitated, then added before getting off the line that he still wasn't going to New York for Thanksgiving.

I wasn't going to fight him on it, and least not then. After Stevie, I talked with Emma, and she no longer felt compelled to tell me how mad she was at me. Instead she spent fifteen minutes reading me one of the books I had sent her, and listening to her do that was nicer than I would've imagined. Fuck, I missed her.

Later that night before heading off for my shift at the nightclub, I told Bambi it would probably be best if she didn't come with me for the next few nights. She wasn't too happy with that and insisted on me telling her why. I didn't want to get into it with her right then, especially telling her what I thought might be going down soon. While I was trying to think of some credible excuse apart from the feeling that there might be some trouble at the club tonight, she let loose with a few suggestions about what I could do to myself since I wasn't going to be doing them to her anytime soon, then slammed the bedroom door in my face. I figured it was just as well and left it at that.

Joel Cohen was as on edge as he was the previous night, maybe even more so. He asked again if I could stay until three, and I told him I would. It was quiet, though. Whatever he was expecting again didn't happen, at least not by the time I left.

When I got back to the apartment I found the bedroom door locked and ended up sleeping on the sofa. Given how wiped out I felt, that was okay with me. The next morning I didn't bother trying to get a fresh change of clothes out of the bedroom. I set up the ironing board and ran the iron over what I had worn the day before, and was out the door before Bambi left the bedroom.

The investigation had the feel of one that was growing cold fast. We had finished interviewing the tenants at the Upper West Side apartment building and had come up with nothing. Hennison was still collecting ballistic samples, but so far all tests were negative, and it was hard to believe we'd catch our killer that way. Three of the detectives on the team were digging into Paul Burke's background and who he'd been sleeping with, and they were getting nowhere. From my vantage point, the FBI was only spinning its wheels like the rest of us. More and more this was looking like the type of case that would crack only if our guy started making noise about what he'd been doing—either contacting us or the newspapers or bragging at bars to strangers. According to the psychological profile Jill Chandler worked up, there was little chance he'd be doing any of that.

I spent part of the day twiddling my thumbs, part of it tracking down an informant lead that went nowhere. That night was only more of the same as the previous one. Bambi was still too angry to acknowledge me and instead let her body language do her talking, especially in the way she banged cupboard doors and threw things around the apartment. Joel Cohen was as much on edge as he'd been the previous two nights and asked me to stay late, and again, nothing happened. When I returned back to the apartment, the bedroom door was locked, and I slept on the sofa. All in all, a night of déjà vu.

Wednesday, October 27, 2004

The following Wednesday I followed Zachary Lynch as he made his way to and from Strombolli's. There was no sign anyone was out hunting for him. That night the Boston Red Sox finished sweeping the St. Louis Cardinals, winning their first World Series in eighty-six years. It was a tough pill for Yankee fans everywhere, but I decided it was just one of those weird aberrations. Fine, let them have their one championship every eighty-six years as long as we had our twenty-six rings during the same stretch. By the time Boston won their next World Series, I'd be dead and buried and wouldn't have to see all those chowdahead fans gloating.

Thursday, October 28, 2004

The next night was when something went down at the nightclub. Joel Cohen asked me to stay late, which had become routine over the past week.

At one thirty two guys entered the club whom I hadn't

seen before and who didn't look like they belonged in the neighborhood, one of them thick-bodied with his hair cut close to the scalp, the other lean and wiry and sporting a well-groomed goatee and long black hair that fell past his shoulders. They both had a hardness about them, as well as a distinctive Eastern European look. From where I was sitting I could see the bulge in the thick-bodied man's jacket. They were both smirking as they made their way through the club. I got up to intercept them and stepped in front of them before they reached Joel's office.

"Do you have a permit to carry?" I asked the thick-bodied man.

He stared at me dully while his partner smirked. "Why don't you go shoo," he said, making a shooing gesture with his hand, his Russian accent as thick as his body. His partner laughed at that.

Up close I could see the scars tattooing his face and that his nose had been broken several times and was bent to the right. I'd already taken my badge out, and I showed it to him.

"NYPD," I said. "Sir, I won't be asking you this again, do you have a permit to carry a concealed weapon?"

He continued staring at me, his eyes dulling to the point where they appeared almost translucent. "Why not mind your own business?" he said. "This not concern you. No reason to get hurt, yes?"

He was smiling thinly, his shoulder muscles bunching. His partner took a sliding step to his right, trying to get behind me.

"Both of you, on your knees now, hands on your head!" I ordered.

The thick-bodied Russian shrugged and for a second looked as if he were going to comply, and then made a move to charge me. Christ, I don't know what he was thinking. I grabbed him by both shoulders and used his momentum to pull him toward me, while at the same time bringing my knee hard into his groin. That took the fight out of him, and he stumbled back, his face purpling as he gasped in air. I had my service revolver out and pointed at him, and he went down to his knees. I then swung the .38 around at the other Russian, whose smirk intensified as he also lowered himself to the floor, kneeling, his fingers interlaced behind his head.

"This is big trouble for you," the thinner, goateed Russian said.

"Shut up!" I yelled back at him, the adrenaline pumping hard through me. This was the first time in more than ten years that I'd had to pull out my service revolver and point it at someone. "Don't you fucking move! Neither of you!"

Joel Cohen came out of his office to see what the commotion was about. He stared deadpan at the two Russians. I patted them down, removing 9 mm Lugers from both of them. With them on their knees and their hands behind their heads, I took my cell phone out and called dispatch, telling them what I had and asking them to send backup.

"Tell your friend mistake he's making," the thick-bodied Russian said to Joel between gasps of air, his eyes still tearing from the blow he'd taken, his face mottled purple and white.

Joel, without a word, went back into his office and closed the door. I started reciting them their rights. The thick-bodied Russian interrupted me and told me whatever I was being paid wasn't enough.

"Are you threatening a police officer?" I asked.

He met my stare full-on; then a dark shadow passed over his eyes. "*Fooking jid*," he swore, spitting on the floor near my feet. I didn't know what he was calling me, but whatever it was it made my ears burn red.

"What the fuck did you just call me?" I asked.

He didn't say anything. All he did was smile at me. An empty smile filled with the promise of violence.

Two police cruisers responded to the scene. They cuffed the two Russians, and I followed them to the Flatbush precinct on Empire Boulevard where the Russians were each charged with illegal possession of a firearm as well as threatening a police officer, and the thicker-bodied Russian also charged with assault and battery on a police officer. Their bond hearing wasn't going to happen until morning, so they were going to be spending the night in lockup. The detective I spoke with agreed with me that the "threatening a police officer" charge wouldn't stick since they didn't make any specific threats, but he'd leave it in since it could bump up their bail.

"It was lucky you were on the scene," he told me. "It might've gotten ugly if you weren't."

"Yeah, well, the club's in the neighborhood. Just having a few drinks."

"Damn good thing you were alert, anyway," he said. He stopped to rub a hand along his jaw. "Is this a place we should be keeping an eye on?"

"I don't know. Those two were making threats, but I don't know how serious they were. Maybe Organized Crime needs to get involved. Find out who these jokers work for and put some heat on their boss."

"Yeah, maybe," the detective said, his eyes dulling enough to tell me that wasn't going to happen.

After I left the Flatbush precinct, I went back to the nightclub. Joel was still there. "Whatever you've paid me I earned out tonight," I told him when we were alone in his office.

"Yeah, you did," he agreed, his eyes glassy. He sniffed, rubbed a hand nervously across his nose. "I won't argue that, but I wouldn't mind having you on the payroll as long as you want to be on it. Give it some thought, Stan. It's good money."

"No, I don't think so. Let's say I'd walked in a minute earlier and caught you snorting coke, I'd be busting you like I did those two Russians."

"Jesus, Stan—"

I held up a hand to stop him. "Don't bother. By the way, do you know what *jid* means?"

"What?"

"One of those Russians called me that."

He smiled sickly at me. "Yeah, I've had enough contact with these Brighton Beach boys to know what it means. These assholes are pure Russian, you know. As anti-Semitic as they come. It's a not-so-nice word to call a Jew. Kind of like *kike* or *yid*, except worse."

"Fucking A," I said. "To think, I could've cracked that fucker's skull open and passed on the opportunity."

"Keep working here, and maybe you'll have another chance."

I didn't bother answering that and left him. I usually don't drink hard alcohol, but I accepted a shot of bourbon from the bartender when he mentioned that it looked like I could badly use one, and then followed that with a second shot. My hands were still shaking from the adrenaline rush earlier.

I was too charged up to go home after that. I ended up stopping for a large coffee and a bag of doughnuts, then driving to Canarsie and pulling off of the Belt Parkway. I sat in my car and stared out in the direction of the ocean. It was too dark to see much, but I could hear the waves coming in. Hours later when the sun started to come up and the sky turned into more of a gray murkiness, I pulled back onto the Parkway and headed to Manhattan.

Later that day Phillips pulled me into his office so I could give him a report on what happened at the nightclub. I gave him the same story I gave the Brooklyn detective. He suggested I take my job more seriously, and not drink late into the night when I had an eight o'clock shift the next morning.

He also added that it would be a good idea not to come to work in the same clothes I slept in the night before.

That night I told Bambi what happened at the nightclub.

"Is that why you didn't want me coming with you?"

"Yeah, I knew something was going down. I didn't want to see you caught in the crossfire."

"Why didn't you tell me?"

I didn't have to answer her. She knew the reason was that I didn't want her worrying. Whatever grudge she was holding melted away, and for the first time in a week I didn't have to sleep on the sofa.

Over the next several weeks the case became ice-cold. The FBI had been looking at other open cases throughout the country, but wasn't able to connect these murders with any of them. Jill Chandler thought there was a chance if we publicly altered this guy's story that he might make contact to correct the record. We ended up leaking a story to the papers that Paul Burke's murder was the result of an argument that had gotten out of hand, and an arrest was imminent. If this ended up getting under our killer's skin, he didn't let us know.

Monday, November 15, 2004

At this point, Jack Hennison was the only detective working the case full-time. Jill Chandler and the other two FBI agents were gone, and the other detectives from the team were reassigned. I was still working the case when I could fit in the hours, but spent most of my time on other calls. I was still following Zachary Lynch every Wednesday as he made his weekly trek to Strombolli's. This had become more habit than anything else, but I'd be damned if I was going to hear about him ending up in the morgue.

Thanksgiving rolled around and Stevie was still adamant against coming to New York, and if he wasn't coming, Emma wasn't either. I didn't fight him on it. I was still calling and writing both of them every day, and my relationship with them was improving, and that was enough for now. Things were also getting better with Bambi. There was less of that dissatisfaction from her about the way we were living and how little money I was keeping from my paycheck each week. We ended up cooking a full Thanksgiving dinner together—a fourteen-pound turkey, mashed potatoes, stuffing, yams, peas and pearl onions, even a pumpkin pie. Mike and his kids were supposed to join us, but at the last minute he bailed on me. It was okay—it was still nice, just the two of us—but shit, we ended up with a ton of leftovers.

The next day I drove up to Cumberland, Rhode Island. Bambi stayed behind in New York, not really wanting to spend several days at a Motel Six and still feeling uncomfortable about being with my kids, and I didn't push hard to change her mind.

Things went better with Emma than with Stevie. Whatever shyness she showed was gone within an hour. Stevie, however, stayed aloof the whole weekend. I tried, though. Saturday I took them to Boston where we spent the day at the Aquarium and later at the Museum of Science, and Sunday to a local diner for chocolate chip pancakes, a movie, and ice skating—which being Brooklyn-bred, I'd never done before, and kept falling on my ass. Mostly all I got out of Stevie were monosyllabic grunts to whatever I asked him, although he did begrudgingly tell me that he liked the books I'd sent him, his favorite being *Conan the Adventurer*. Still, while things didn't go perfectly, it was hard leaving them when I did Sunday, and I felt a heaviness welling up in my chest as I drove back to New York.

The first week in December my mom suffered a major stroke. It had been hard enough seeing her over the last few years, but it was heartbreaking seeing her in the hospital barely a shell of what she'd once been. The Alzheimer's had robbed her of so much, and the stroke took away the little she had left. One of the nights I was visiting her, Mike showed up. It was the first time I'd seen him in months. We talked for a little while. He was still on disability, and with him still missing twenty percent of his lung capacity it didn't sound as if he'd be getting off of it anytime soon. He didn't look good. I couldn't help feeling as if things were slipping away from him. It had been bad for more than three years, ever since 9-11, but this was worse. He apologized for missing Thanksgiving and promised he'd make it up the following year. When I tried asking him if things were getting any better between him and Marcy, he cut me off short and left.

The following week a couple of detectives from Organized Crime talked to me about what happened at Joel Cohen's nightclub. If they suspected me of being on Joel's payroll they kept it to themselves. Anyway, it was a brief talk, and they wanted to know if I had contact with any associates of the two Russians I arrested. I told them so far I hadn't, and one of them hinted that with some luck it would stay that way.

By the end of December I was officially off the murder investigation. I was still watching over Zachary Lynch each week, but that was strictly my own time. Jack Hennison was still working the case part-time, and even that, you could tell was taking a toll on him. He didn't want to give up on it. None of us did. But sometimes these damn cases just can't be solved no matter how much you pound away at them.

Chapter 20

Tuesday, January 18, 2005

Acting on a tip, detectives from Major Crimes broke into the basement of a building on Wooster Street. The building had once been a textile factory, later converted to office space, and had been abandoned since suffering fire damage in 2003. The detectives found, in a sealed-off area in the back, one Gerard Fiske and seven young children. The children, all between the ages of five and eight, were locked up in dog cages. Fiske had abducted them from parents who were illegal immigrants and, as the investigation later showed, were too afraid to come forward about the abductions. Three of the children were girls, the rest boys. The news only reported a small part of what Fiske had done to those children—and that was horrifying enough. I talked later with one of the detectives on the case and he gave me the full story, which was far worse than anyone could've imagined.

The day the story broke and I saw Fiske on the news, something about him seemed familiar. It bothered me throughout the night. I kept trying to remember where I'd seen him before.

The following day he was still being held at the Tombs, and I took a trip over there to get a look at him in person. While I stood outside his cell, Fiske sat on his cot with his head bowed. It was minutes before he realized I was there, and when he did he told me to go fuck myself, that he wasn't talking to the police.

"I'm not here to talk to you," I said.

He looked up at me then. "What are you here for then?" he asked, his curiosity getting the better of him.

I didn't bother answering him. While he was wearing a jail-issue jumpsuit and not the grayish-blue pinstripe suit I'd first seen him in, I recognized him. He was the same person Zachary Lynch nearly went catatonic over outside his apartment building.

Throughout the day I kept playing over in my head the way Lynch reacted when he saw Gerard Fiske. That afternoon I went to the New York Public Library and searched through newspapers dating back to 1972. When I found what I was looking for I sat for a few minutes saying a silent prayer for the memory of a twelve-year-old from back then who had lived in our neighborhood, Chucky Wilson. Afterward, I headed back to Central, where I dug out an old police report, then searched through DOC records, infuriated by what I found.

That night I watched over Zachary Lynch like I'd been doing every Wednesday, then drove to the studio apartment Mike had moved into after his separation from Marcy. We talked for a while, mostly about what had happened outside of that fish market when I was seven years old. Later, when I was alone in my living room, I forced myself to remember what it was I saw that day, and I wrote it down. I didn't sleep much that night.

Thursday, January 20, 2005

I was up early the next day and by five o'clock was sitting impatiently in my recliner waiting for the sun to come up. At seven I called in sick, then went to a diner and killed more time. I waited until nine o'clock before heading to Zachary Lynch's apartment. It had been almost two months since I last contacted him, and he seemed surprised to see me. It looked like I had woken him—he answered the door in a robe, his eyes squinting, a pillow-crease impression showing on his cheek. I told him I needed him to look at someone.

"I really don't have time this morning," he started. "I have a contract that I need to finish today—"

"This is important," I said. "I wouldn't be here otherwise."

He squinted his eyes shut against the light filtering in from the hallway. "Let me make a phone call," he said.

I followed him into his apartment. He called whoever it was he had a contract with and arranged for an extension. After he did that, he told me he'd take a quick shower and be ready in a few minutes. I opened the shades to let some light in and sat down. The living room had been cleaned up since I was last there. Books and papers had been put away, and the room aired out. It was more than that. A new sofa had been added, as well as a small but new dining room table, which even had a vase of flowers sitting on it. When Lynch came back wearing an old pair of jeans and a flannel shirt, with his long hair wet and hanging off his head like knotted string, I mentioned how he had redecorated. He gave an embarrassed smile and told me he'd picked up a few things online.

Fortunately he didn't ask me about my new suspect, so I didn't have to lie to him. I stopped off at a bakery nearby and bought him a Danish and coffee for breakfast, then headed off to Staten Island. An hour later I pulled up to a housing project for the elderly on the northern end of Staten Island, off of Tompkins Avenue. Lynch looked confused when he realized where we were, but he didn't say anything about it. I talked with the security guard working the front desk, showing him my badge and telling him I was there on official business, then led Lynch to a room on the second floor. When I found the room I was looking for, I knocked hard on the door and could see Lynch tensing while we waited.

"Are you sure this is safe?" he asked.

"Don't worry."

A fit of asthmatic coughing came from inside the room, then the sound of something being dragged along the floor. I felt the muscles along my jaw tightening as I stood there. The door opened enough to show a withered old man looking out. Zachary Lynch sucked in his breath at the sight of him and whispered to me that he wasn't the shooter. I ignored him and stood frozen, staring straight ahead.

The old man, with his hollowed cheeks and dead eyes, looked like he could've been the work of a taxidermist. He eyed me silently, grasping onto a walker for support, holding it tightly with two thickly veined and gnarled hands. An oxygen tank attached to the walker fed a thin tube into each of his nostrils. Even though his face was wasted and there was barely any flesh left on him, I recognized him. It had been thirty-two years, but I recognized him. Every few seconds his labored breathing reminded me that what was in front of me was still flesh and blood, no matter how dead his eyes looked. Eventually he recognized me also. He didn't say anything, just pushed the door shut, but there was a glint in his eyes and a faint trace of a smile letting me know that he knew who I was. It was almost as if that smile were telling me about what could've been if only I had followed him into the back of his fish market all those years ago. There was no doubt in my mind that if he was capable of it he'd be looking for another young boy to chop up.

"Why'd you bring me here?" Lynch asked.

I couldn't answer him, not then anyway. For a long moment I couldn't do much of anything other than feel my hands clenching and unclenching. When I could, I turned and made my way quickly out of the housing project and back to my car. Lynch was out of breath as he ran to keep up with me.

When we were in the car I asked Lynch what it was he saw when he looked at that man. My voice sounded foreign and strange to me, and my tone scared him. I could almost feel him shrinking from me. In a breathless whisper he told me that this person wasn't the one who killed Gail Laurent, and what he saw didn't matter.

"Just tell me what you saw."

He wasn't going to. I sat back, a wave of exhaustion hitting me. I described to Lynch the image I had forced myself to remember. I told him about that thin cobra-like body, the obscene hole where a nose was supposed to be, the enormous gaping jaw overflowing with jagged dagger-like teeth, the long blood-red talons where hands should've been. Zachary Lynch sat stunned hearing all that.

"How?" he asked.

"When I was seven years old, he tried to lure me and my brother into the back of a fish market with the promise of five dollars," I said. "For a split second I saw him the way I just described him."

"If you hadn't seen him like that . . ." Lynch muttered, shaking his head. "If you had gone with him . . ."

"I know what would've happened. He was later found chopping up the body of another boy he was able to lure back there." I swallowed hard and rubbed my hand across my jaw. "He was in Attica until recently. The DOC released him two months ago because he's dying of emphysema, although not soon enough if you ask me."

Lynch started crying. It was mostly a noiseless sob, his eyes squeezed tightly shut. I could see him struggling hard to stop it.

"I'm so sorry," he said. "This is embarrassing. But you have to understand. For six years I've been living with this nagging fear that maybe I am insane, that what I'm seeing really are just hallucinations and not what I think they are. But you seeing what you did—even if it was only for a split second—proves otherwise."

"What is it you see?" I asked.

"I'll . . . I'll tell you, but first, how'd you figure this out?"

"You must've seen the news stories about Gerard Fiske? The guy found in Tribeca with those children locked up in dog cages?"

Lynch nodded slowly.

"He's the same guy you saw that time with me when you nearly went catatonic. It was that first time I was taking you to the precinct, when we were walking to my car."

A heaviness came over his face as he remembered Fiske.

"You saw something that day," I said. "Just like I saw something outside that fish market when I was seven. So what is that we saw?" My voice caught in my throat, and I had to clear it before I could ask, "Are they some sort of monsters?"

"Monstrous, but not monsters," he said softly. An off-kilter smile twisted his lips. "Detective Green, I guess you can say I see people the way they really are. Not how they are physically, but spiritually. Their essence. Their true selves. This is what I've been living with ever since being brought back from the dead, and it's not much fun."

We both sat quietly. I expected something like that, so what he told me wasn't a surprise, but still, I had to sit and digest it.

"What is it you see when you look at me?" I asked.

"Detective, it's not important—"

"Bullshit," I said. "I'm the guy with holes instead of eyes, remember? What the fuck do you see?"

"What difference does it make? You're not a monster, if that's what you want to know."

"Yeah, all I do is make you flinch and nearly swallow your tongue every time you see me."

"Come on, detective," he said, trying to joke it off. "I haven't done that in ages."

"I need to know. Zachary, as a friend, just tell me what it is."

He sucked in a lungful of air and blew it out an explosive breath. "You really need me to tell you what you already know?" he asked.

"Yeah, I need you to."

His mouth weakened as he nodded. "Okay," he said. "You're not a monster, Detective Green. You're not spiritually ugly or deformed. But what I see is so much swirling confusion and rage inside you that it's hard to take. At least it used to be, but I guess I've gotten used to you."

He was trying hard to smile. "That's ridiculous," I said, "I'm a calm person. I almost never express rage." But I knew he was right. He only told me what I already knew, what I found myself fighting against almost every waking minute, at least since Cheryl dropped her bombshell on me more than two years ago.

He touched me lightly on the shoulder and forced himself to look at me as he maintained his smile. "People can grow spiritually," he said. "Not the completely broken ones, not people like that man in there or Gerard Fiske or the one who I saw shoot that woman, but the rest of us can."

"Of course what you're telling me is a load of horseshit," I said.

"Of course. Just ask my neurologist."

I nodded, my jaw clenched shut. I put the car in drive. Neither of us said a word to each other while I drove us back to Manhattan. It wasn't until I parked in front of Zachary Lynch's apartment building that I told him that what he had was a gift.

He laughed sourly at that. "Some gift. Please, show me to the exchange window so I can trade it for a pair of socks."

"No, it is. If we knew ahead of time about people like Gerard Fiske and could be watching them, maybe what we discovered the other day never would've happened."

"It's not that simple," he said.

"Sure it is. You knew when you saw him on the street that day what he was."

"Who would I have told?" he asked, his voice breaking into a soft whisper. "Who would've believed me?"

"I would have."

He pulled awkwardly at his lower lip as he considered that, then smiling sadly asked, "And who would believe you?"

It was a good question. I tried to think of some way of answering him, but drew a blank.

"That's the problem," Lynch said. "Even if I pointed out these monsters to you, you wouldn't be able to do anything about it. And there are so many of them out there. You wouldn't believe how many there are. Although not many like Gerard Fiske. Or that man you took me to see today."

"There's got to be something . . ."

"Sadly, detective, there isn't. Even if there was, I wouldn't want to do it. I don't think it would be right for me to be the one to determine whether someone's soul is monstrous enough to warrant investigation."

"But if you saw someone like Fiske again—"

"I wouldn't. I almost never look up at people on the street."

"But if you did . . ."

"What would I do then? I wouldn't be able to describe the person to you, at least not his physical appearance, and I don't think describing his soul would help you much."

"I'll buy you a digital camera. You can carry it around

and take pictures of these people when you see them."

He blanched at the prospect of doing that. "I don't think so," he said. "I couldn't make a promise like that. It's so hard looking into people's souls, harder than you'd imagine. It takes so much out of me."

"But not when you look into Lisa's."

He pulled some more on his lower lip, shook his head. "No, not when I see hers," he agreed. Flashing his crooked smile, he asked, "Would you like to see what her soul looks like?"

I nodded, finding myself more curious about that than I would've imagined. "Yeah, I would," I said.

He seemed both genuinely pleased and nervous over the prospect of sharing that with me. I followed him into his apartment and waited while he brought up a drawing on his computer screen. The woman in it was amazingly beautiful, and almost physically the opposite of the Lisa Williams I'd seen at Strombolli's. Tall, lean, with long, flowing golden hair. But I could see the resemblance with Lisa in the soft hazel eyes and the warm smile. While I looked at the drawing, Lynch stood next to me, anxiously watching for my reaction.

"I haven't really done her justice," he said. "I've been working on the drawing for several years, but I'm not an artist and Lisa's much more beautiful than that. But it gives you an idea of what she looks like. Her true essence, that is."

"I can see her in the drawing," I said. "I can see her in the way you drew her eyes and smile, and you captured the same soft kindness she exudes."

"Really?" he asked, nearly beaming with pride, his eyes fixed on the drawing.

"You have a date with her, don't you?"

A light pink mottled his cheeks, which was all the answer he gave me.

"Come on, Zachary, I'm a detective. I can figure stuff like

this out. You've cleaned up the place, bought some new furniture, and, my guess, also some new clothes. So when's the big date?"

I didn't have to guess about the new clothing. The last few times I'd followed him to Strombolli's he was dressed up in what looked like a new wardrobe, and looking damned uncomfortable in it

Zachary's blush deepened, and he told me she was going to be having dinner with him Friday night.

"Tomorrow night, huh? You haven't told her yet about what happened to you and what you see when you look at people?"

He shook his head.

I asked for a piece of paper, then wrote down my cell phone number. "If you want, you can have her call me after you talk to her. I'll back you up and make sure she knows you're not crazy. Or at least leave her thinking we're both crazy."

He nodded silently and took the paper from me, relief washing over his long, thin face. Of course, that was why he invited me up to see his drawing of Lisa; he was hoping I'd make that offer. It must've been scaring the hell out of him, wondering how'd she react to something like that.

"I'm also getting you a camera," I told him. "Who knows, maybe you'll see someone whose picture you should be taking."

"I can't promise I'll ever use it," he said, "but I'll try to bring it with me when I go outside."

"Don't worry, I won't be going broke over this. I'll buy you a cheap one. Good luck tomorrow." I moved to the door, pausing with my hand on the doorknob. "Zachary, can you tell me what you saw when you looked at the killer?"

"Why? How can that help you?"

"I don't know. But knowing what this guy is really like

can't hurt. Maybe it will help me connect the dots somewhere else along the line."

A pained expression washed over his face, like he was suffering a bad stomachache. "Who will you be telling this to?"

"No one. I'll be keeping this to myself."

He closed his eyes, nodded. Thin lines creased his forehead as he concentrated to dredge up a memory from almost three months ago. "He was something out of a nightmare," Lynch said. "The man was enormous, and when he leaned over that woman's body his back arched like a feral animal's. It made me think of a wolf. When he turned around and faced me, he was grotesque. It was like he had a snout instead of a nose, and when his jaw opened and unhinged it was massive. Those are the things that stuck most in my mind. I'm sorry, I can't picture much more about him."

"But you'd know him if you saw him again?"

Grim-faced, he nodded, his eyes still closed.

"All right. Thanks, Zachary. I'll be in touch."

I was halfway out the door when his voice stopped me.

"Detective Green," he said, his voice low, faltering, "you're the only person I've ever told any of this to."

"I know," I told him.

I left then.

Sunday, January 23, 2005

Over the next several days I thought a lot about Zachary Lynch, about what it must be like seeing the things he did, seeing what people really were beneath the skin. I thought a lot also about his description of the killer, about how huge and grotesque the killer's soul was, and how that seemed to add up with Jill Chandler's profile of him being a full-blown narcissist.

I never got a call from Lisa Williams. If Lynch followed through and told her his secret, she either believed him or thought he was completely nuts. In either case, she didn't bother getting my take on it.

That night I took Bambi to the West Village for dinner. Instead of sticking with beer, I ended up joining her with vodka martinis, and I probably had more than one too many. After dinner I dragged her to Tribeca with the excuse of meeting a new buddy of mine. Standing outside of Lynch's apartment, Bambi was nearly falling over giggling. I had to lean against the door frame to keep myself upright, and I rapped my knuckles hard against his door, a big, dumb silly grin stretched across my face. Lynch asked who it was, and I yelled out for him to open the door. When he did, and he caught a glimpse of Bambi and me waiting for him, his face turned wooden, but I wasn't able to catch any other reaction from him.

"So this is your new friend," Bambi said, giggling harder and nearly falling over in her stiletto pumps.

"Yep, this is my good buddy," I said. Still grinning stupidly at Lynch, I added, "Zach, let me introduce you to my significant other, Bambi Morrison. We were in the neighborhood, thought we'd drop in, see how you're doing, maybe talk you into going out for some coffee."

Seeing the disappointment in Lynch's face sobered me up quickly. Very softly so Bambi couldn't hear him he told me we needed to talk alone.

"What's he saying?" Bambi asked suspiciously, no longer giggling, her lips freezing into a hard smile.

"Just a minute," I told her. I stepped into Lynch's apartment and he closed the door behind me.

"You can't do this," he said. "It's inappropriate. It's also not fair."

"What?"

"Bringing your girlfriend here for me to look at her. This isn't a parlor trick I do."

"Chrissakes, that's not why I came here," I said.

He didn't bother responding, just stared woodenly off into a corner of the room.

"Okay, so maybe that was part of the reason," I admitted. "We were in the neighborhood, so I figured why not. Fuck, if I had you to look at my first wife sixteen years ago you could've saved me a lot of money and aggravation. So come on, what's your verdict?"

He shook his head, his mouth clamped tightly shut.

"Zach, what's the big fucking deal?"

"I'm not invading her privacy like this," he said. "You shouldn't be asking me to."

My grin had long since turned plastic. I let it drop and rubbed a hand across my jaw to wipe off any remaining remnants of it. "How about a simple question then," I said. "Would you date her if you could?"

"Please don't ever come here for something like this again," he said.

I gave him a pleading look and he returned it unfazed. "Okay, sure," I said, sighing, waving my hand loosely in front of my face. "Ah, fuck, I'm sorry, I guess had too much to drink tonight. I wasn't thinking clearly."

We both knew I was being disingenuous, that I had this idea of bringing Bambi to see him ever since I knew what it was he saw. It wasn't an accident that Bambi and I ended up in Manhattan that night. Or that I switched to vodka martinis so I could use the excuse of being drunk. I won't say I felt ashamed about what I did, but I regretted invading Lynch's privacy and trying to take advantage of him, even if it was in a way that shouldn't have mattered that much to him.

"What can I say," I added half under my breath. "You're a man of principle. I apologize."

I left him to rejoin Bambi. She still had a hard smile frozen on her face, but I could see the anger in her eyes. She had sobered up also.

"What were you two talking about?" she demanded.

I shook my head. "Nothing important."

"That was unbelievably rude, leaving me out here like that," she complained.

"Yeah, well, Zach's kind of an eccentric. He wasn't up to company right now. Let's go get some coffee, maybe some dessert also."

"Your friend's a goddamned freak," she said, still fuming. "A pug-ugly stick figure like him acting snooty to me. *Eff* him!"

We walked out of there and took a train back to the West Village, where we found a restaurant to have some dessert and espresso. I had a piece of pecan pie, and Bambi had something chocolate and gooey, but it didn't help her mood. She was still smoldering by the time a taxi brought us back to Flatbush. It didn't get any better that night.

The next day I returned back to Lynch's apartment bringing him the digital camera I had promised. We talked some over coffee and doughnuts that I had also brought along, and I promised him I would never again pull a stunt like I did the night before. He accepted my apology, and as we talked more, he confided in me that his date with Lisa went well. He further told me he didn't give her my cell phone number; that she not only seemed to believe what he told her, but it was almost as if she were expecting it. His off-kilter little smile reappeared for a moment as he told me she was going to be coming over for dinner again Friday night. I was happy for the guy, maybe even a little jealous.

Chapter 21

Thursday, February 10, 2005

Phillips ended up assigning Hennison and me to partner together. This happened the first week of February after Hennison's old partner, Joan Lahey, decided not to come back after her maternity leave ended, and neither Hennison nor I could come up with a strong enough objection to keep us from partnering.

I had gotten up early that morning and was on my way to the precinct when Hennison called at seven o'clock to tell me about a dead body found in SoHo. I ended up meeting him at the crime scene: a back alleyway behind a restaurant. The victim had been stabbed to death, and when Hennison and I saw the savagery of the murder, as well as the missing fingers, we looked at each other, both thinking the same thought.

"Yeah?" Hennison asked, trying to get me to commit first.

"Hell, I don't know," I said. "It could be our guy, even if a gun wasn't used. Maybe the ME will be able to match up the knife. Fuck, though, it's going to be a bitch identifying him."

"Yet one more thing that points this to the same psycho sonofabitch," Hennison said.

The victim was a middle-aged male, and while it was hard to be precise with the way he was crumpled up in a fetal position, I would've guessed he was about five foot ten, two hundred and thirty pounds. In addition to the missing fingers, his throat had been cut, his eyes gouged out, and his mouth caved in as if it had been stomped on. His face was stabbed enough times to make it unrecognizable. The victim was also missing a coat. Maybe he had one and it was taken off him, or maybe something caused him to rush into the alley. As cold as it was the other night, he should've had one on. His clothing was so torn and bloodied it was hard to figure out from that whether he was a street person or someone well-off, but his shoes gave him away. He had money. While a knife was used instead of a .40 caliber with hollow-points, it felt familiar, as if the killer were trying to obliterate the man's face as much as the psycho who had butchered Gail Laurent and Paul Burke.

The patrolman who called in the body was standing off to the side. Hennison waved him over to get a rundown of what he knew. The restaurant didn't open until eleven and the patrolman was checking the back area to make sure there wasn't any prostitution activity, something he had been alerted to a week earlier.

"Employees were coming out here to dump garbage and finding a pro servicing her clientele," the patrolman said. He stopped for a moment to blow on his hands. He'd been out there for a while, and it was turning out to be a bitterly cold February morning with the wind beginning to pick up. "The owner called the station on it," he continued. "Since then, I've been back here a few times each day, making sure it wasn't still going on."

Hennison grimaced as he looked around the alley, his jaw muscles tightening. "What a load of sick bastards in this city," he said. "Just what you need to get yourself in the mood, standing in a filthy rat-infested back alley in the cold and, for good measure, breathing in the smell of rotting garbage." He fixed his stare back toward the patrolman. "Any recent activity?" he asked.

The patrolman shook his head. "Not since I've been checking."

"Anyone checking at night?" I asked.

"I'd have to think so, but you'll have to call the station about that. But if an officer was back here doing a quick check, I don't think he'd see the body."

He was right. Late at night the body would've been in the shadows of the dumpster. Unless a patrolman swept the area with a flashlight, he would've missed it. A restaurant employee throwing away garbage wouldn't have seen it either.

"You know the pro working back here?" Hennison asked.

"Not a hundred percent, but we have an idea who she is. Her street name's Ashlee Smith—her real name's Willie Howard. She's a he. Let me call the station and get a last known address, not that there's much chance he'll still be there."

He got on his two-way, and after a short conversation with dispatch and then what sounded like his desk sergeant, he gave us an address in the Bronx.

We were pretty well hidden back there. The restaurant wasn't going to be opening for another few hours, and there wasn't any foot traffic, and not much chance that anyone other than a vagrant was going to be stumbling onto the crime scene. Hennison told the patrolman he didn't have to stick around, that we could maintain the area ourselves. The officer nodded and stared hard in the direction of the corpse. "Fucking brutal what was done to this guy," he said before leaving.

Once the patrolman was out of the alley I told Hennison we were going to have to hunt down Willie Howard. He made a face but reluctantly agreed.

"Who knows?" Hennison said. "Maybe he's also our guy for Laurent and Burke."

Several vans pulled into the alley, and I nodded to a forensics team member I knew as he exited one of the vans, and watched as the evidence collection team emptied out of the other vehicle. I told Hennison I'd get us coffee and left him there to fill in forensics. It took me ten minutes, and by the time I returned to the crime scene the body was being loaded into the back of an ambulance and forensics was methodically going over the alley. I handed Hennison a large coffee. His ears bright red from the cold, he told me he'd put in a call for a canine unit and also to get Willie Howard brought in. While we waited, a call came in over his two-way to tell Hennison that the address in the Bronx wasn't any good, that Howard hadn't been seen there in months.

"This is going to be a pain in the ass," Hennison grumbled partly to me, mostly to himself. "Worse than a bad case of hemorrhoids."

The canine team arrived with two beautiful full-breed Belgian shepherds. They were led up and down the alley and then brought next to the dumpster, neither of them showing any agitation. With the way the dogs reacted, the odds were small that the missing fingers or eyes were left in the alley; still, though, forensics was going to have to have the dumpster carted away and painstakingly searched through. The dogs were taken out of the alley to search a radius of several city blocks for the missing body pieces.

It was ten o'clock before we were able to get the manager of the restaurant, Thomas Langlois, to show up. He was in his late twenties, on the heavy side, with thinning blond hair, and looked both tired and disheveled as if he'd just crawled out of bed and hadn't fully woken up yet. He explained that he'd locked up the restaurant the night before and didn't leave until four in the morning, and that he wasn't planning on returning to work until four that afternoon.

"Is that usual for you?" Hennison.

"Every day for the last three years. I'll tell you, I could use some coffee bad, I mean real bad. How about I make you guys some also?"

I wasn't about to refuse the offer, and neither was Hennison. We were sitting at a table, and Hennison shrugged and told him if it wouldn't be any additional bother we'd join him for coffee. Langlois said it wouldn't be. We all moved to the bar area where they had a very expensive-looking espresso machine. Langlois got behind the bar and fired the machine up.

"Espresso, cappuccino?" he asked us. "I can make you regular if you'd like."

"Espresso sounds good," I said. Hennison grunted, indicating he'd take some also. While we waited for the machine to warm up, Langlois explained that he didn't hear or see anything the other night, that if he had he would've called the police. "Any of my people, they would've told me. I can guarantee you no one working here saw or heard anything."

He poured a double-shot of espresso for himself, then the same for me and Hennison. His hands shook as he drank. "It's like I'm a junkie," he explained. "You wouldn't believe how much of this I go through each day."

"You've had some prostitution activity out back of your restaurant," Hennison stated.

"Yep," he nodded. "Three times last week employees saw sex acts being performed out there. I called the police about it each time."

"Anything since then?"

He shook his head.

"Did you use the dumpster last night?"

"We use it every night. After we clean up in the kitchen, we throw the refuse out."

"What time would that be?"

Langlois thought about it. "Last night, around three o'clock," he said.

"Did you do it?"

"No, it would've been one of our busboys. I think Leonard would've done it last night."

"Anyone else step out back?" I asked.

Langlois shrugged. "Not unless someone was catching a smoke. Like I said before, if anyone saw anything they didn't mention it, at least not to me."

"We'll need names, phone numbers, addresses of everyone working last night," I said. "If you've got illegals working here, please include them also. You'll only get everyone in more trouble if you leave their names off the list."

"I don't have illegals working in my kitchen," Langlois said, insulted.

"Glad to hear it. If you remember later that you do, don't leave their names off. This isn't going to the INS. After you get the list made up, you could do us a huge favor by calling your employees and getting them over here so we can interview them. It would be better if we can talk to them now instead of when you're busy later tonight."

"Sure, of course," Langlois agreed, nodding.

"Good. We appreciate your cooperation. We're also going to need a customer list from last night. Whatever names you can pull off your reservations, credit card receipts, or anyone you remember seeing here."

Langlois looked depressed at providing us that. "Most of our business is repeat," he said. "I hope you're not planning to harass my customers."

"Nope," Hennison grunted. "We're going to be checking to see if they're still alive."

Langlois looked blankly at Hennison. I explained we needed to make sure that the victim wasn't one of their customers from the other night.

He swallowed hard at that thought and told us he'd be willing to take a look at the body and tell us if he recognized him as one of his customers.

"That won't be necessary," Hennison said.

"No, really, I'm willing to do it."

"It wouldn't help us," I said.

He gave us a questioning look but didn't push it further; instead he told us he'd get started on the lists we asked for. "Not all of our customers pay by credit card," he added. "More than you'd think pay cash, but I'll try to work on as complete a list as I can. Is there a problem with me opening today, at least for dinner?"

"There shouldn't be," I said. "The alleyway behind the restaurant is being maintained as a crime scene, and I'm not sure when we'll be releasing it, but it shouldn't stop you from opening up. Until further notice, your back entranceway has been taped off, and we also had to remove your dumpster. We'll be returning it as soon as we can."

He gave me a puzzled sideways look. "Why'd you take our dumpster?" he asked.

"We need to search it," Hennison said in his best tight-lipped manner.

The puzzlement clouding up Langlois's face faded as it dawned on him what we might be searching the dumpster for. He left to go to the kitchen area. While we waited, one of the forensics team members knocked on the front door. I let him in.

"Just what I expect from you prima donna detectives," he said, smiling grimly at the half-drunk espresso in front of Hennison. "Sitting around drinking coffee while we're outside freezing our asses off collecting every bit of muck we can."

"And?" Hennison asked.

"And we're done out there. The scene was pretty much

a mess with rodent droppings and other assorted garbage, but we scraped up all the blood we could, and we'll see if any of it came from a second party."

"Anything else?" I asked.

"Nothing surprising," he said. "There's been too much foot traffic out there to pick up a clean shoe print. All the blood was contained around the area of the corpse. There was some splatter, but not a lot given what was done to the victim, which makes me think most of the wounds were inflicted post-mortem. We'll let you know if we find any surprises inside the dumpster. You can let the restaurant know the area's open and they can use the back door if they want."

He left, and I was out the door shortly after him, leaving Hennison behind to collect the restaurant manager's lists and interview the employees as they arrived. Both Hennison and I shared the same vibe that this was our killer giving us another chapter to his story, but until we had any hard evidence to take to Phillips we were going to have to handle this routinely, making Willie Howard our chief suspect.

The first thing I did was call in an APB for Howard, then headed back to the precinct to pull up his sheet. He was twenty-seven years old but looked more like a teenager, only five foot four and a hundred and twenty pounds. They had taken his wig off for his mug shot, but he still had on thick layers of mascara and an even heavier coating of lipstick. Even with his slight build, it would be hard to imagine he'd fool too many people regardless of how he was disguised. He just had that look of a tough kid from the Bronx that no amount of makeup or fake wigs would hide.

He had quite a sheet. His arrests went back over ten years, and four of those years were spent in prison, including what must've been two hard years at Dannemora. His arrests were mostly for prostitution and drug offenses, with his drug of choice being heroin, but there were also assault and battery charges mixed in. There were a few times where his johns were beaten up badly enough to send them to the hospital. I was surprised to see that over the last three years all of his charges were dropped before trial, especially given the violence involved, and it made me think he must've become somebody's informant. It also made me think it was possible that he killed our latest victim, and if he did that one, maybe he also did the other two.

I contacted a detective I knew working Vice and asked him for any leads finding Howard. "Do me a favor and see if he's on your payroll," I asked.

"You think he's somebody's snitch?"

"Yeah, I think so. If he is, I'll owe you big if you can find out whose."

"I'll get back to you."

Forty minutes later he called me back and told me I was right about Howard being an informant. He gave me the name of a detective out of Organized Crime who was working him.

"You're kidding me," I said.

"Nope, I kid you not. It wasn't easy getting that, but one of our guys who got fed up last year seeing Willie back on the street days after kicking the shit out of a john was able to dig that out."

"So he's as violent as his sheet says?"

"Yeah, that's what I'm being told. Personally, I never had the pleasure. In the past he worked mostly out of the Bronx, although I've heard he's been working in SoHo the last few months."

I thanked him for the information, then got on the phone until I was able to track down the detective in Organized Crime whose name I was given. He sounded annoyed when I asked him about Howard, and he told me that they cut him loose about six months ago. "Let's just say he got into a beef with a guy we needed him close to, and then discovered he was stringing us along with most of the shit he was feeding us. Why the interest, what's Willie done?"

"We're looking at him for a homicide, maybe two others."

"Doesn't sound like him," the detective said. "Manslaughter maybe, but not homicide. How'd this shit happen?"

"Knife, .40 caliber."

"I think you got the wrong guy. Willie's got himself a temper, but I've never known him to carry blades or guns."

"A body was found last night where he's been doing business lately. Whether he's our guy or not, we need to talk with him."

"Hang on and I'll dig out some addresses."

When he came back he gave me a list of places in the Bronx where I might find Howard—known shooting dens, as well as adult bookstores and theaters where Howard might be working.

I drove to the Bronx and visited the bookstores and theaters first. None of the people working there knew Howard, or at least claimed they didn't, but I went through the places anyway and felt like I needed a shower badly after each one.

Next on my list were the shooting dens. Two of them were in abandoned buildings; one was a residence, and I was going to need a warrant pulled before going to that one. I was also going to need backup. While I waited across the street from the first address—an abandoned two-family house that had seen far better days—the medical examiner's office called. The knife used in the murder was military, but it wasn't the same make and model used in the other two killings. The forensics technician told me that they counted forty-eight stab wounds in the face, another sixty-two to the torso, all done post-mortem. The jugular was also severed post-mortem.

"What was cause of death then?" I asked.

Over the phone I could hear him clucking his tongue. "Shame on you, detective, jumping to the conclusion you did and not examining the body carefully enough. Cause of death was blunt trauma to the back of the skull. He was hit hard with something flat and with a rough surface. I would guess a brick."

Two squad cars had pulled up behind me and four uniformed officers were getting out of the vehicles. I held up a hand, indicating I needed a minute. I asked the technician if they found anything else.

"Time of death was between nine thirty and ten o'clock last night," he said. "The victim ate within fifteen minutes of his death. Contents showed what looked like Indian food. Most likely his last meal was lamb saag—rice, spinach, and lamb. One more thing, he has a tattoo on his right biceps. A heart colored in red with the name Gretta written inside with yellow ink."

Sometimes you catch a break. The tattoo was a big one given how badly the victim's face had been torn up. I got forensics on the phone to ask if they'd found a brick in the dumpster. They hadn't. As far as they were concerned, they didn't find anything pertaining to the murder inside it. I had spoken to Hennison by phone a half hour earlier after he had finished interviewing the restaurant staff. A few of them had gone out back the other night to smoke but none of them had seen anything. He also let me know then that the canine team came up empty. I called Hennison back and relayed to him what the medical examiner's office told me, including the technician's guess that the victim's last meal was Indian food.

"I remember seeing an Indian restaurant on the same block," I said.

"I'll check it out," Hennison said, "Fucking shame the same knife wasn't used."

"He could've ditched his knife and gun after Lynch witnessed him killing Gail Laurent. He could've rearmed himself recently."

"This is going to make it a bitch selling the idea to Phillips that we have the same psycho at work," Hennison said. "By the way, I located the patrolman who was supposed to be checking the restaurant last night. He didn't. He got too caught up with a convenience store robbery. You still out looking for Howard?"

"Still am. I'm in the Bronx now, got a few more addresses to visit before heading back to Manhattan."

I got off the phone with Hennison, then left my car to join the four uniformed officers who were standing impatiently waiting for me. A Sergeant Henry Jackson was supposed to pull a warrant for a Melrose Avenue address. I asked which one of them was Jackson, and he turned out to be a big hulking guy with a thick horseshoe-style mustache. He handed me the paper.

The first location we searched was empty. The stench inside was bad enough I had to fight to keep from gagging. Every room had been used as an outhouse by the addicts visiting there, and there were plenty of signs of recent activity: broken needles, empty lighters, and other paraphernalia and garbage left behind. At the next location there were a half dozen addicts lying around in different stages of shooting up, but no Willie Howard, and no one willing to say they knew him. None of them even seemed to care much when we arrested them and loaded them into a waiting van.

At the Melrose Avenue address, we were greeted at the door by a skinny guy with a shaved head and tattoos covering most of his face and neck. I handed him the warrant, and while he looked it over a dog inside the house went ballistic.

"This is bullshit, man," he said angrily, handing me back the warrant. "My home ain't no known shooting gallery. And I don't know no Willie Howard. Never heard shit of the guy."

His eyes were glazed enough to show that he was high on something. I told him we were going to have to search his residence regardless. His face contorted to show his disgust at that. "Let me get hold of Lucy first," he said. "I don't want none of you hurting her."

He opened his door enough for him to squeeze through the narrow opening. and it looked like he fought something back as he did so. When he opened the door again he had a pit bull held tightly at the end of a choke collar. The animal was near apoplectic as she tried to lunge at us, thick strands of drool pouring out of her jaws. One of the patrolmen held his revolver out in case the animal got loose. I let my hand drop to my holster flap.

"Why don't you lock her in a room?" I asked the owner.

He shook his head. "I ain't doing that. Someone lets her out, and you assholes end up using her for target practice. No fucking way."

We followed him into the house, making sure to give his pit bull a wide berth. Inside it was a mess, and while we found a number of stoned out people throughout the residence who looked like they must've shot up recently, we didn't see any drugs out in the open or any other paraphernalia. Also no sign of Willie Howard. The owner kept a short lead on the pit bull, and the animal didn't let up for one second. You would've thought she would've choked herself to death with the way she tried to get at us. I kept a wary eye on her the whole time I was in the house, and could feel cold sweat building on the back of my neck. When we were leaving, I asked the owner why the name Lucy for such a hell-bent beast. He grinned at me, told me it was short for Lucifer.

I was glad once we were outside and breathing in fresh air and had a door separating us from that dog. The other officers looked just as relieved.

"You need us for anything else?" Sergeant Jackson asked bluntly when we were back at our cars.

"No, we're done," I said. "Thanks for all your help. Just make sure I get called first if you catch wind of this guy."

I watched them get into their patrol cars. None of them looked too happy about wasting the afternoon. I wasn't too happy about it either. After they drove off, I got into my own car and headed back to Manhattan, glad to be putting the Bronx behind me.

Chapter 22

Hennison was on the phone when I arrived back at the precinct. His eyes were hard glass, his expression locked in rigid attention. He noticed me and signaled for me to wait for him. After a few grunts into the phone, he scribbled down some notes and hung up. When he looked back up at me his eyes were glistening.

"I might have a lead on our dead guy," he said.

"Yeah?"

"Yeah. You were right, there is an Indian restaurant on the same block, and our victim might've eaten there." Hennison shook his head over a private thought, a hard grin tightening his mouth. "The owner there claims he remembers everyone who eats there, so I give him a rough time estimate and general description, and this guy's eyes light up and he tells me what our dead guy was wearing, even down to the shoes. Then he pulls out a credit card receipt for one James Solinski and claims that's who I was asking about."

"How about a coat?"

"Supposedly he wore one to the restaurant. Double-breasted camel hair topcoat. I just got off the phone with Solinski's credit card company, and have a home address and phone number for him. Poor sap's from Cleveland, Ohio."

Fuck, a tourist. That was all we needed. I took a deep breath, let it out slowly.

"How high are you rating this?" I asked.

"Very. That owner's some kind of freak. He even had the brand of the shoe right."

"You're going to have to call Solinski's home."

"Yeah, I know. Any luck finding Howard?"

He already knew the answer to that. He was just gloating over his own discovery and my failure at locating Willie Howard. I shook my head and stood watching as Hennison called Solinski's home number. From his end of the conversation it was clear he had gotten the man's wife. He asked her whether her husband had any distinguishing marks, and I could hear her voice over the line turning shrill and nearly hysterical as she described her husband's tattoo, the one on his biceps with a red heart and her name, Gretta, written in yellow ink, and then asking why he needed to know that. Hennison, his voice flat and detached, explained what happened, told her where and when her husband's body was discovered, and asssured her that someone would be calling her back soon with more information.

He got off the phone and turned to me, his expression somber. "We know who we got in the morgue," he said.

"What was he doing in New York?"

"Business. Christ, he must've been killed minutes after he ate dinner. You know how the owner of that Indian restaurant described him? *Jolly* and *gregarious*. How'd this poor shmuck end up in that alley?"

"He could've been lured back there."

Hennison made a face. "We've got the same psycho at work. I don't buy it's some tranny cocksucker doing this murder."

"You read his sheet?"

"Yeah, I read it, and I still don't buy it. How many times was Solinski stabbed? Over a hundred? Three fingers cut off? Mouth bashed in? This has the same stench of overkill as the other two." Hennison started banging his palm impatiently on his desk, his lips curling back to reveal badly stained teeth.

"Fuck this," he said all at once. "I'm talking to Phillips."

He jumped to his feet and stormed off, presumably to

convince Phillips that this murder was connected with the other two from back in October. I didn't bother joining him, instead waiting by his desk. I didn't have to wait long. Two minutes later he came back holding a cup of coffee. He shook his head and told me until we had something solid, or at least could cross Willie Howard off, Phillips didn't want to hear about it.

"Fucking cocksucker," Hennison muttered under his breath.

I wasn't sure whether he was referring to Phillips or Howard.

The local news that night ran Willie Howard's mug shot, reporting that we were looking for him in connection with the murder of an out-of-town businessman behind a SoHo restaurant. I was glad we were able to keep Solinski's name out of the story; as it was they had a field day with the story given Willie Howard's past arrests and their speculation on how the victim ended up in that alley. We needed to get Howard's picture out there, as well as the tip hotline we set up, but I just hoped none of Solinski's family saw any of the stories, because if they did I'm sure they'd be able to put two and two together.

Later, after dinner, I got a call from Earl Buntz. He wanted to meet, said it was important.

"How important?"

"Important enough. Half hour, okay?"

He told me where to meet him. Bambi asked me if it was someone from work calling. I shook my head and told her I was heading out.

The tavern where Earl wanted to meet was a hole-in-the-wall dive in East Flatbush. A four-step walk-down led me into a dimly lit room that smelled faintly of stale beer and body odor. An oak bar took up the right side of the tavern, and it was badly chipped and worn and had clearly seen better days. Half a dozen tables were scattered about on the other side of the room. A few hardcore drinkers were sitting at the bar, no one at the tables. Earl wasn't there yet. None of the customers paid any attention to me as I walked up to the bar to order a drink. The bartender barely paid any attention to me either. He was a raw big-boned man with thick forearms and had the look of someone who'd done a lot of brawling in his younger days, at least from all the dents and scars along his face. He didn't look too enthused about being there, at least no more so than any of his customers. I asked him for a Bud, and at first he acted as if he didn't hear me, then reluctantly, as if it pained him greatly to do so, he pulled a bottle out of a cooler and handed it to me.

"Three bucks," he said, his lips barely moving. I laid a five dollar bill on the bar and walked away with the beer. I didn't bother waiting for him to ask if I wanted my change. Something told me I'd be waiting a long time for him to do that.

I sat at a table facing the street. Earl didn't keep me waiting long. Within minutes, the door opened and he walked briskly in, rubbing his hands together to try to warm them. He spotted me, gave me a short nod, then continued on to the bar to get himself a drink. Earl went to high school with Mike and graduated in the same class. Ever since I'd known him he was always a roly-poly type with a face as round as a beach ball and a mop of orange hair topping his head. He was a damn good athlete in his younger days with quick reflexes, lighter on his feet than you'd expect from someone his size. He joined me at the table, beer in hand. His hair was cut shorter than I remembered it, and more gray than orange.

"What's this about?" I asked.

He looked uncomfortable sitting across from me. In all

the time I'd known him, his cheeks were always red, but now they were colorless. He adjusted himself in his chair before looking at me.

"Those Brighton Beach boys you arrested a few months back," he said. "Their pretrial hearing is next Tuesday."

"Yeah, I know. I'll be there testifying."

Earl had been looking more over my shoulder than directly at me. His eyes slid sideways to meet mine.

"Maybe it might be a good idea to change your story," he said. "Maybe remember that you forgot to identify yourself as a police officer."

"You're asking me to perjure myself?"

"I'm not asking you to do anything. Don't put words in my mouth."

"Bullshit. What the fuck's going on?"

"Watch your tone with me," he warned. "I'm here as a friend. That's my only involvement in this. So don't fly off the handle at me, okay? You do that again, I'm walking out of here."

"Yeah, sure." I took a deep breath, held it for a ten-count before letting it out. "What's going on?"

He took a drink of his beer and wiped a hand across his mouth. "Someone reached out to me and suggested it might be a good idea for you to change your story, and I agree."

"Who's this somebody?"

He shook his head. "I'm not saying, Stan, and it wouldn't make any difference to you if I did."

I felt a pulse start to beat along my temple. "Tell this person to go fuck himself," I said.

"It could be worth some money to you," he said.

"Yeah, what am I supposed to do? Say that I lied on the arrest?"

He shrugged. "Mistakes happen, especially in the heat of the moment. You remember differently now. That's all."

"It wouldn't matter. They'd still have those Russians on weapons charges."

"Maybe, maybe not. Your statement gets brought into question, it all could end up being thrown out of court."

I sat back, finished off my beer and placed the empty bottle on the table. "Thanks, but no thanks," I said.

"You should give it some thought," he said.

"Is there a threat involved?"

"I don't know." He shifted his gaze away from me. "These are the type of guys you're never quite sure about. I don't like it, Stan. I think you should take the money and bite the bullet on this. Your career can take the hit."

"Thanks for your concern, but I think I'll pass."

He nodded, finished his beer, and placed the empty bottle next to mine. "I should've known this would be a waste of time," he said. "But don't say I didn't try."

"You sure you can't give me a name?"

He shook his head, a thin smile showing. "Want to hear the funny part of all this?" he said. "Remember when you wanted those baseball tickets and I was trying to get a favor instead of the money? The favor was to have you working Cohen's nightclub just like you ended up doing all on your own."

That pulse beating on my temples was now a tom-tom. "You don't say?" I said.

"Yeah, that was it. Back then I bought into the story that Cohen was being leaned on for protection by those Russians."

Almost like a switch had been thrown the pulse died and a coolness filled my head.

"What's the real story?" I heard myself asking.

"Some sort of beef over disputed turf, but I'm not going into specifics," Earl said. He pushed himself to his feet and gave me a hard look. "I hope you had Cohen pay you a nice sum. That John Travolta wannabe was offering me twenty-five grand to deliver you to him or anyone else I could from NYPD." He took a step away, then turned to warn me to be careful. "You really should think about laying down on this one," he said while buttoning his coat. "All the great ones have taken a dive now and then. No reason you can't."

I didn't bother saying anything; instead I watched as he fit his two beefy hands into a pair of calfskin gloves, then bulled his way out the door and into the cold night's air. I sat at the table for several minutes before I trusted that I'd be able to control myself, then left also, heading to Joel Cohen's nightclub.

Joel was whispering into the ear of a young twenty-something blonde, the fingers on his right hand moving lightly along her hip. From the way her face was flushing she seemed to be enjoying the attention.

I tapped Joel on the shoulder. He turned to me with a big breezy smile, his eyes dull. As he recognized me, his smile lost some its luster but stayed frozen in place.

"Stan, good to see you," he said, offering me his hand. I kept my own hands in my jacket pockets, and he pulled his back.

"We need to talk," I told him.

"Sure," he said. "Go ahead."

"In private."

He hesitated for a moment but nodded. He leaned back over to the blonde, nuzzled her ear, and whispered something to her that caused her to throw her head back laughing. He then turned to me and asked me what I was drinking. I could feel that same pulse from before beating along my temple. I didn't answer him. He gave up waiting for me to and asked the bartender for a couple of Michelobs, then led me back to his office. Once inside he tried handing me a beer and I let the bottle drop to the floor.

"Fucksake, Stan! What'd you do that for? Now I'm going to have to get Jenny in here to mop up this mess. A perfectly good beer. Shit!"

"Fuck the beer," I said. "Tell me about those Russians."

"Sorry, I'm confused here."

"They weren't leaning on you for protection payments. So what the fuck was all that about?"

He froze for a moment, then sat down on his red leather sofa and crossed his legs. When he looked back up at me he flashed me something between a smirk and a fuck-you smile.

"I can't tell you, Stan," he said. "You're too much of a Boy Scout. If I tell you you're likely to repeat it to someone, maybe even when you testify against those two dumbasses next week."

Looking at him, I barely recognized him from the old days. It was more than just his good looks from years ago being tarnished by age and extra weight. Much more than that, more even than the dead paleness to his eyes. There was something cold about him, something that made me think of a rattlesnake.

"What's to stop me from cuffing you and arresting your sorry ass right now?"

He scratched leisurely around his ear before giving me more of his fuck-you smile, his eyes crinkling with amusement.

"What would you arrest me for?" he asked. "You don't know anything. All you're doing is guessing at shit. And Stan, if you arrested me, how'd it look with you being on my payroll back in October?"

"You hired me to do a security job," I said. "Nothing else."

"Yeah, well, you could try telling them that story. I guess there's a chance they'd believe you. Me, though, I'd tell them something completely different. You see, Stan, I'm not the same Boy Scout you are. I don't have the same compulsion to play fair and tell the truth all the goddamned time."

He grinned widely, then started laughing at a private joke.

"Those crazy Russian muthafuckers," he said, shaking his head. "I told them I had you in my hip pocket and if they showed up you'd arrest them. You know what those fucking morons actually told me? That you'd have enough brains to know better than to do something like that. What a bunch of dumbasses!"

"You used me, you son of a bitch."

The amusement dried up quickly from his face, and what was left behind was as hard as granite. "I don't know what you're getting so worked up about," he said. "You're a cop, you saw a couple of mofos walk into a club carrying concealed weapons, so you arrested them. Big fucking deal. So what's the problem? You don't think I paid you enough? You're probably right. I'll kick in another couple of grand if that will make you happy."

I wanted to arrest him. More than anything I wanted to snap the cuffs on him and drag him out of his club and let that blonde at the bar see what a piece of shit he was. But I had no reason, not yet anyway. I was going to have to dig around and watch his club. Later I would get my chance, but not now.

"You can keep your money," I said.

He showed me that damn cocksure smile again. "A genuine Boy Scout, huh? You had no problem taking my three grand earlier, but you don't want my money now, fine. How about I give you some information instead—and don't worry, I'm not trying to work you with this. This is something you'll thank me for. That hot-looking skirt you brought in here back in October, you're still with that, right?"

He waited for me to answer him. When I didn't he continued. "Okay, so you're still with her. She disappeared on you for a few days around then, right?"

"What are you trying to get at?"

He shrugged, his smile now more of a smirk. "Just helping you out, Stan. For old time's sake, you know? She was shacked up with some other dude then. And don't bother arguing with me. It's reliable. I got that from someone who recognized her. If you want a name, leave me your cell number and I'll call you in a couple of days."

"Go to hell."

His smile came back in full force. "Why would I lie to you about that, Stan? Ask her. Or better yet, wait a couple of days and I'll dig up that dude's name and you can ask him yourself. Unless there's something else, I've got someone waiting for me out there."

He got to his feet and brushed close enough past me so I could catch a full whiff of the musk cologne that he had doused himself with. He opened the door, then stopped to tell me that I could stay there as long as I wanted, but to shut off the lights and close the door on my way out.

"What's to stop me from finding out who those Russians work for and letting him know you don't have any NYPD in your hip pocket, and that you never did?" I asked.

He laughed at that. "It wouldn't matter," he said. "Any issues we had have been worked out. Besides, I don't think he'd believe you. See you, Stan. Drinks on the house anytime you want them."

I watched him walk away from me.

The sonofabitch . . .

I knew he'd told me the truth about Bambi. He had no reason to lie to me about it, and in my heart I knew it was the truth. But as I told myself months ago when she fed me her story about staying with her friend Angela, it didn't matter. We weren't married. I had no claim on her.

There was a buzzing in my ears as I left Joel's office. I realized I was breathing hard, and I held my breath to try to get it under control.

It didn't matter . . .

What was done was done—it was over. She was back with me now and that was all that mattered . . .

As I walked through the club something made me look to my left and I froze, seeing Joel Cohen in a corner of the room getting cozy with the same blonde as before. At that moment all I could think about was pulling him away from her and beating the crap out of him. Without even realizing it I noticed my hands had balled into fists. I took a step toward him. All at once I saw myself in my mind's eye, except it wasn't the way I really was but the way Zachary Lynch would've seen me—a swirling storm of rage and fury. It only lasted a second, if that, but it stopped me. I turned away from Joel and left the club.

While I drove home I kept rationalizing about Bambi. We weren't married and she had every right to move in with some other guy if she wanted to. So what happened? It must've turned to shit fast on her, but she knew she had me waiting in the wings. Or maybe it wasn't like that—maybe she realized she had acted impulsively and made a mistake . . . But still, she must've been working this other guy for months to move as fast as she had.

But I kept telling myself it didn't matter. Whatever happened with her it was over now . . .

I parked behind my building and walked up the six flights of stairs to my apartment, not bothering with the elevator. When I entered the apartment and Bambi saw me her face went sort of funny. I didn't say anything to her. I went to the kitchen, got myself a beer, and brought it back to the living room, where I sat in my recliner. Bambi stood silently watching me, her arms looking unnatural the way they hung at her side.

I kept trying to tell myself it didn't matter, but I realized I was only kidding myself.

"Tell me about the guy you moved in with last October," I said.

Her mouth turned brittle as she stood watching me.

"What's wrong with you?" she asked.

"Just tell me about the guy."

"I told you before. I stayed with my friend Angela. You can call her and ask her if you want."

I felt completely drained right then. I dropped my forehead into my left hand and slowly rubbed my eyes.

"I know you weren't with Angela," I said. "Joel Cohen told me someone at his club recognized you."

"He's lying."

"No, he isn't."

I raised my head slowly. It took just about every bit of energy I had. Bambi's face had changed subtly, but enough to where she was no longer beautiful. Not even attractive. There was a hardness to her face, her eyes becoming small and calculating.

"He's lying, and you're going to believe him over me? *Eff* you!"

"If I call him in a couple of days he'll give me the guy's name so I can talk to him myself. Do I have to do that?"

I saw the shift in her eyes as she made a decision.

"You're making a big deal out of nothing," she said. "We didn't even sleep together."

She was lying. I could see that with the way her mouth tensed, but there was no point in arguing it with her

"Who's the guy?" I asked.

Her eyes moved away from mine. "Someone from work," she said. "You're making a big deal out of nothing. I was so mad at you for ditching me in that hotel, I wanted to get back at you. After I cooled off I realized how much I missed you. Nothing happened."

Her eyes and mouth had gotten so small I could barely recognize her. I was never sure what we had before, but I knew now. I took a deep breath and told her it was over between us. It had to be. Maybe I hadn't made enough of an effort with her and was more to blame than she was about what happened, but after what I'd gone through with Cheryl I couldn't go through something like that again. It mattered that she lied to me and was willing to swap me for the first guy she could.

Her eyes grew even smaller as they fixed on me. "Fine," she said, her voice dripping with resentment. "It's not like you're such an *effing* bargain. If I can't do better than some pathetic out-of-shape middle-aged cop who's always broke, put an *effing* bullet in my head."

"How much time do you need to move out?"

Her mouth compressed into a tiny oval. I wasn't sure whether she was fighting to hold on to her composure or to keep from unleashing a tirade against me. Whichever it was, she succeeded in her effort. "Two weeks," she finally said.

I nodded, pushed myself out of the recliner, then took a suitcase from the storage closet and brought it into the bedroom. Bambi followed me and watched as I packed socks, underwear, and shirts into the suitcase.

"This is stupid," she said. "You don't have to leave. Why don't you stay in the second bedroom until I'm out?"

I shook my head. "It will be better this way."

I finished packing up the suitcase. I grabbed an extra suit from my closet, then carried that and the suitcase out of the room. Bambi followed me.

"You've been looking for an excuse to break up with me for a long time," she said.

"You might be right. I don't know."

I opened the door and was halfway out of the apartment

when she told me I wasn't going to do better than her. "You know that, don't you?" she said.

"It doesn't matter," I said. I closed the door behind me.

I thought about asking Mike if I could stay with him, but he only had a small studio apartment. It would be cramped with the two of us there, and besides, I knew he didn't want any company these days. I knew Marcy would put me up in their guest room, and it would be kind of nice to spend some time with my nephews, but I'd feel funny staying there with Mike having moved out. Likewise I knew Joe Ramirez would put me up, but I didn't want to impose on him for two weeks. I made a few calls and ended up renting a room at the Y.

Chapter 23

Friday, February 11, 2005

I don't think I slept more than an hour that night. The mattress was maybe an inch thick, and I couldn't shake this sensation that bugs were crawling over me. I know they weren't, that I was just feeling itchy from the cheap polyester sheets and even cheaper wool blanket, but I couldn't get that thought out of my head. Maybe I was in too weird a state of mind after breaking things off with Bambi; even if I'd been back in my own bed I would've been too restless to sleep. Somewhere around three in the morning I gave up the pretense of trying and rolled out of bed. I thought I'd take advantage of being at the Y—lift some weights, jog around the track, maybe use the sauna—but when I went to the gym I found that it was closed until six AM. I tried talking the security guard manning the front desk to open the gym up for me, but he wouldn't. I ended up going back to my room and doing thirty push-ups, struggling badly with the last three. I thought of doing some sit-ups, decided against it, and got up and took a lukewarm shower using the communal bathroom down the hall. After that I dressed and headed back to Manhattan. As it was I was at my desk by four in the morning.

I spent the morning and a good chunk of the afternoon tracking down leads for Willie Howard that had come in from informants and the tip hotline, and none of them went anywhere. At ten minutes to four in the afternoon I got a call from the city morgue to let me know they had Willie Howard as a resident.

"Since when?" I asked.

"Since a week ago last Wednesday. His body was found in Central Park. Heroin overdose."

The papers were going to have fun with this—us launching a citywide manhunt for a guy who'd been dead and in our morgue for more than a week. I thanked the attendant for the call, then got on the phone to Hennison to give him the news.

"We've been chasing our fucking tails the last two days," he complained. "I told you before we've got the same psycho sonofabitch at work."

"As long as you can convince Phillips of it."

"I'll convince him of it. Don't you worry. You coming back to the precinct?"

"I don't think so. I've been on the job since four this morning. I'm calling it a day."

"Fucking lightweight," he muttered under his breath before hanging up, not bothering to hide his disgust.

With this most recent development I knew Hennison wanted me back at the precinct to put in more overtime, but I wasn't going to. We had no leads worth a damn and I'd just be spinning cycles. Besides, early that morning I'd made up my mind how I needed to spend the weekend. I'd brought my suitcase with me so I didn't need to head back to Brooklyn and the Y to gather up my stuff. Instead, I got in the car and headed to Rhode Island.

I waited until I was on I-95 North to call Cheryl and let her know I was on my way to Cumberland to see the kids. She hesitated for a long moment before telling me I could stay in their guest room if I wanted to. That threw me. When I could find my voice again I thanked her for the offer and told her I'd like that.

I wasn't sure I really did. In a way I was glad I wasn't going to be alone in a motel room that weekend, but I felt funny about staying in their house, and wasn't sure I was up to seeing Cheryl and Carl together as a married couple all weekend. The thing was, Cheryl and I were starting to turn the corner in our post-marriage relationship, and if I refused her offer it would only set us back. I'd been keeping my promise to myself about calling my kids each day, and also had been routinely sending them long letters and additional packages of books and other personal items of mine. It felt good doing that; it made me feel more connected with Stevie and Emma, and I guess it also had the side benefit of loosening up Cheryl's attitude toward me. As anxious as I was feeling about staying in Cheryl's house, I was also excited about being able to squeeze in some extra hours with my kids.

Traffic was mostly light and I was able to get to Cheryl's house in time to take the kids out to dinner. Things were mostly good with Emma and me, and were better with Stevie than they had been. He was still aloof at times, but only gave brief hints of the hostility he'd had before. Later that evening when I had them back at their home, Cheryl played videotapes of Stevie's hockey games. Even though Carl had left the room, I had a heaviness fill my chest knowing that he'd be there at future games and not me.

The next two days went by fast. By Saturday afternoon, Emma was either in my arms or on my lap whenever she had the chance, and it was like the way it had always been with us. With Stevie, we were closer to the old days—not quite there, but closer. I had them out of the house as much as I could, and in the evening Carl had the decency to find things to do in other rooms so I didn't have to see him much other than in passing.

My plan was to leave at four AM Monday morning and drive straight to the precinct. Sunday night I was having trouble sleeping and ended up wandering into the kitchen around one in the morning. I was in the middle of making a grilled cheese sandwich when Cheryl walked in wearing a robe over her pajamas.

"Can't sleep?" she asked.

I nodded. "Must be my guilty conscience," I said.

She peered over my shoulder to see what I was making. "You want to make me one also?"

"Sure."

I gave her the first grilled cheese sandwich when it was ready, then joined her at the kitchen table when the second was done. It was the first time we'd been alone together, not only that weekend but since she told me she was leaving me. We ate quietly at first but it was a comfortable quiet. When I looked at her she seemed relaxed in a way I hadn't seen her be for several years. I'd forgotten how pretty she could be, especially when she was just out of bed with her hair down past her shoulders and no makeup on.

"You still make a mean grilled cheese sandwich," she said.

"Yeah, I've had a lot of practice."

She put down what was left of her sandwich and gave me a sympathetic smile. "Stan, I am sorry about how things ended up between us," she said. "And I'm so sorry to hear about your mom."

I nodded, a lump forming in my throat. I hadn't told her about my mom's series of strokes, but she still had friends in Brooklyn. Someone must've filled her in.

"How have you been, Cheryl?" I asked.

"Mostly good."

"You don't miss Brooklyn?"

She shook her head, her smile turning more wistful. "I'm glad to be out of there," she said. "I've grown to appreciate the quiet and calm I've got here. I needed the slower pace of life, you know, Stan?"

I nodded again, in a way understanding the allure of her new life, although I think I'd go nuts living in the cow pasture of a town she had chosen. I didn't want to upset this newfound peace we had slipped into, but a question was nagging on the back of my mind about whether she regretted giving up her dream of acting. Throughout our marriage she always had this frustration burning inside her about never getting her big break, and it was hard to believe that she was no longer auditioning for roles. Ever since I'd known her she'd been running to every audition she could, barely slowing down even when she was pregnant with Stevie and Emma. I couldn't help myself. I had to ask her about it.

"I'm okay with it," she said. "At some point you have to get realistic about things. If it didn't happened after fifteen years of busting my ass, it wasn't ever going to. But I'm doing community theater now, and I'm content with that. In fact, guess who's going to be starring in our local production of *Cabaret*?"

"No idea."

She stuck her tongue out at me, then broke into a self-conscious grin. "The play's running the first week of April. Any interest in coming?"

"I'll be there. You can count on it."

If this had been four months ago she would've rolled her eyes, or made some snide comment about how much she counts on any of my promises. Now, though, she nodded as if she believed me. There was something else nagging at the back of my mind, something I had picked up on earlier over the weekend. I asked her how things were with Carl. She hesitated for a slight moment before telling me that they were good.

"You'd tell me if they weren't?"

"Of course," she said, but from the way her face hesitated for a second, I wasn't so sure she would. "How about you, Stan?" she said. "You haven't told me how you've been."

I swallowed back the trite answer that I had planned earlier in case she asked me something like that and shrugged instead. I wasn't going to tell her about Bambi, about us breaking up, but I mostly leveled with her.

"It's been tough," I said. "With you and the kids gone, and with my mom, and what Mike's been going through." I looked away from her, then added, "I don't know. For the last couple of years I've been feeling like I'm only drifting along in life. I can't quite get a handle on where I fit in or what I should be doing next."

I could feel her staring at me, and when I looked back at her there was only genuine concern in her eyes. We just sat like that for several minutes, neither of us talking, but feeling a comfort with each other that we hadn't felt in a long time. Cheryl broke the quiet first.

"Things will get better for you, Stan," she said, a moistness clouding her eyes. "I know they will. And I'm glad you came this weekend. And I'm proud of you for the effort you've been making with Stevie and Emma since October."

I heard some rustling behind me and turned to see Carl stumbling into the room, his eyes squinting badly against the kitchen light. "There you are," he said to Cheryl, his voice raspy as if he had something stuck in his throat. He smiled awkwardly at me before turning back to his wife. "You coming back to bed?"

She nodded, mouthed the word *sure*, then followed him out of the room. I sat for several minutes collecting my thoughts. There didn't seem to be any point in waiting until four in the morning; now seemed as good a time as any to drive back to Manhattan. I pushed myself to my feet and spent a few minutes looking in on Emma and Stevie. After that I packed up my suitcase and left.

Chapter 24

Monday, February 14, 2005

Hennison had had no luck that past Friday convincing Phillips to link Solinski's murder with Gail Laurent's and Paul Burke's. Unless we had something concrete, Phillips wasn't going to do it, which meant he wasn't going to be bringing the task force back together and giving us the extra resources.

That morning we met with Jill Chandler and went over the details of James Solinski's murder with her. She thought it was possible it was the same guy, but she didn't have enough to say it was definitively so.

"How about saying it's *highly likely*?" Hennison asked, barely controlling the exasperation in his voice.

"I can't do that," Jill said. "There are similar elements with this murder to the others—the type of knife that was used, cutting off several fingers, and the overall savagery of it—but this one was so much more so. What this murder speaks to is an uncontrollable rage. His gouging out the eyes of the victim is different also. It's almost as if the killer couldn't stand being looked at by his victim and had to destroy any vestige of it. While it wouldn't surprise me if it turned out to be the same killer, it also wouldn't surprise me if this was a completely different one and that the killer knew his victim and targeted him, or maybe even something that started off as a simple mugging."

"This was never any mugging," Hennison said, his voice strained. "And about it being someone who wanted Solinski dead, I've looked into that angle and there's not much chance of it. Look, you wouldn't be committing to anything, but you'd be doing us a solid if you could just use the two words *highly likely* in your report."

"I'm sorry," she said. "Unless you give me something more, I can't do that."

"Any idea why Solinski's coat was taken?" I asked.

She smiled at me. It was a nice smile, warm, inviting. Earlier I had noticed her giving me an odd look, almost as if she knew what was going on in my life. Damn her profiling training!

"Who knows?" she said. "The killer might've needed a coat or just liked the cut of the material. Or maybe he was being careful, suspecting his own clothes were going to end up blood-splattered and he would need something to cover himself. Whatever the reason, I wouldn't put too much significance in it."

"So we're done here," Hennison grumbled hastily as he got to his feet and made a quick exit out of the room. I shrugged, gave Jill a halfhearted smile by means of an apology for Hennison's lack of tact, and followed him out of the room. On the way back to my desk I stopped off for some coffee. Jill Chandler joined me there.

"I'm really sorry I couldn't help," she said. "If you find anything else, give me a call and maybe I'll feel better about connecting this murder with the ones back in October."

"It sure seems like the same guy," I said.

"I don't know," she said. "Why wait almost four months between this murder and the others? And why change his method of killing? This could've started off as a mugging that turned into a brutal killing."

"About why our guy could've waited four months, I think he was running scared after being spotted by Zachary Lynch. I'd bet he's been hiding since then. I'd also bet he dumped his gun and knife and only recently rearmed himself.

This last murder is just him picking up his *story* where he left off. And about this being a mugging that got out of hand, how many muggers cut off their victim's fingers? Or stab them more than a hundred times?"

"Not too many," she admitted, "but it's possible that that's what happened. And it's possible we have the same killer at work, but without more to work with, I can't say it's anything more than a possibility."

When she had walked into the meeting room earlier, she was all angles and hard lines. Now there was that same inviting softness about her. She hesitated for a moment and looked like she was going to ask me something, and I found myself hoping she would, but instead she only smiled pensively and told me she'd be in touch. I nodded and watched her walk away.

The rest of the day Hennison and I checked out some bum leads that came in from our informants. Since we also had to work the angle that the killing could've started off as a street mugging, we searched pawnshops throughout the five boroughs for the camel hair topcoat Solinski had been wearing, as well as shelters for any residents who appeared to have recently come into some money. We came up empty.

I took a break at six o'clock to call my kids and get some food. I wasn't too eager to head back to the Y and ended up staying on the job until two in the morning. None of the leads I checked out went anywhere, not that I was overly optimistic that any of them would.

Tuesday, February 15, 2005

The pretrial hearing for the two Russians was scheduled for ten in the morning. I arrived to the courthouse at nine thirty to meet with the prosecuting attorney. After talking with her, I waited until ten o'clock to enter the courtroom. The two

Russians were there, both dressed conservatively in gray suits, and both still looking every inch like the thugs they both were. The thicker-bodied Russian—the one with his hair cut close to the scalp and the scarred face—glared blindly at me, his facial muscles unflinching. Looking at him, I couldn't help thinking of a marble sculpture that had been nicked up. The thinner Russian had gotten a haircut. He stared straight ahead, ignoring me.

I was brought to the witness stand, and the prosecuting attorney had me tell what happened. Both Russians were being defended by the same lawyer, a short, square-looking man with a flat, pan-shaped face and maybe the thickest, bushiest eyebrows I'd ever seen. He made a show of approaching the witness stand, all the while glowering at me under those thick eyebrows. After loudly clearing his throat, he asked me in a booming voice wasn't it true that I had failed to identify myself as a police officer.

"No, sir," I said, squarely meeting his eyes. "The first thing I did when I approached your clients was to identify myself as a member of the NYPD, as well as show them my badge."

That took him by surprise. He must've been told that I was going to be recanting my statement. He cleared his throat again, his stare losing a bit of its forcefulness, and asked if I was sure about that.

"Yes, sir. They both heard me and they both looked at my badge. Their response to me was for me to mind my own business."

He had recovered enough from his surprise to launch into a series of questions trying to shake my version of the events. Once he realized he wasn't going to get anywhere with it, he changed tactics and tried to suggest that Joel Cohen had hired me to plant guns on his clients. The prosecutor jumped at that, objecting strenuously to these allegations, and the judge sustained, refusing to allow that line of questioning without evidence. The defense attorney was stuck. My folder was clean, I had never been the subject of an Internal Affairs investigation, and he wasn't going to be able to uncover any hidden bank accounts or unexplained money. Reluctantly, he gave up trying to impugn my testimony. Neither of his clients bothered taking the stand. The judge denied his motions to dismiss the charges, and a date was set for when the trial would begin.

Both of the Russians gave me dead-eyed stares as they got up to leave the courtroom. They were both out on bail. I didn't like that, but the prosecutor told me she didn't have enough to revoke their bail, even with the vague threat that I had received through Earl Buntz.

Thursday, February 17, 2005

The investigation for Solinski's murder was going nowhere. We had no witnesses, no leads, and no prospects for getting any. Late that morning I had dug out all the paperwork for it, and was going through it sheet by sheet trying to divine some inspiration. When I looked over the customer list the restaurant manager had provided us, one of the names stopped me. James Longo. The name sounded so damn familiar. I knew I had seen it before. I dug out my notes from Gail Laurent's murder and had to smile when I realized where I had seen that name. He was the guy who owned the bookstore right outside where Gail Laurent had been murdered. I read over what he had told me—how he had frozen up after the gunshots so the killer was already gone by the time he looked outside—and felt my smile tighten across my face.

I looked over the tenant list for the apartment building where Paul Burke's body was found and couldn't find Longo's name on it. We were going to have to question all the tenants again to see if any of them knew him. I felt it was a long shot, but I called the apartment building and asked the manager there whether James Longo had ever lived there. He didn't even have to look it up. He remembered that Longo had moved out of the building September thirtieth. I hung up the phone and sat thinking how convincingly that sonofabitch had lied to me, and how I bought it.

Christ, I wanted to kick myself for not getting a search warrant for that bookstore. It made sense in so many ways. It explained why the killer was conveniently out of sight by the time Longo looked outside his shop, and why we couldn't find any witnesses seeing anyone arriving or leaving the murder scene in a Mets sweatshirt. I thought of how Zachary described the killer's spiritual essence resembling that of a ferocious wolf, and as I pictured Longo with his stooped shoulders and hunched back and his lanky body I could see the wolf in him. It also fit with Jill Chandler's profile; what I took as Longo's haughtiness could've easily been narcissism. After selling so many other people's stories, the sonofabitch wanted to tell one of his own.

I called Longo's bookstore and was told that he had left on a personal errand and wouldn't be back until three o'clock. I considered telling Hennison about Longo, but instead called Lynch. I told him I had someone for him to look at.

"Is this another wild goose chase, or do you really believe this person is the killer?" he asked.

"Zach, this time it's real. I have good reason to think he's our guy."

There was a long hesitation on his end, then, "Will this be safe for me?"

"It will be safe."

Very softly then, "Okay."

I could hear the fear in his voice. It was only a few minutes before eleven, and I didn't want him sitting around for hours making himself sick with fear. I told him I'd bring lunch over after I saw a judge about a search warrant, and would explain more when I saw him.

I took out my cell phone and checked the time again. It was three fifteen. We'd been camped out across the street from the bookstore since two thirty and still no sign of Longo. Lynch sat rigid, his color a sickly milk-white, his face frozen in the type of expression you might see on a bad actor in a very bad horror movie. I could just about smell the anxiety coming off him like cologne. I called the bookstore, and when I recognized James Longo's stilted voice answering the phone, I asked what their hours were and hung up. Damn, he must've slipped in the back door. I was hoping Lynch would be able to see him from the safety of the car and not have to be brought up so that Longo could see him also. Swearing softly to myself, I put the phone away. It couldn't be helped, I had to bring Lynch into the store.

I turned to Lynch. "He's in there. Let's go."

He gave me a dazed look before collecting himself and nodding in a harsh, almost violent fashion. We both left the car, and as we walked across the street and up the steps to the bookstore, I told Lynch all I wanted him to do was get a look at Longo, tell me whether he was the killer, then leave the store and wait for me by the car. He nodded in response. I doubted at that moment whether he was capable of speech.

We walked into the store. There were a half dozen customers milling about, one employee stacking books, another at the cash register, but no James Longo. I moved deeper into the store and spotted Longo making his way in from a back room, his arms loaded with books. Lynch, who was standing just behind me, gasped, then squeaked out, "That's the killer!"

James Longo's appearance was similar to the last time I'd seen him; same tweed jacket with the leather patches, same trousers, his long hair giving him a shaggy appearance. I could see something almost feral in him now, and I moved quickly toward him. When he looked up and saw me he became startled and dropped the books he was carrying. From behind me I heard Lynch screaming, "What are you doing? What are you doing?"

I turned around and saw Lynch standing petrified, his expression frozen as if he were about to scream for his life. The man he was staring at, though, wasn't James Longo, but one of the store's customers—a guy in his thirties, about average height and weight—and from the way he was staring at Lynch he recognized him also. The man stood maybe twenty feet away from me. An almost animalistic snarl had come over his face, and I noticed he had taken a gun out of his jacket pocket and was leveling it at Lynch.

I grabbed the closest thing to me—a thick hardcover book—and threw it tomahawk style at him, hitting him on the side of the face. The impact was enough to knock him off balance and keep him from shooting Lynch. I charged him then, throwing myself at him from about five feet away, and ended up knocking him to the floor. We grappled for a minute or so over a pile of books that had also been knocked over. He fired his gun once, but I outweighed him by a good fifty pounds and was able to get him in a submission hold and force him to let go of the gun. After that I cuffed him and dropped his gun into my coat pocket. It was a .32 caliber.

I looked up briefly to make sure Zachary Lynch was okay and hadn't been hit by the random shot, then turned back to the suspect. Breathing hard, I told him he was under arrest for the murders of Gail Laurent and Paul Burke, then read him his rights. The man's eyes were filled with such an intense fury that it was hard to look at him. He wasn't paying any attention to me or Lynch, and I glanced over my shoulder to see who he was staring so intently at. It was James Longo, who stood nearby looking completely startled.

"You smug bastard," the man swore at Longo, his voice seething with contempt.

"Do you know this person?" I asked Longo.

James Longo shook his head. "I've seen him in the shop over the last few weeks, but I've never spoken to him. I have no idea who he is."

"If you'd read my manuscript instead of lying about it, you'd know who I was!" he yelled at Longo, his eyes shining with a mix of triumphant glee and insanity.

"I don't know what he's talking about," Longo told me.

"Of course not! Because you're a liar!" The man turned his madness to me. "I sent this lying piece of shit a manuscript I wrote. My book is beyond brilliant. I spent over three years polishing it to make it more perfect than anything he's ever seen, and you know how this shit responds back to me: '*Thank you for letting me see your manuscript. You have quite a handsome package here—and have done a nice job with your cover art—but unfortunately that is the only value I can find in what you sent me. I regret that I can't offer more encouragement, but I'm afraid your work doesn't merit it. Good luck with your efforts to find a publisher for this. Miracles do happen.*'"

He was staring at me as if he had made some revelatory statement. "I don't get it," I told him.

"I had to prove that lying piece of shit never read my novel. And I proved it all right!"

"I still don't get what you're saying."

He shifted his gloating, triumphant look back to Longo. "If he'd read my novel he would've known who it was killing those people."

"How?"

He looked at me as if I was dense. "Because they were done exactly as they were in my book."

"Let me get this straight, you murdered two people to test whether some guy in a bookstore read something you wrote?"

His expression turned extremely smug. "Four people," he said. He glanced down at me, smiled, and added, "With a little luck, maybe five."

James Longo muttered something about not knowing what this person was referring to. "I have so many hopeful writers sending me their manuscripts. My staff reads them and responds back," he said. His eyes grew wide as he looked at me. "Detective Green, you're bleeding."

I had thought I'd pulled a muscle during the scuffle. I touched my side where it hurt and saw blood covering my fingers. That sonofabitch had shot me. With the adrenaline rush wearing off, I started to feel woozy. I asked James Longo to call 911.

They took me to the Downtown Hospital on Williams Street, which was just on the other side of City Hall Park. The guy I arrested turned out to be named Allen Cowler, and I was lucky he had switched from a .40 caliber with hollow-points to a .32; otherwise he would've blasted away a good chunk of me. The .32 slug went cleanly through me without causing any internal damage. According to my doctor, a quarter of an inch to the side and I would've been in serious trouble. It bled a lot and hurt like hell, but it was not much more than a glorified flesh wound. I probably could've just been stitched up and released, but the doctors wanted to keep me overnight, maybe longer, and I was groggy enough from anesthesia and the pain medication not to fight them on it. Anyway, the hospital bed was a hell of a lot more comfortable than what I'd been sleeping on at the Y.

Hennison was waiting for me when I was brought out of surgery. His eyes narrowed as he studied me, and then he told me that I deserved to take that bullet for not bringing him in on this.

"It couldn't be helped," I told him, my voice sounding weaker than I would've thought it would. "I don't think I could've gotten Zachary Lynch to come with me to that bookstore if you were with me. Has Cowler said anything about James Solinski?"

"Yeah, that psycho's proud of himself. He told us all about killing Solinski and gave us the location for another body that he claims he buried upstate. A retired cop from Trenton who stopped when Cowler was shooting those dogs. Cowler's going to be disappointed when he hears about you. He was hoping to add another notch to his belt."

I gave Hennison a puzzled look.

"The sonofabitch actually has four notches carved on his belt," Hennison said.

"Did he tell you about his book?" I asked.

"Yeah, he did." Hennison paused for a moment. "How'd you piece this together?"

I wasn't going to tell him that I suspected Wooten and had pulled a warrant to search his shop. Instead, I told Hennison how I'd made the connection between Wooten and all three murders, and brought Zachary Lynch to the store so we could keep an eye out in case the murderer showed up. It was a white lie, but one I could live with.

Hennison chuckled at that. "That psycho sonofabitch. If he only knew that your oddball friend can't even describe him he might've been able to keep his cool instead of giving himself up the way he did. You want to know why he didn't shoot Lynch when Lynch witnessed him killing that woman?"

"He was out of bullets?"

"Nope. I gotta give that FBI profiler credit. She nailed it.

Cowler couldn't pull the trigger because his book only had one killing happening then. Fucking nutcase."

Hennison stopped and gave me a long look. While he did this his face hardened and his lips compressed into two tight lines. "You got lucky today, Green," he said at last.

I nodded. I was going to say something, but I felt so damned tired all of a sudden, and my eyelids started drooping shut. I guess Hennison must've left then. Next thing I remembered was Phillips pushing me awake. Blinking, I looked at the clock on the wall and saw that it had been three hours since I'd conked out.

"Good work, detective," Phillips said gruffly. "You up to talking to the media?"

I took a drink of water to clear my throat and told him I was. Phillips waved to someone standing beyond the door, and the room filled up quickly with cameramen and reporters. I gave a brief statement with Phillips making sure to stand next to me so he'd be in the shots. I ended up taking questions for about ten minutes before I started drifting off again, and one of the nurses cleared the room of reporters. Right before I fell asleep, Phillips grunted something again about me doing good work but that it was damn careless of me to go to that store without backup, and that if it were up to him I'd be written up for breaking protocol. I tried to give him the finger, but I think I was too tired to lift my hand.

The next time I woke up I realized Joe Ramirez was standing next to my bed.

"Stan," he said when he saw my eyes open.

"Hey, Joe." My voice was raspy, not much more than a croak. "What time is it?"

He looked at his watch and told me it was ten past one in the morning. That didn't make sense. He should've been in the middle of his shift. I woke up completely, a coolness filling my head. From the way he was looking he wasn't there to congratulate me, and all at once it hit me what must've happened. A sickish feeling flooded through me as I waited for him to tell me that those fucking Russians had enacted their revenge on me by breaking into my apartment and killing Bambi while she was there all alone and helpless. Joe was having trouble getting his words out, and it was agonizing waiting for him.

"Stan," he said finally, "there's no easy way to tell you this. Your brother was found murdered tonight."

I stared at him dumbly because it wasn't what I was expecting him to say. When I finally made sense of what he was telling me, I felt myself sink into my bed, a numbness taking over my body.

"Where was Mike found?" I heard myself asking him.

"In his apartment. One or more persons had broken in. We're not sure yet whether the motive was robbery or murder, but death was caused by blunt trauma to the back of the head. They think a hammer was used."

"It wasn't robbery," I said. "Mike had nothing in that apartment."

Joe sighed deeply and nodded. "The homicide detective working this out of Brooklyn is outside waiting. Are you up to talking to him?"

"Yeah."

Joe brought the detective into the room. He wanted to know if Mike did drugs or had any enemies or ongoing beefs with anyone that I knew of. I told him it wasn't anything like that, then explained about the Russians and the veiled threat they had made.

"You know who made the threat?"

"I'll find out. It was relayed to me by a third party."

"And this third party's name?"

I shook my head. "If I give him to you he'll shut down on us. I'll talk to him. In the meantime, you know the two Russians I arrested. Talk to Organized Crime, get the name of their boss."

"Yeah, okay, I'll see if this leads anywhere," he said without much enthusiasm. "Right now we've got nothing. It could be what you're saying, or it could turn out to be something completely different, so don't get yourself too worked up over these Russians, and for fucksake, don't get yourself involved any further than talking with your friend." He hesitated, then added, "Your brother was a fireman, right? A decorated hero? We're going to get whoever did this, I promise you."

I nodded and barely noticed as he left.

Chapter 25

Friday, February 18, 2005

When morning came, my doctor wanted me to stay another day, and I told him I was checking out instead.

"That's really not advisable—"

I stopped him with a look. "My brother was murdered last night," I said. "With tomorrow being the Sabbath, I have to make the funeral arrangements today if I'm going to bury him Sunday."

"I see," he muttered, clearly shaken by what I told him. He took off his glasses and wiped them slowly, buying time to collect himself. "Isn't there any other family member who could do this?"

"No."

He put his glasses back on and nodded solemnly. "I can't keep you here against your will, but you'll be putting yourself at serious risk leaving today. I have to ask that you check yourself back in at the first sign of a fever. You'll also have to come back later as an outpatient to have your bandages changed."

He unhooked an intravenous drip from my arm, and I gingerly swung my legs around and lowered my feet to the floor. That damn bullet wound left me feeling as if someone had shoved a lit book of matches into my side. I asked the doctor if he could write me a prescription for some heavy-duty painkillers and he handed me a prescription for Oxycontin that he'd already written out.

After he left, I got myself dressed and called Marcy. As I expected, she was too exhausted from mourning Mike each day over the last three years, and she asked if I could make the arrangements. I told her I would.

I had to go back to my apartment to get the paperwork for a family plot my dad had bought thirty years ago at Cypress Hills, and when I got there I saw that Bambi had already moved out. She'd left a note on my pillow that I was going to find myself missing her. There was a chance she was right.

That afternoon I met with Earl Buntz. He promised me that if he heard anything about what happened with Mike he'd let me know. "I'm going to be asking around about this, Stan, you've got my word on that. I'll always have a soft spot in my heart for your brother. He was a great guy, and a hell of a shortstop when he was younger. He should've tried for the pros."

"Those damned off-speed pitches always got him," I said. I asked him for the name of the guy who passed that threat to him, and he gave it to me without hesitation.

"Who do these assholes work for?"

He only hesitated for a second before giving me the name Yuri Gorkin. "From what I hear he's some sort of ultra badass who used to be a colonel in the KGB back in the day. Stan, I don't know that these Russians had anything to do with Mike. They might not have. I promise you I'll be looking into this, but you've got to stay calm in the meantime and not do anything stupid, okay?"

I grunted out that I'd watch myself and struggled for a moment to push myself to my feet. Earl told me he saw me on the news the other day. "Maybe Mike had a chance to see you also. It would've made him proud if he did."

I fought back the urge to tell Earl that Mike would have had nothing to be fucking proud of me over, but I left it alone.

I drove back to Manhattan and found out what I could about Yuri Gorkin. There wasn't much about him in the system, but there was a little. At least I knew the name of the restaurant he owned on Brighton Beach Avenue. I also found a picture of him and knew what he looked like.

When I drove back to Brooklyn, I kept driving until I found myself across the street from Gorkin's restaurant. I sat out there for hours and watched as he walked in. I had my .38 special with me, and I thought long and hard about following Gorkin in there, but I ended up driving away. If it weren't for Stevie and Emma, maybe I would've, but I had my kids to think about. I had to give the system a chance to work things out.

I didn't plan to go Joel Cohen's club. I wasn't even consciously aware of it when I parked on the same block. It was only when I was walking into the place that I realized what I was up to.

As it usually was for a Friday night, the place was jampacked and blasting some crap synthesized disco music. It took a moment for my eyes to adjust to the light; then I squeezed through the crowd looking for Joel. I spotted him talking to a couple of young girls at a table. They didn't look twenty-one to me. I pushed my way to their table. Joel looked surprised to see me. He started to offer his condolences about Mike, and I held up my hand to stop him.

I took my badge out and showed it to the two girls at the table. "Let's see some ID." From the looks the girls exchanged with each other, I knew they were underage.

Joel started to excuse himself, and I told him to stay where he was.

One of the girls made a show of looking through her pocketbook before telling me she must've left it at home. The other girl just smiled at me. I picked up their drinks and sniffed them. One of them was drinking rum and coke, the other a cosmo.

"Serving alcohol to underage drinkers?" I asked Joel. "Turn around."

"Cut the shit, Stan," he said, smiling nervously. "You don't work Brooklyn."

I shoved him hard around and had to grit my teeth when I felt the stitches rip in my wound. He stumbled over, and before he could regain his balance I had his arms pulled up behind his back, cuffing him. I took a notebook and pen out and turned to the girls. They gave me their names, addresses, and real ages, and I knew they were too scared to be lying to me. I growled at them to beat it. They didn't think twice. They got up from their table and ran.

"What the fuck you doing, Stan?" Joel demanded.

"I'm arresting you for serving alcohol to customers under the legal drinking age. Now move it."

I shoved him hard, and he stumbled forward. A path quickly cleared in front of him.

"You're making a big mistake," Joel said once I had him outside. I didn't bother answering him, just kept pushing him until we got to my car. Then I had him get in the back seat.

"I had nothing to do with what happened with Mike," he said.

I turned on the ignition and put the car in drive, then slowly pulled the car onto the road.

"This is stupid. It will take my lawyer all of five minutes to bounce these charges. Worst case, we're talking a few thousand dollars in fines."

He uttered the latter more as a question, being just smart enough not to offer me an outright bribe in a way that I could arrest him for it, at least not if I told the truth about what he said. I looked in the rearview mirror and could see him sweating badly. It wasn't over him worrying about me charging him with serving alcohol to underage drinkers. At that moment he wasn't sure whether I was taking him to a precinct or someplace quiet to put a bullet in his head. The more I looked at him the less I knew myself which it was going to be.

"Jesus, Stan," he said, a panic creeping into his voice, "you don't know what happened to Mike had anything to do with us."

I didn't answer him. If I allowed myself to, I would've hit the gas and kept going straight instead of turning onto Empire Boulevard. Peering in the rearview mirror I could see the relief washing over his face when I pulled into the back lot behind the Flatbush precinct. Fuck, I wish he had had a heart attack on the way over. I brought him in there and handed him to the desk sergeant for processing. After that I drove to the nearest emergency room to have my stitches redone.

Sunday, February 20, 2005

It was a miserable, rotten day. Gray overcast skies, sleeting rain, just plain miserable. I visited my mom before Mike's funeral. I didn't tell her about Mike. I don't think she would've understood me, but I didn't want to take the chance of taking away the little she might have left.

The funeral service was held graveside. It was well attended by people from the neighborhood, policemen I knew and firemen from throughout the city. A third of Mike's company had died on 9-11, but the surviving members made sure to be up front and center. Most of the crowd shielded themselves with umbrellas, but I didn't and the firefighters didn't. I thought of Mike the way he was before 9-11 and how he was afterward. He never really survived that day, not entirely. It fucked up his lungs and sucked so much of his life out of him. Whatever chance he had to recover and lead a normal life was now gone.

Marcy and my nephews stood next to me during the service. I hadn't seen her in months, and she had aged so much since then. My nephews were only twelve and fourteen, but they stood stoically, both biting hard on their lips to keep from crying.

After the rabbi finished his service, one fireman after the next got up front to say a few words and give his remembrances of Mike; then friends of Mike's from the neighborhood followed. When one of Mike's buddies tried to get me to say something, I shook him off. I couldn't do it. Eventually the crowd dispersed, and it was just me, Marcy, and my nephews left standing by the grave. After a while Marcy touched my arm, then left with my nephews. I couldn't move. Not then.

I don't know how much longer it was, maybe five minutes, maybe ten, but someone approached me and held an umbrella over my head, then touched me lightly on the shoulder. It was Jill Chandler, smiling sadly.

"You're going to get sick if you keep standing out in the rain like this," she said.

I nodded and accepted the umbrella from her. I wanted to thank her, but I couldn't talk. She gave me another sad smile and left me.

It was a long time before I left the grave, and I was surprised to see Zachary Lynch off in the distance waiting for me. He wasn't alone; as I got closer to him I was able to make out that the woman with him was Lisa Williams from Strombolli's. I knew how hard it must've been for him to show up like he did. When I got up to him, I held my hand out. He took it, shivering and blanching badly as he did so.

"Detective Green," he said, his voice cracking on him and becoming something guttural, "you can't let your rage consume you like this. Please."

Before he turned away, Lisa Williams offered her condolences, and even though I didn't know her, I could tell they were heartfelt.

As Zachary walked away, I was able to find my voice, and I thanked him for showing up. He turned briefly and offered me what must've been meant as a reassuring smile.

Chapter 26

Tuesday, April 12, 2005

I ended up on disability and off the job for five weeks because of that bullet wound. Zachary's comment to me had its effect; I sought out an anger management workshop instead of spending every minute of those five weeks obsessing over Joel Cohen and Yuri Gorkin. It wasn't just what Zachary said to me; it was also thinking of Stevie and Emma standing at my grave the way Mike's kids had. Still, I have my bad days, days when I am so overwhelmed with thoughts of Mike that I find myself driving to Brighton Beach and parking for hours outside of Gorkin's restaurant, keeping tabs of who's coming and going. I've been making more of an effort lately to attend the anger management workshops, and the techniques I've been learning are starting to help. At least so far they've kept me from walking into Gorkin's restaurant and putting a bullet between his eyes.

Two weeks into my disability leave, Jill Chandler visited me at my apartment to discuss the case and also give me a copy of the manuscript Allen Cowler had sent the bookstore. She looked beautiful that day, dressed in jeans and a leather jacket over a yellow cotton sweater, her blond hair left down and falling just enough over her face so she kept having to brush it away from her eyes. I almost asked her out for dinner. I wanted to, but at the last moment I lost my nerve.

Jill had been right about almost every aspect of her profile on the killer: Cowler worked in a coffee shop, held an MFA in creative writing, and lived in a two-bedroom apartment with his mother in Queens. The book was obviously the work of an extreme narcissistic personality. It turns out Cowler got the sleeping pills he used on the dogs from a prescription his mother had. While Jill was right about why he didn't kill Zachary that day outside the bookstore, I was right about why the murders stopped for four months. Cowler was terrified we had a description of him, and he kept himself holed up until his rage over James Longo got the better of him. That was the same reason he dumped his .40 caliber and military knife into the Hudson. I was lucky that when he rearmed he did it with a .32 caliber, and the only reason that happened was because he was afraid we'd have informants out looking for anyone trying to buy a .40 caliber, or anything else of that type of firepower. When he was still talking before shutting himself down, he kept going on about how much he hated having to carry a pussy gun like a .32 instead of the real deal like he'd originally had.

Whoever on Longo's staff wrote that letter to Cowler about the book's packaging wasn't kidding. The guy had spent a good deal of money professionally binding it and having a graphic artist draw him a cover for it. On the back were all these unattributable quotes claiming the author was the next James Ellroy, which I assumed must've come from Cowler himself. The shooting of the dogs and murders identical to Gail Laurent's, Paul Burke's and James Solinski's all occurred in the book, which also detailed six additional murders, each more grisly than the last. The next one would've involved a hatchet, and sure enough, we found one hidden in his bedroom closet. At least we stopped him before he was able to act out the whole book.

I've always read a lot of novels, but usually they're science fiction, Westerns, or fantasy. I tend not to read crime fiction—it hits a little too close to home. I have read a couple of James Ellroy's books, though: *The Big Nowhere* and

White Jazz. Cowler is no James Ellroy. The tone of his book was unbelievably condescending and smug, and the events that unfolded made no sense. It just seemed like one poorly written, violent, and gory scene after the next. I'm sure in Cowler's mind it's all brilliant, but to me whoever wrote him that letter on Longo's staff was being kind.

It's been in the papers recently that one of the large New York publishing houses wants to publish Cowler's book and that the families of the victims are fighting to keep that from happening. Personally I'm hoping the book gets published. Cowler is going to spend the rest of his days locked up and he'll never see a dime of the money, so let them publish it. Understanding that psycho the way I do, the crap reviews the book will generate will eat away at him until his last breath, and while it's not enough, at least it would be some justice.

I ran into Jill Chandler a month ago, and this time I didn't chicken out. I asked her out for dinner and we've been seeing each other ever since. We're trying to take it slow and haven't slept together yet, but I think that will be changing soon. She's been suggesting as much. I find myself thinking about her a lot during the day, and am genuinely happy when we're able to get together. Every time I see her, she seems more beautiful.

The trial for those Russians I arrested was two weeks ago. They were both given eighteen months for the gun charges, and I doubt they'll end up serving more than six months of it. There's still nothing as far as Mike's murder. I'm still spending some of my off hours looking into Gorkin and also into Joel Cohen's activities, but I'm trying to limit how much of my life I dedicate to it, and also trying hard not to go off the deep end over it. I know I must be doing something right. I've been seeing Zachary every Thursday, ostensibly to see if he's taken pictures of any more monsters out there. Last week he told me he could now see my eyes—that they were no longer being obscured by rage. The guy is also amazingly intuitive. Out of the blue he showed me his off-kilter smile and volunteered about how attractive he found that FBI profiler who had talked to him months ago about hypnosis—how if he wasn't already in love with Lisa he'd be thrilled to be able to date her. I never mentioned to him that I was seeing Jill; somehow he just knew it. Last week he also gave me a photograph of a man he saw in the street. The man was in his fifties, mostly nondescript. According to Zachary, this person's soul is even more broken and corrupt than Cowler's or that of the child killer I took him to see on Staten Island. I've been keeping an eye out, but so far haven't had any luck identifying him.

Last week I went to see Cheryl's opening night performance in *Cabaret*. She was amazing as Sally Bowles. On Jill's suggestion, I brought a dozen red roses for Cheryl. I was glad did. When I handed them to her, it brought tears to her eyes.

Yesterday was opening day at Fenway Park, and as luck would have it, they had the Red Sox playing the Yankees. I was able to score four tickets for the game, and took Jill and my kids to it. It was the first time Stevie and Emma met Jill, and while they were standoffish at first, by the end of the day all of them were fast friends. Stevie had an absolute blast at the game, especially with the Yankees having to stand and watch the Red Sox players get their World Series rings, and the World Series championship banner being unveiled. The fact that Boston beat New York eight to one didn't hurt either.

I had a good day yesterday, and have been having more than my share of those lately. Not every day has been perfect. I still have those days where I find myself anxious about Mike. I know one way or another I'll get justice for him, that I just have to be patient. For the time being I have to give the detective working the case a chance to do his job. I keep telling myself I have to focus on the good days and not let myself be overwhelmed by the bad. Easier said than done. But the thought of having Zachary blanching at the sight of me during our weekly meetings has been enough to keep me on track, so far.